THEY STARED AT EACH OTHER, THE AIR CRACKLING AROUND THEM, LOVE AND HATE DUELING TO THE DEATH.

"Get out of here," Luna whispered. "Leave!"

It was almost worse seeing him now than it had been on the Capitol steps. At least then it had been so quick, it was almost like a figment of imagination. Not so now . . . here . . . in her small office. He loomed over her, bringing the memories flooding back. Damn his tall good looks! She hated blond hair streaked with silver; his bourbon-colored eyes were so beautiful, they seemed sinister. Once he had ripped her apart emotionally and now he was doing it again.

"No." Dray Lodge closed the door behind him. "I'm staying until you listen to me."

"What do you want?" she asked, terrified by her desire to throw herself into his arms.

"You."

QUANTITY SALES

Most Dell books are available at special quantity discounts when purchased in bulk by corporations, organizations, and special-interest groups. Custom imprinting or excerpting can also be done to fit special needs. For details write: Dell Publishing, 666 Fifth Avenue, New York, NY 10103. Attn.: Special Sales Department.

INDIVIDUAL SALES

Are there any Dell books you want but cannot find in your local stores? If so, you can order them directly from us. You can get any Dell book in print. Simply include the book's title, author, and ISBN number if you have it, along with a check or money order (no cash can be accepted) for the full retail price plus $1.50 to cover shipping and handling. Mail to: Dell Readers Service, P.O. Box 5057, Des Plaines, IL 60017.

Brief Encounter

Helen Mittermeyer

A DELL BOOK

Published by
Dell Publishing
a division of
The Bantam Doubleday Dell
Publishing Group, Inc.
666 Fifth Avenue
New York, NY 10103

ISBN 0-440-20135-7

Printed in the United States of America

Published simultaneously in Canada

October 1988

10 9 8 7 6 5 4 3 2 1
KRI

I dedicate this book to my daughter,
Captain Ann Mittermeyer, JAG, who was
the inspiration for my spunky heroine.
                                        —H.M.

Chapter 1

Washington, D.C., was putting on its best face. It was the last day of March, cool, a trifle breezy, but the sun shone out of a bright-blue sky, glinting down on the government buildings, casting them in the golden illusion of ancient Athens.

Senator Perrin Draper Lodge was bored and more than a little irked. He had told his assistant that he didn't want to deal with Skinner anymore, but the man had accosted him and Haddon March while they were having coffee in the Capitol coffee shop.

Haddon had been silent since the lobbyist had approached him. He was too canny to converse openly in front of a well-known information monger.

Damn! Dray, as the senator had been called since childhood, had waited a week to see Haddon and now they'd been interrupted. Letting his eyes rove over the beautiful building that was the seat of government, Dray saw a movement beside one of the columns as a woman came into view who seemed to be looking their way. He was more intrigued than wary when she began to run toward them. People approached him all the time.

Luna McAfee spotted her quarry and took a deep breath, not taking her eyes off him, scarcely noticing his two companions. She wished, not for the first time, that the firm could afford a regulation process server, but until then . . .

Approaching Chuck Skinner, who was a well-known lobbyist, considered by friend and foe to be a formidable adversary, took a certain chutzpah, maybe the panache of a kamikaze, but it had to be done. Luna was determined. The man had eluded every messenger they'd sent with the summons, and the court date was coming up fast . . . and their client Veli Skinner was being deprived of her monetary rights. Her civil rights were in jeopardy as well. Delinquent in making his alimony payments, Chuck Skinner was in danger of denying his ex-wife the use of her home, which had come to her in the divorce settlement and which she might lose by default if she didn't keep up the payments. He wasn't going to get away with it! Skinner was a wealthy man with even wealthier clients, some with less savory reputations than others. Not only was he making money over the counter but he was reputed to be dealing under the table as well. He could damn well afford to pay his just debts, and she, as Veli's lawyer, was going to make sure that he did.

The moment the three men began to descend the steps of the Capitol, Luna stepped from behind one of the huge Grecian columns and positioned herself. She'd been a swimmer and distance runner in college and she still worked out as much as she could. Being in shape for this encounter was one thing, but she needed a bit of luck too. Inhaling, Luna readied herself. Timing was everything! She had to deliver the summons at the exact moment when one of the men accompanying Skinner put out his hand in parting.

Luna started to run, her eyes never wavering from her objective.

As Skinner was about to place his hand in an outstretched one, his palm flat, his fingers curled as though to grasp, Luna skidded to a stop in front of him and slapped the summons into his hand. "Charles Payson Skinner, you have just been served with a subpoena to appear in court in . . ." The rest of what Luna said was drowned in a cacophony of shouts and epithets.

"What the bloody hell . . . ?" Skinner grabbed her arm, dropping his briefcase. His other hand, which was clutching the summons, was aimed at her face.

Dray was paralyzed by recognition for a moment, then his hand shot out defensively. "Not so fast, Skinner." Dray grasped the hand aimed at Luna McAfee, the woman he had been searching for so many long months. Then he turned, in the same motion almost dropping his own briefcase. "Luna? Is it really you? Wait."

Dray released the fulminating Skinner, putting himself between Luna McAfee and the lobbyist, turning to clutch at the woman who'd been walking through his dreams for months now. "Please, don't go. I've been looking for you."

Luna saw stars; her stomach heaved in sickening realization of and rejection at whom she was facing. Why hadn't she noticed him standing with Skinner? Damn it to hell, why hadn't she taken the time to scan Skinner's companions!

That smoothly planed face with the Nordic cheekbones was the same. Viking in a Savile Row suit, that was Dray. Those bourbon-colored eyes were still a jarring sexy contrast to the streaky blond hair with its touches of silver. She was sure the very shock that twisted his strong features was doing the same to her own. Then those eyes showed the smooth heat of desire, mule-kicking her memory of them, together, loving. God! It had to be a nightmare that had come to life here in the Washington sunlight!

"No! Let me go." Without thinking, she struck out with her foot, catching the junior senator from New York in the shinbone. Then she was running back the way she'd come, as if all the hounds of hell were at her heels.

"Luna! Wait!"

Luna didn't look back. Running hard, she passed others in the Capitol area who barely looked at her. Joggers were a common sight around the Capitol. She prayed that Gretchen had kept the car running. Luna rounded a corner and headed straight across the strip of grass and trees that separated her from the parked, rather battered VW, throwing herself at it, grasping the door, and hurling herself into the seat. "Drive!" she commanded.

Gretchen floored the gas pedal, pulling out into traffic and almost colliding with a mail truck. The driver, blowing his horn, had to veer and correct in order to avoid being hit. Again the air was filled with invective and fist shaking.

"You . . . almost . . . hit . . . that truck," Luna said, out of breath, air coming painfully from her throat. Dray Lodge! What a nightmare! What had made her think that she could hide from him when she was on his turf . . . Washington, D.C.

"*You* said to drive," Gretchen pointed out haughtily. "I did." Gretchen hunched over the wheel, not lessening speed as they screeched around a corner. "You acted like the Devil himself was after you."

"He was."

"Huh?"

When Gretchen turned to look at Luna, the VW sailed up on the sidewalk, approaching a walking tour-group, who, en masse, stared openmouthed at the car for a moment before they leapt in every direction, allowing the vehicle a clear path.

"Gretchen, for God's sake." Luna looked through the spaces in her fingers as she covered her face.

"Did you see that woman dive into those bushes? Isn't it amazing what senior citizens can do today? I'll bet she works out," Gretchen pronounced firmly, steering the car in a haphazard fashion back to the roadway again.

"Amazing." Luna exhaled in relief when they were off the sidewalk again, mentally hurrying Gretchen despite the misgivings she had about her friend's erratic driving. "Haddon March, whom I've been trying to see for weeks, was with Skinner."

"Was he the devil?"

"No." Not even with a good friend like Gretchen could she discuss Dray Lodge.

After many backtracks, twists, and turns, they were on the avenue taking them to Silver Spring, caught in a bumper-to-bumper traffic jam. Gretchen had a predilection for getting lost.

Luna put her head back on the seat, the crack in the vinyl upholstery biting into her neck. Dray Lodge! The impossible had happened. All the time she'd been in the Washington area she'd assured herself that it was a chance in a million that she would see him . . . and now she had.

"Oh, oh, Luna, I think we're in a gridlock."

Not now! Not when she was fighting her mind and the memory that wanted to take her back to Germany.

Chapter 2

West Germany, 1984

Zweibrucken Air Force Base was considered a small base by most standards, certainly not a large, important one like Rheinman, outside Frankfurt, but Luna McAfee had been happy there for the two years that she'd been a JAG—a judge advocate general—on the base. There had been bases in the United States that she had worked on and liked, but none of them had intrigued and delighted her as much as the German base.

Europe had been an adventure. She'd traveled in Greece, Spain, France, all of Germany, even the eastern sector. Visiting Russia and the Scandinavian countries had been a thrill, and she'd even managed to buy a Saab, a Swedish car, which would be ready for her to ship home when it was time to return to the United States. The walking tour she'd taken of the British Isles had been memorable, the Lake District of Wordsworth a stellar "spot of time," as the poet himself would have phrased it.

Luna had only six months to go on her tour of duty, then she would be going back to civilian life, ready to take the Philadelphia legal community by storm. The experience in trial work that she had garnered since joining the Air Force would be invaluable in the private sector.

When her friend from law school Samuel Lopez, called Uel by his friends, phoned long distance to invite her into his storefront law office, she told him that.

"Your tour of duty is up soon, and Washington is where the action is, Luna. With all the experience you've gained in trial law there, you'll be right at home. Trial work is a large part of our cases."

"Thanks, Uel, you're a darling, but I think I would like to try Philadelphia even though I have no family there anymore. It was home to me when I was a child. And you know what they say about Philadelphia lawyers."

"Not really. I'll go along with you, friend, but I want you to think about it. My bride sends her love and says that a letter follows. Take care. Remember, we love you."

"I love you both. Good-bye." Luna had shed a few tears at the end of the call. Sometimes she was lonely for her old friends and wanted to see them so much she ached with it. She was an only child and both of her parents had died years ago. The few distant cousins she had didn't keep in close touch, so she valued her friends very much.

If her military trial-work hadn't been so interesting, she was sure she would have gone out of her mind at times. Loneliness was a big factor in a foreign country. There were friends in Germany but no one she was as close to as Uel and Barb.

Being a JAG, for the Air Force in Germany had proved to be an exciting career choice, and she had done everything she could to hone her skills as a lawyer. There were times, even, when she was tempted to make the military her career. Certainly, at this point in her life, it was less chancy than the private sector. Once she was a civilian she would have to set about studying for and passing the Pennsylvania bar. She had already passed the D.C. and the Maryland bars, and that could be a help to her.

All that ran through her mind as she drove up the winding road leading to the air base, which overlooked the countryside. It was a cold February morning, but she didn't mind that. The coming weekend she and some new friends would be going to Switzerland to ski, but for now she had a very intricate and intriguing case that filled her mind to the exclusion of all else.

Luna acknowledged the airman on duty who saluted the sticker on her battered Fiat that designated her an officer.

Then she drove to the parking space allotted to her in the JAG area of the base.

"Good morning, Captain McAfee. The colonel would like to see you at once." Helga Braun, her assistant, was a pretty blond woman who spoke excellent English, as did most of the civilian personnel.

"Thank you, Helga." Luna smiled when Helga grimaced. Colonel Encorvado was not the most popular person in the JAG unit, but he was the CO. "Have I time to go over the notes I gave you yesterday?"

Helga shook her head. "I don't think so. He's pawing the ground in there. He has someone from the States with him and he's frothing."

"Oh? Someone from the Defense Department?"

"I think it has something to do with the Hetty case."

Luna frowned, and glanced into the small mirror she kept in her desk drawer, checking to see that her uniform was in order. "I shouldn't be too long. Go over what we did yesterday and make some notes."

Luna walked down the short corridor and rapped once on the door, then opened it. Sergeant Dobbs, who clerked for the major, indicated with a jerk of his head that she go straight into the office.

Taking a deep breath, she grasped the handle, turned it, and pushed in the door. "Sir? You wanted to see me?"

Dray Lodge rose to his feet slowly, the voice of the colonel fading in his ears. She was tall, but so slender and well formed, with a fragile strength that made his blood chug into life. Desire flickered in him as it always did when he saw a beautiful woman, but never had he felt such a rush of protectiveness along with it. Was her hair blond or red? Or both? It was pulled back in a tight bun with not a wisp out of place, but she hadn't been able to control the hint of waviness in her hair. Those eyes were a sapphire-blue with dark rings around the irises, the gold rays in them picking up the glints in her hair. Gorgeous even in that damned blue uniform that fitted her well but had all the charm of a prison matron's garb. "What? Oh, pardon me. How do you do, Captain McAfee?"

"Mr. Lodge." Luna McAfee had blushed, and that fascinated Dray. "I will be glad to fill him in, sir, if that's your wish, but I don't see why he doesn't contact Captain Billings, who is—"

"Yes, yes, I know who the defense lawyer is, Captain. Mr. Lodge has spoken to him and now wishes to speak with you."

"Very well, sir, if that's your wish."

"It is."

Luna McAfee turned to look at the man, who was a full head taller than the colonel. "Would you come this way, Mr. Lodge. My office is just down the hall."

"Right behind you, Captain." And what a lovely, graceful sway she had to her walk. Her hips were small but she had the most beautifully rounded bottom. Dray's hands itched to cup those cheeks.

When she turned to face him with her desk between them, Dray smiled. "Have dinner with me."

Luna blinked at him. "Mr. Lodge, you're here because . . ."

"Because Gil Hetty asked me to look in on this case involving his son, since I was coming to Bonn anyway. From what I've been able to garner from your CO, the charges are pretty serious, and the evidence pretty conclusive."

"You're a lawyer."

Dray nodded, and took the seat opposite her, listening as she gave him a bare-bones sketch of the case. His attention was pulled from his scrutiny of her by the sheer force of her arguments and the volume of hard evidence she had. "Rape . . . assault and battery . . . drugs." Dray frowned at the papers he held and shook his head. "I think you've got him."

Nearly an hour later, Luna rose to her feet. "I do have another client to see, Mr. Lodge. If you'll excuse me . . ."

"Of course. I'll see you this evening."

Luna hadn't answered him. She had no intention of seeing him again. When she went through the gate that evening she was tired and eager to get to the *Schwimmbad* and exercise. She didn't take notice of the black Mercedes following her until she was almost in the small town of Homburg, where her apartment was located.

"Hi." Dray Lodge got out of the Mercedes, which had parked next to hers, and folded his arms on the top. "You're very beautiful, Captain McAfee, and I think I'm in love with you. How do you feel?"

Luna couldn't seem to close her mouth or focus her thoughts. "I'm going swimming."

"Me too."

Luna was sure he wouldn't be able to get into the *Schwimmbad,* but when she went out to do her laps he was already in the water, gliding up and down his lane like an Olympic contender.

She was into her third lap when she felt hands underneath her and a face appeared under hers. When he kissed her, blowing air into her mouth and still managing to swim, she almost drowned.

As quickly as he had appeared he left her, going back to his own lane and beginning the hard stroking he had been doing since his entrance into the pool.

Now Luna was out of breath, disoriented, having to struggle to regain her own rhythm.

When she'd done her eighty lengths of the standard-sized pool, she paused at the end to catch her breath.

"You swim very well, Captain McAfee."

Luna turned to look at the handsome hard-muscled man next to her. "Thank you. If you ever try your cute tricks on me again, Mr. Lodge, I'll call the *Polizei.* Believe me, the Germans would make you think twice about accosting a woman."

"Was I doing that? I thought I was giving you a message that I'm yours if you want me."

Splashing water in his face, Luna turned and hoisted herself up the side onto the surround in one easy motion, not looking around when she heard the low whistle at her back.

Dressing as fast as she could, she hurried out of the *Schwimmbad,* greeting the persons she recognized in fluent German. It had not taken her long to master the language, since she'd studied it in high school and college, but at first she had been very slow. Now she was quite fluent because she had made it a habit to mix with the German people in her area.

"We can go in your car if you like, and I can have mine picked up and taken to my hotel."

Luna swung around at the sound of Mr. Lodge's voice, the sound like velvet steel. "I am going home to eat and sleep, Mr. Lodge."

"That's what I have to do too, but since we both have to eat, you could direct me to a good place, couldn't you?"

"Mr. Lodge, I told you that I wouldn't discuss the Hetty case any further with you, and I meant it."

"Fine. No talk about the case. I hate eating alone. How about you?"

"I'm used to it."

"Then have a change of pace, dine with me."

"You look like a little boy begging for candy."

"Take pity on me."

"Just for dinner? No conversation about the case?"

"Right."

Luna directed him to follow her. She drove to the Romerhaus, a quaint stone structure across a narrow road from Roman ruins, hence the name. The cuisine was first-rate, not the heavy fare of Bavaria but the light, pleasing dishes that abounded in the region bordering France.

"This is very nice, Captain McAfee."

"Would it make it easier if you called me Luna?"

"Yes, and please call me Dray. So you're a moon lady, are you?"

"Yes. My father was a professor of astronomy and Mother was a professor of English literature at the same university. They were in love and very devoted to each other. I was an only child so they gave me a romantic name. My father died when I was fifteen and my mother was killed in a car accident a few years ago.

"That's rough."

Luna looked into his eyes and saw the sincerity, and all at once her eyes flooded with tears. "For-forgive me. I don't know what's come over me. I dealt with my mother's death three years ago when it happened."

Dray had hitched his chair around so that he was blocking her from the rest of the room. "I understand, really I do." Dray kissed her forehead, talking softly to her until she'd composed herself. Luna hadn't felt so relaxed with a person in a long time.

After dinner they savored their strong coffee and sipped schnapps.

Luna never recalled having had such an evening. It had a glow to it.

Dray followed her home at two in the morning, then walked to her door with her. He kissed her nose lightly. "See you tomorrow, moon lady."

The next three evenings were similarly wonderful. Though they went to other restaurants, on the fourth evening they were together, they came back to the Romerhaus.

Luna felt as though she'd bared her soul to Dray, though he'd kept to his promise and not asked her again about the Hetty case.

When he took her home it was before midnight. Shadows were magnified by the cold moonlight touching the world.

"That's your namesake." Dray turned her so that she had her back to him, his arms loosely around her, her head back against his chest. "Are you getting a message from her?"

Luna's heart thudded against her chest as though it would bull through bone and tissue to be free.

"Darling, let me come in with you. I want you so much."

"Yes." Luna's life had become a pink bubble encasing her in the wondrous secrets of the ages. She had found the man she would love to eternity and beyond.

The night sounds of Germany faded into a heavy silence as

they went into her apartment. Their breathing was the only sound on the planet.

Luna wore a silk dress, and the whisper of it was like a caress around them as it slithered to her feet.

Moonlight streamed through the one large window, hitting the queen-size bed like bands of silver.

Dray caught her hand when she moved to turn on the light. "I want your namesake to touch us in that bed, Luna. That's the only cover we need."

Luna's body tingled with awareness as he removed his shirt, his eyes on her as she stood in front of him donned in a slip. He leaned down and kissed the skin bared to him over and over again. He eased her to a seated position on the bed while he undressed quickly. Firing the rest of his clothes at a chair in careless abandon, he sat down beside her, leaning back and pulling her with him.

"You're beautiful, moon lady." His mouth closed over one breast, his lips kneading the flesh under the slip, teasing the nipple gently.

Leaning back from her, he let his gaze run down her body, noting the garter belt she wore instead of panty hose. His thumb slid under the taut silky elastic. "Those garters are very erotic, moon lady."

Luna let her fingers thread through his hair, loving the crisp, healthy feel of it. Then her hands slid downward until she was playing with the chest hairs that peppered his strong torso, loving the feel of his flat masculine nipples.

Dray gasped, then uttered an expletive, his hand tightening on her breast before it moved down in slow, exquisite exploration on her silky midsection. "You are very beautiful, moon lady."

His whispered words ruffled the very fine hairs of her abdomen, the sensation causing her to gasp.

"Am I hurting you, Luna?"

"No." In restless passion she reached, cupping his head and trying to pull it up to her.

"Let me love you, Luna."

"Weren't you doing that?"

"I am now." In sweet discovery his lips coursed her form, reaching the apex of her body, where reddish curling hair abounded.

Luna pulled back in rejection. Though she was no virgin, she felt a sense of shock, a gentle violation.

Dray lifted his head, his eyes heavy with passion, their lustrous bourbon color like hot brown velvet. "I won't hurt you, darling. Let me love you; if you don't like it I'll stop."

Luna's being jerked in reaction, then there was a surrender, a giving over of herself to a very special man. Years of being on her own had taught her the value of independence; honed a measure of aloofness, of being chary of commitment. Dray Lodge was burning all her barriers, melting them with a passion that made her his.

When his tongue entered her body and began a slow, tingling rhythm, she couldn't control the hoarse cries that burst from her throat. His breath created an aura of emotion in her that she'd never imagined anyone could experience, her body beginning to undulate in an age-old feminine response.

Luna sank her fingers into his head, her own thrashing on the pillow. Her toes arched into him, beginning a massage of their own against that strong muscular body.

Tidal waves of feeling swept over them, raying through her from the point of contact with his mouth. She felt as if she were floating on the ocean of love and happily gave way to the overwhelming sensations.

Dray felt her limbs tremble with the release beginning in her. His own control was fast slipping. Never in his life had anyone brought him to such a pulsating crest. He wanted Luna more than he'd ever wanted anyone, but more than that he wanted to take care of her, to cherish and nurture her.

In slow entry he took her, awed and shaken when she clung to him and took him deeper into her.

They cried out together as the passion built and exploded, fragmenting them and putting them back together as one.

"Never, never was there anything like that, Luna, darling."

"I agree."

Dray cuddled her close to him. "I want to stay the night with you."

"I want that too, but isn't this bed too short for you?"

"It's the best bed in the world."

Never had Luna felt so wanted, so filled with happiness. She found herself whistling all the time. Once she'd even caught herself humming when she was in court. Perrin Draper Lodge had changed her life for all time.

Though her work still consumed her and there was lots of it, Dray was always in the back of her mind.

Evenings spent with him were an explosion of discovery and delight.

"Cooking is one of your many accomplishments?"

"Certainly. Here, taste this sauce." Dray held a wooden spoon out to her.

Most of the time they spent alone, not wanting or needing the stimulation of other people.

One evening, when they were sitting on the couch, cuddled close together and listening, the music of Rudolf Serkin in the background, Dray leaned down and kissed her. "Isn't tomorrow the day you're going to interview your star witness?"

"Yes, but don't ask me any more about her, I won't tell you."

"I won't ask, but I would like you to let me drive you. You said that she lives some distance from here?"

"Yes, outside Frankfurt actually, but it's no problem for me to drive there."

"I'd feel better if you let me drive you."

Luna shook her head. "No, it wouldn't work. I've promised Stenzi that I would come alone, just as I did the first time we talked. She's very frightened, Dray."

"I can understand it if she was as badly beaten as you say."

"She could have died."

After listening to Dray's admonitions about driving safely,

Luna left the next morning, making her way on that insanity of German driving called the Autobahn. Even though she was traveling at seventy miles per hour, it seemed as if she were standing still. The cars that whizzed by her rocked her car with the force of their speed, but no one slowed for anything.

Stenzi's apartment was not in a high-rent district but the building, which had four apartments, was clean. Stenzi answered on the first ring, looking around Luna to see if anyone else was there before gesturing her inside.

"I do not like coming for the trial, Captain McAfee." Stenzi's English was stilted but clear enough.

"I know, but you will be on the base, where you will be protected, and Hetty is going to be put away for a long time."

"And what if that doesn't happen? Then he will come to kill me."

Luna touched the blond girl's arm. "I will protect you, I promise."

Luna looked at the fading discolorations. Though her arm was still in a sling from the compound fracture and her hair was still very short from being shaved after her skull fracture and she had undergone neurosurgery, Stenzi was slowly coming back to health. She only worked half-days, but she was expected to make a full recovery in time.

"I hope you can keep your promise, Captain. I have had phone calls from people who don't leave names, warning me not to be a witness."

One afternoon, when the trial was only a few days away, Luna received a phone call from the United States. It was a little after three in the afternoon and she was immersed in her study of the Hetty case. "Who? Oh, Mr. Hetty, you're Airman Hetty's father. I'm sorry, sir, you have the wrong extension. I'm sure you want your son's defense lawyer. What? You're wrong, Mr. Hetty. Your son will get a fair hearing. I don't care to say anything else about the case. I hope that doesn't constitute a threat, Mr. Hetty." Luna replaced the receiver, more shaken than she wanted to admit. The man was a raving lunatic! Trying to free his son by intimidating the prosecution. Ridiculous. Perhaps she should speak to her commanding officer about it. Then she shook her head. Colonel Encorvado was not known for supporting his JAGs. Expediency was his strong suit.

Luna looked up, blinking at Master Sergeant Nichols, who was the NCO IC for their area. The noncommissioned officer in charge was usually a great help to the JAGs in getting their jobs done. Luna didn't know Nichols all that well, nor had she had many dealings with the man. "Yes, Sergeant, what is it?"

"I'm sorry, Captain, I knocked. You wanted to check on the evidence that we have for the Hetty case."

"Oh, right. It's in the locked cupboard." Luna was about to hand him her key when he showed her his. "Would you bring it in here, please? I want to go over it, then I'm going to lock it in my file cabinet tonight so it will be easy to get to in the morning."

"I'll get it right away, Captain."

There was a fair amount of material, plus the depositions that she'd been able to get. Going through it and cataloguing and numbering it had taken time, but it had been worth it. Her case was airtight. "I thought Sergeant Beams was going to help me with this case. Aren't you tied up with Captain Avery's case?"

"I had some free time and Sergeant Beams was busy, Captain. How did the interview with Fräulein Heilmann go, Captain?"

Luna stared at the expressionless man across the desk from her. "How did you know about that, Sergeant? I've kept that under wraps."

"You know what the grapevine is like, Captain."

"Yes, I do." He hadn't answered her, but she didn't pursue it, since he didn't ask any more questions about Stenzi.

They worked for several hours steadily. When they were finished, Luna felt like a damp mop. "Whew! That's enough. We're ready. Thank you, Sergeant."

"Do you want me to lock these in your file drawer, Captain McAfee?" Sergeant Nichols put the work together with systematic speed, so that there was a neat pile in front of him in no time.

"Ah, all right." Luna handed him the key and watched him while he went across her office to the recessed file cabinet that acted as a safety vault for the documents she wanted kept confidential. "There's a folder at the front with the name on it."

"I have it." Sergeant Nichols didn't turn around when he spoke to her, continuing to place the material he had placed on an adjoining table into the file. "There. That's it, all in place and secure, Captain." Sergeant Nichols swung around, his back to the cabinet, the key dangling from his hand."

"Thank you." Luna reached up to take the key from him as he approached her desk again. "I'll see you in court, Sergeant."

"That you will, Captain."

Luna was almost at once immersed in the notes she was making for herself for the next day and barely noticed when the door closed behind the noncommissioned officer.

The trial was to begin early Monday morning.

Luna arrived an hour beforehand and called her secretary to come into her office. "I think we'll give our documents the once-over and make sure that everything we'll be using is tagged properly." She handed the key to the woman, removed her outer coat, and sank into her chair.

"Captain McAfee, there's nothing here on the Hetty case."

Luna shot to her feet and was around the desk and next to her at once. "What?" "The evidence and papers should be right on top!"

Chapter 3

"There's nothing here."

Luna tore through the file, then she opened all the drawers in all the cabinets, scattering papers every which way in her effort to track down her work. "Get Sergeant Nichols in here, on the double."

The secretary ran from the room, but Luna didn't look up; she was too busy tearing apart her once neat office.

"You wanted to speak to me, Captain McAfee?"

Luna whirled around, staring hard at the expressionless man facing her. "Where are the Hetty papers and the evidence?"

Nichols blinked at her. "Why, right in the file drawer, Captain. You saw me put them there then lock it and give you the key. Did you happen to remove the evidenciary work and forget where you put it?"

Luna felt as though she'd been punched in the solar plexus. "You know that didn't happen, Sergeant. Where are the papers? The evidence?" The raspiness in her voice sounded strange in her ears.

"I don't think you should pass the buck to me when it would seem you're the one who had the key to the file."

"Your back was to me. For all I know you left the file unlocked so that you could come back later and take it, or you took it with you when you left my office yesterday." Luna was drowning and there was no lifeline.

"Those are harsh accusations, Captain. I won't stand still for having my record besmirched because you're not efficient or . . ."

"Or what, Sergeant?"

"You've been pretty cozy with a man who came here to help in Hetty's defense. By tomorrow people will be saying that you destroyed the evidence to help your lover, Captain."

"That's insubordinate and inflammatory, Sergeant. Your stripes could be in question here."

"I'll swear on a bible that I locked the evidence away, Captain. It's your word against mine." Nichols saluted and spun around and left the room.

With shaking hands she sank into her chair and dialed her own number. It rang twelve times, but there was no answer.

Her secretary came into the room again, her face creased in worry. "I haven't been able to find out a thing." She leaned across the desk. "There's a man named Lodge outside."

Luna jumped to her feet. "Send him in, hurry." She was around the desk and waiting when Dray strode into the room. Avoiding his outstretched arms and the puzzled look on his face, she stared at him. "Where is the evidence and all the papers pertaining to the case?"

"What are you talking about?"

"Stop acting. I want my evidence."

Dray's glance touched the chaos in the room. "Your work has disappeared?"

"As though you didn't know."

"I didn't."

"Whom did you collude with? Nichols? Hetty's father? Damn you to hell for what you've done."

"Wait a minute, Luna . . ."

"Take your hands off me, or I'll call the guard and have you tossed off this base."

"Listen to me. I don't know what happened to your evidence, I swear it. Believe me, Luna. I wouldn't do that to you."

"You came here as an advocate for Hetty. I was a fool to trust you. Why didn't I even suspect that this could happen? I'm three kinds of a fool, aren't I?"

"Luna, darling, listen."

"Get out." She went to the door and pulled it open. "I have to be in court in twenty minutes. With no evidence I'll have the fight of my life. So, get out and give me time to think. Go."

Dray was taut and watchful. "After the trial we'll talk."

"Get out."

Too soon she was in the courtroom, floundering through her case.

"But, Your Honor, I've tried to tell you that most of the evidence I have against this man is missing. . . ."

"Captain, we feel for you, but we cannot admit this testimony without corroboration."

Luna called Stenzi Heilmann, but the woman didn't appear.

In slow, painful shards, the case against Hetty shattered around Luna, piercing her soul and reputation.

When Corporal Hetty was found innocent, he looked at her with a cold expression of triumph in his eyes. Luna felt as if she were being buried in ice.

"Maybe you should find another line of work, Captain McAfee."

"Get out of my way, Hetty, and stay out of my way."

Luna tried to remain impassive when her CO called her on the carpet.

"And that was no way to handle the prosecution, Captain."

"I told you, Colonel Encorvado, that my evidence disappeared and—"

"Don't try my patience again, Captain, by trying to implicate Sergeant Nichols. There is nothing to substantiate your charge."

"I would like the matter investigated, sir."

"There will be an investigation, but I think it will just turn up what I already suspect, that you didn't do your job, Captain. I would hate to think that the investigation would show that you arranged for the evidence to disappear. That would warrant a dishonorable discharge."

"Sir! I have never stooped to criminal activity of any kind, and I resent your implication."

"Watch your temper, Captain. Mr. Gilmore Hetty has informed me that he feels you tried to railroad his son."

"Sir, the information against his son was there for you to see at any time. In fact you had a complete report of what I was going to do. . . ."

"Yes, yes, I know all that. Keep yourself available for questioning, Captain."

Luna left the base early that day. When she saw Dray's rental car at her apartment, she almost turned around and returned to the base.

He was in the apartment when she opened the door.

"I'd like my key back, and would you please leave my apartment."

"Luna, I had nothing to do with what happened today."

"You came to Germany ostensibly on business, stopping here to see if you could do anything for Hetty. Well, you've done it. Now, I want you out of here. I will not listen to any of your lame excuses. If you're not out of here in five minutes, I will call the *Polizei.* I mean that."

Dray nodded. "All right. I admit it looks bad, but, Luna, you must know I wouldn't do anything to hurt you. We've come to mean a great deal to each other—"

"Out! Now!" Luna's voice rose to soprano level.

Anger limned Dray's features, his hands flexing at his sides. "Are you saying that I'm guilty by association? That because I know Gil Hetty I must be the one who lifted your evidence?"

"I'm saying my career is hanging by a thread, and you have not proven to me that you weren't involved in a scheme to whitewash that rapist."

"I didn't think I needed to do that. I was a fool to assume that you would know I'm innocent."

"I don't know what you are. Get out of my apartment. I never want to see you again."

Dray slammed out of her place, as angry as she was.

For days he tried to contact her, often being at her apartment when she returned in the evening; but Luna never let him in, nor did she talk with him.

Finally she arranged to move onto the base and close her apartment in order to avoid him.

Eventually Dray went back to the States.

Luna refused all the calls he made to her and kept a low profile on base until it was time for her to return to the United States. There was no more thought of making the military her career. The whispers and rumors followed her like a nest of midges, buzzing and circling round her head.

Philadelphia was almost as alien and unfriendly as Germany had been to her. Passing the Pennsylvania bar had not been enough. Law firm after law firm turned her down, many refusing to grant her an interview.

"Come to Washington, Luna. We want you and we know how good you are. You have both the D.C. and the Maryland bar, just what you need. You could even get the Virginia bar at some time in the future." Uel Lopez had been talking long distance to his law school friend for over thirty minutes. "We love you and need you here, Luna. Storefront law is never dull, and you had a good record as a JAG until that Hetty setup. You were a crack prosecutor, and we could use you in the firm with the legal record you have."

"Even with a little cloud over it?"

"You went up against some big guns, Luna. Doing that at any time, in the private sector or in the military, can bring trouble. Gil Hetty is one of the toughest men around, and that NCO you suspect colluded with him is pretty powerful in his own right. Sometimes it's impossible to go head to head with people like that. You know you can't count on justice and the American way. To beat people like that you have to get down and dirty."

"I guess you're right. Someday I might just discover what happened."

"Atta girl."

"Sometimes I think you're a cynic, Uel."

"I'm a realist, having been a double minority, black and Hispanic, all my life, I know about fairness and justice. Those words have different meanings depending on your strata in society." Uel took a deep breath. "Come to us, Luna. I'm not talking any longer, it's too expensive. Just remember those law firms that turned you down have checked on your background, Luna. They know about Germany."

"Have you enough business to support the three of us, Uel?"

"We'll get along and save the world the way we always planned to do when we were in law school, kid. Barb misses you and so do I." Uel paused. "I know something else happened to you over there, Luna."

"Yes, I'll tell you about it when I come to Washington."

Uel whooped and turned to tell Barb what she'd said. "Barb says we're going to knock the capital on its ear."

"Give me two weeks and I'll be there."

She had very little memory of the rest of that day. Being rejected in Philadelphia was a raw hurt. Remembering Germany was agony. Like a zombie she prowled her rooms trying to figure out what went awry in her life. Leaving it all behind and joining Uel and Barb in Washington was the only bright light in her future.

Chapter 4

"Luna? Luna, are you asleep? I thought you said my driving made you crazy. It must be more relaxing than you thought. We're almost back at the office." Gretchen grinned at her.

Luna blinked, trying to orient herself. She was back in Silver Spring, not far from their storefront office . . . and she had just been eyeball to eyeball with Dray Lodge, whom she hadn't seen in two years.

Perrin Draper Lodge was no longer just a well-known lawyer. Since Germany he had run against an incumbent from his home state of New York and had become a United States senator.

When Luna had read about him in the newspapers she had been concerned that she might see him, but little by little she'd shucked that worry. Washington was a busy place, and she and Dray certainly moved in different circles.

Luna's eyes snapped open again when the car swerved. "What happened, Gretchen?"

"Some man tried to run in front of me when I went through the light."

"Green or red?"

"Yellow, I think." Gretchen grinned and maneuvered the car into a space in front of the law offices.

"Dever? Yes, it's Senator Lodge. Remember that investigation I had you on in Philadelphia? Right, Germany too. Well, I think Luna McAfee is in Washington. Oh, of course I still want you to find out what you can. I realize it's been a great many dead ends, but something could surface. Thanks." Dray replaced the receiver and buzzed for his assistant.

"John, get in touch with Haddon March. I want to talk to him right away."

Dray was staring out his window reliving his confrontation with Luna when the buzzer rang, signaling that his call was through. "Haddon? Yes, what do you know about Chuck Skinner and his ex-wife? Nothing. Okay. No, I was just playing a hunch. Yes, I knew the process server. Right, it is a small world."

Luna and Gretchen peered through the large glass window with the firm's name scrolled on it, LOPEZ, MCAFEE AND LOPEZ.

"Full house again." Gretchen sighed. "Those twenty-dollar consulting fees really bring in the clients."

"And clients bring in fees that pay the rent."

"Yeah. It ain't luxury, Maw, but we're eating."

Luna smiled at the other woman. Gretchen was an asset to the firm, not just as a receptionist but also as a fledgling lawyer who was clerking for her degree in law. Unmarried and the mother of two, she also cared for her parents, who lived with her. "I like being busy, Gretchen."

"With the three of you going all over D.C. and Maryland to the courthouses, you should keep your offices in your cars."

Barb Lopez, Uel's wife and Luna's fellow student at law school, saw them enter as she was interviewing a prospective client in the waiting room. Excusing herself, she approached Luna, following her into the back area where the offices were. "Well? Did you get him?"

Luna nodded, her smile crooking when her friend whooped.

Uel looked out at them from his office, making tutting noises and glaring at them.

Barb grinned at him impishly. "Sorry."

Uel looked first at his wife, then long and hard at his friend.

Returning to his desk, he murmured something, then rejoined the two women in the small anteroom behind the reception area that fronted four offices. "You got your man, I can tell by Barb's smile . . . but something else happened, didn't it?"

Barb's head swiveled from her husband to her friend. It was uncanny how Uel and Luna could get vibrations from each other. Then she noted the tight lines around Luna's mouth, as though she were hanging on to her self-control by a thread. "Did it, Luna?"

Luna nodded, walking into her office, which wasn't much larger than a walk-in closet, but it had a window that looked out on a small garden in the back of the building.

Barb and Uel took the two straight chairs in front of her desk when she slouched into the swivel chair behind it.

Barb stared from her husband to Luna. "What is it?"

"He was there when I served the subpoena, Uel." Luna had told her friend about the lawyer who had come from the United States and had been a friend of Airman Hetty's father. Though there were some intimate details that she couldn't even tell a good friend like Uel, he was the only person privy to most of what had happened to her in Germany.

"Jee-zus." Uel reached out to take her hand, which was now clammy and trembling slightly. Luna's lips quavered, telegraphing the tight rein she was keeping on herself. "It's a damned coincidence, Luna. You know that, don't you? God, with all the people in Washington . . ."

"I know, it would seem impossible that I would ever see him. And I hardly move in his circle." Luna's lips twisted upward. "Stop looking so stricken, old chum. It wasn't your fault, just a nasty quirk of fate." She snapped in half the pencil that she'd been holding, barely glancing at the two pieces. "And I'm not running. We have a good business here. We're practicing real down-to-earth American law in this office. Of course we'll never be rich, but we are doing very important work and making it."

"Not if you and Barb keep telling our clients they can pay

our consultation fee by a dollar down and a dollar a week."
Uel glared at his wife and Luna.

"We only did that once." The two women answered at the
same time.

"Then in came the uncle, the cousins, the aunts, the second
cousin once removed, the brother-in-law who never sat with
his back to the door. The damned family was related to Jesse
James, I'd swear to it," Uel grumbled, ticking off their misde-
meanors on his fingers and rolling his eyes when they laughed
at him.

"Get out of here, you two. I have the Wixel brief to go over
before tomorrow," Luna told her friends, feeling less tense
than when she'd entered the office.

Uel rose to his feet, smacked his wife gently on the bottom
after she'd done the same to him, kissed her, and turned her
toward the door.

Looking back at Luna, he smiled. "I'm glad you got Skinner, but I never had any doubt. See you in court, Counselor,
and remember, there is nothing we can't handle." Uel gave
her a thumbs-up sign.

Luna stared at the closed door after her friends had left, her
thoughts far from the Wixel brief that she would have to go
over before giving it to Uel for his input.

Washington, D.C., seemed light-years away from West Germany and the person she had been then, with high hopes of
getting as much trial experience as she could get by doing
military tribunals. After her tour of duty she thought she'd
have the choice of signing over or taking the Philadelphia
legal community by storm. Wasn't the private sector just crying for a very able litigator like Luna Terence McAfee?

But the case of Airman Hetty, which at first had seemed so
simple to her, had turned into a nightmare and irrevocably
changed the course of her legal career. The nasty experience
still remained somewhat of a mystery to her. Whatever had
happened to Stenzi Heilmann? Had she fully recovered from
the terrible beating Hetty had given her? Why hadn't she
come forward the day of the trial? Where had all the evidence

gone? The same old questions ran around her head as though she had just returned from Germany yesterday. Dray had brought everything to life again.

Perrin Draper Lodge had come into her life at a critical moment . . . and betrayed her in all the ways a man could betray a woman. If at times she had doubts that he had betrayed her, she buried those. Hadn't she given over enough of herself to that man without whitewashing his actions in Germany? Besides, it was ancient history now.

Luna picked up the Wixel file, forcing her mind to follow the words on the paper, smothering thoughts of Dray Lodge as she had learned to over the past two years.

Luna shook herself from her reverie, doggedly working through the Wixel file, then grabbing for the Skinner file and opening it. The words danced in front of her eyes, making no sense. In front of her brain was the vision of herself with Dray, the two of them writhing on her bed in uninhibited feeling, passion entangling them, making them one.

"God!" Luna leaped to her feet, pacing her small office, the Skinner folder clutched in her hand. "I will not let that cheating lowlife get at me again. It's over! I learned a valuable lesson. . . ."

Her door opened and Gretchen stuck her head in. "Hi. Is someone in here with you?" Gretchen stretched her neck, a puzzled frown on her face. "Could have sworn I heard something."

"No one is in here," Luna said woodenly. "What is it, Gretchen?"

"Ummm . . . it's gone clean out of my head. Now let me see . . ."

Luna took the door and began edging it closed. "Why not come back when you've thought of it?"

"I have it." Gretchen's features brightened. "We have a client in the front who has to speak to you at once. Emergency."

"Oh? Who is it?" Luna spoke to empty space. Gretchen had wheeled around and retraced her steps across the anteroom and out to the reception area. "Damn! I don't have time to consult with anyone at the moment." Luna checked her calendar. There was no one listed for a consultation. She sank back in her chair, opening the folder in front of her, elbows on the desk, her chin resting on her clasped hands. When the door opened again, she didn't look up. "Gretchen, get the person's name and give them a day next week. If they really feel it's an emergency, tell them to come back about seven this evening. I'll see them then."

"I think it's an emergency." The soft New York Yankee twang curled through the air, snapping Luna's head up and bringing her to her feet so fast she almost tumbled her chair backward.

"Get out of here," she whispered, her mouth and throat dry. "Leave."

It was almost worse seeing him now than it had been on the Capitol steps. At least then it had been so quick it was almost like a figment of imagination. Not so now . . . here . . . in her small office. The bad memories came flooding back. Damn his tall good looks! She hated blond hair streaked with silver, his bourbon-colored eyes were so beautiful they seemed sinister. The pain of seeing him had her gasping. Driving a wooden stake through his heart should kill him, drawing and quartering him seemed too kind. He had ripped her apart and he was doing it again.

"No." Dray Lodge closed the door behind him. "I'm staying until you listen to me."

"What do you want?"

"You."

Luna picked up from her desk the paperweight in the shape of a law book and threw it right at him.

Dray ducked easily, and it struck the door with a loud thud.

They stared at each other, the air crackling around them, love and hate dueling to the death.

Gretchen managed to push the door open again, though Dray didn't give her much leeway. "What happened? Did something fall? Did you sock him, Luna?" Gretchen smiled when Dray looked down at her. "Luna did that once. A client's husband tried to drag the wife he'd been battering out of the office, and when he slapped the poor woman Luna uncorked one and hit him right in the eye. He tried to sue but the judge told him to take a—"

"Gretchen! Nothing was broken. It's fine."

Gretchen stared at Luna. "Why do your eyes look so glassy? And you're flushed. You coming down with a cold?"

"No." The raspy word did sound as though she had throat trouble.

"Oh." Gretchen turned to Dray, who looked from Luna to her. "Most of our clients are the off-the-rack type. We don't usually get custom-tailored." Gretchen went out and closed the door behind her.

"Unusual receptionist," Dray murmured, watching Luna, seeing the conflicting emotions chase each other across her expressive features.

"Don't make fun of Gretchen. She is struggling to raise two children alone and helping her aging parents too. She barely makes enough here to get by," Luna told him stiffly.

"I wasn't making fun of her." Dray faced her across her desk, watching her eyes dart toward the door. "You have to talk to me. I searched Pennsylvania for you."

"Terrific." Luna took deep breaths, trying to steady herself. He wasn't going to dismantle her emotions a second time. It had taken a long time to put herself back together and no one would get to her again. "I should take up with you, Senator. What a chance for revenge!" Luna laughed mirthlessly. "United States legislator from New York kanoodles with lawyer involved in scandal in Europe. That should shake up your constituents. I should hook up with you just to put you on the front pages of the tabloids."

"For whatever reason you choose."

"Leave, you bastard. Get out of my life."

"No. It's taken me all this time to find you. We have to talk, and you know it. I'm not losing this chance to set the record straight."

"You lost me in Germany . . . irrevocably and completely." And she'd almost lost her mind and spirit. No more!

Dray shook his head. "No way, Luna. That's histrionics, and you as a lawyer should know that. We need time together to discuss what happened. I want to meet the people important to you, and you can meet mine."

"Not on your life. Your friends and way of life would make me gag."

His face reddened with anger. "Luna, I didn't know about Hetty's son's background. The drugs, the beatings, were all a surprise to me, I swear it. And I would never have set you up by stealing your evidence or being a party to anything so underhanded."

"Really? Talk is cheap, Senator."

Dray's mouth tightened. "I happen to be a lawyer too. The law is as precious to me as it is to you."

"Great. You've said what you have to say. Now leave."

"No, I won't. We haven't gone into this and . . ."

"I have several hours of work, Senator. I don't have a staff to do it for me, nor is this firm wealthy enough to hire a battery of stenographers, as I'm sure yours can, so if you don't mind . . ." Luna let the sentence hang between them.

It terrified her that she wanted to throw herself into his arms, at the same time not dimming her murderous thoughts of him. Dray Lodge was a weapon of destruction.

Anger made his strong, mobile mouth harden. The muscles tensed beneath the Savile Row suit that fitted his six-foot-four-inch frame like another skin.

Luna wished she had forgotten how the gold rays flashed in his eyes when he was irked. Damn his eyes for being a shade deeper than the thick blond hair that the sunlight streaming in the one window threaded with auburn. It was wrenching, tearing, and disruptive to be with him.

* * *

Dray saw the myriad flashes of pain on her features, the slight sway of her body, as though she'd just sustained a punch. Inflicting anguish on her had not been his plan, but he wouldn't let her disappear from his life again. Never again would they be separated. "I'll let you do your work, Luna, but I'll be back."

He wheeled around, wrenching open the door and firing through it, slamming it behind him so that it rattled in its hinges, and the frame holding her parents' picture fell forward onto the desk.

"Damn you to hell, Perrin Draper Lodge." Luna sounded out each word like a knell, her eyes burning with unshed tears, her hands clenching and unclenching at her sides.

The door opened slowly, Uel shooing Gretchen and Barb away from it before closing it behind him. "I thought I would stay and get the Skinner and Wixel briefs hammered out with you," he said slowly, noting the blind way in which she was looking at him. "That was the other trouble you had in Germany."

Luna's head went up and down like a robot's.

Uel sat on the corner of her desk, his hand opening in an expressive way. "He isn't going to get you. He has to go through Gretchen, Barb, and me first. We have a good business. We're not rich, but we're doing better than last year and we'll do even better next year. I was able to get a new carburetor for my car. I don't know too many people who can say that."

"True," Luna breathed on a shaky sob.

"Barb and I are going to start a family this year—God willing. Gretchen was able to put a down payment on that little house four months ago. We have a lot going for us."

"Yes." Luna fought to control the quaver in her voice.

"If he bothers you again, we'll push him in front of a bus."

"Up the rebels." Luna's voice sounded croaky but she managed a smile.

Uel stood and went around the desk, hugging her, exhaling

in relief when she hugged him back. "Now, let's get on the Skinner and Wixel tangles."

"Right."

"Dray? It's Gil Hetty speaking. I was wondering why you haven't returned my calls. I wanted to speak to you about that little item Chuck Skinner is lobbying for. . . ."

"Save your breath, Gil. From the little I've read I would say that the concept isn't good for New York."

"Now, wait a minute, Dray. Let's lunch with Chuck and . . ."

"No dice. One more thing. I didn't think I could make it plainer than I did when I returned from Germany that I didn't want any more to do with you. Not only don't you have the good of the state in mind, I think you allowed a criminal to escape justice by tampering with evidence, and I am talking about your son's court-martial. I can't prove anything, but I don't want you around me again . . . and don't call here."

"Would you like to be sued for defamation of character?"

"Sue away."

"You're making a big mistake, Senator."

Dray slammed down the telephone, vowing to get his private number changed.

Chapter 5

The three partners in Lopez, McAfee and Lopez worked until eight o'clock. It was their policy to send Gretchen home promptly at five because she had the children, but Barb, Uel, and Luna often labored until the briefs were in the best shape the three of them could make them.

When Luna entered her apartment at the Blyer Towers in Silver Spring the phone was ringing. "Yes," she answered, a little out of breath.

"Will you have dinner with me tonight, Luna?" Dray's voice was a stab wound, making her flinch.

She replaced the receiver, breaking the connection, then she removed it from the cradle and left it on the table, the buzz of the dial tone sounding like a warning in her ear.

Food didn't interest her, but because she'd skipped lunch, she had a glass of skim milk, an apple, and some crackers.

Digging into her briefcase, she attempted to immerse herself in work but she couldn't focus on the contents.

Television was a bore. The newest, highly touted best seller, which she'd bought in paperback, was a turnoff. Settling for a very hot bath, Luna prepared for an early night, finally replacing the receiver on the phone.

It rang at once.

Luna stared at it as though it were a cobra. It rang fifteen times before it stopped.

Sleep was a mishmash of waking, fitful dreaming of Germany; Dray; the Hettys, father and son; Sergeant Nichols and Stenzi Heilmann; and Colonel Encorvado. She tossed and turned over and over, getting up at last to get a glass of hot milk. Finally at dawn she slept, to waken at seven heavy-eyed, feeling sticky and restless.

A long shower helped to revive her, and she was able to eat half a grapefruit and down a glass of orange juice and vitamins.

When she opened up her apartment door to get her paper, the flowers were there. Two dozen cream-colored roses! Her first inclination was to tear them to pieces and throw them in a trash can. Luna didn't need to look at the card to see who'd sent them. Not too many people she knew could have afforded roses at seventy-five dollars a dozen, let alone two dozen of them.

Scooping up the fragrant blossoms with the green paper still around them, she couldn't resist a deep breath of their fragrance as she strode to Mrs. Finnerty's door and knocked loudly. The dear old woman was almost deaf and quite alone in the world. The door opened on the chain and one eye peeped out at Luna. "Here, Mrs. Finnerty. These are for you. Happy Easter."

The door opened wide and the elderly woman reached for the flowers, tears beginning in her eyes. "My dear, how beautiful. Are you sure they're for me?"

"Positive. Have a happy holiday." Luna was glad she remembered that it would soon be the vigil of Easter.

"Oh, thank you, thank you." Mrs. Finnerty's face was pressed into the blooms even as she closed the door to her apartment.

Luna had the card crumpled in her hand as she entered her own place, fully intending to fling it in the trash can. Somehow her traitorous fingers unfolded it and she read the short message.

> LUNA, HAVE A HAPPY DAY. WILL YOU HAVE DINNER WITH ME TONIGHT?
>
> LOVE, DRAY.

"No, no, no." Luna crumpled up the message and tossed it in the trash.

Hurriedly she readied herself for work, swallowing another glass of juice for energy. Then she dressed herself in a linen suit that a client who had had very little money for a divorce had made for her in lieu of cash payment.

Gillian Roth hadn't had the money to pay her when she'd first filed for divorce, so she'd paid with her talent. Since then Luna had shown her work to other friends, and little by little Gillian was building a clientele. She and her sister had a store down the street from Lopez, McAfee and Lopez's law offices. Luna, Barb, and Gretchen shopped there.

When Luna went out to the parking lot of her building to get into the VW that was almost a twin to the bashed-in one that Gretchen drove, she was feeling a little better. She took a deep breath of the crisp, sunny air.

"You need a paint job."

Luna stiffened, dropping her ignition key to the ground and swinging around to face Dray. "What are you doing here? I'll sue you for harassment."

"I'm not harassing you, darling. I just want to date you."

"No."

"Did you like the flowers?"

"I gave them away." It gave her black satisfaction to see anger and hurt flash in his eyes. "The woman lives alone and has no one." She didn't even know why she told him that, but it made her heart bump when his smile flashed over her.

"Still saving the world."

"Someone has to protect it from piranha like you." Stung by his words, she lashed back at him.

The errant muscle under his eye jumped, signaling his irritation. "Luna, someday you'll have to be fair enough to listen to me, to hear my side of what happened in Germany."

"There is no side. There was betrayal, and that's a round, circular thing that closes you in, squeezes you, and chokes you, and you were a big part of that."

"Luna! No, I didn't tamper with your case against Hetty. God, darling, I never wanted you to be hurt that way."

"Bull chips, you always know what you're doing, Senator. You're a very calculating man." Jabbing her key into the lock, she worked it until it turned.

"Let me drive you."

"No." Luna fastened her seat belt and prayed that her car would start on the first try. The VW coughed into life. Looking over her shoulder, Luna reversed the car, her shaking hands gripping the wheel.

She headed down the avenue, checking her rearview mirror, her heart flopping over when she saw the sleek black car reflected there. What gall! A United States senator driving a Ferrari! Whatever happened to "Buy American"?

When Luna reached the office, she didn't park her car in front, on the street, as she usually did. Instead, she drove into the narrow driveway between their building and the one next door and pulled to a stop at the rear entrance.

She hadn't realized she was holding her breath until minutes passed and Dray hadn't driven up beside her. Then she exhaled with relief. Entering the firm by the trade entrance, she traversed the hall that led her past the small bathroom and shower room that occupied one side, opposite the utility room housing the cleaning equipment and the sundries for the office.

Luna was able to push Dray from her mind for a moment in the pleasure of looking at the spotlessly clean surroundings. Everything sparkled. One of their clients ran a small professional cleaning service, and when she and Uel had been able to bring about a satisfactory conclusion in a lawsuit, Consuela and Manuel Torres managed the fee and court costs by giving them nightly cleaning service. Manuel and Consuela had insisted on doing it that way, but Uel and Luna had every intention of keeping them on after the slate was wiped clean.

"Hi." Barb looked along the hall from the anteroom. "I thought you'd be on your way to the courthouse."

"I am, but I left some papers here and I'll need them. Uel gone?"

"Yes. He has to face Judge Winters this morning so he wanted to get there early."

"I don't blame him."

Barb followed Luna into her office. "Is something wrong? You look a little washed out, and I'm not trying to insult you."

"I think I put on the wrong shade of foundation this morning." Luna smiled at the other woman weakly, thinking, not for the first time, that Barb had the most striking color combination with a beautiful coffee-with-cream complexion and eyes like brown velvet. No wonder Uel worshiped the ground his wife walked on, she was lovely on both the outside and the inside.

"Sure, and pigs fly over the Capitol." Barb shook her head, her arms folded in front of her. "Well, I hope you know you have a friend you can talk to, if you want to."

"I know that you and Uel are not just friends but my family, and if I need to talk, there's no one else I would come to but you two."

"You're avoiding telling me what has made your hand tremble."

Luna sighed, nodding. "I can't talk about it yet."

"Uel knows about some of it, but I won't ask him, Luna, because he's your friend and wouldn't want to break a confidence. Someday you'll tell me, and when you do, I'm going to strangle the person who hurt you."

Luna saw the sheen of tears in her friend's eyes. "Thanks, but maybe we should back my VW over him."

"Fine with me. Take care, Luna, and good luck today. I know you'll drive Skinner into the ground."

"I have every intention of doing just that," Luna told her grimly. "Not that Veli Skinner has that much confidence about getting her husband to do his duty."

"What? Doesn't she know that you're one of the best lawyers in the D.C. area? That nobody can go head to head with you in a courtroom?" Barb's eyes flashed brown sparks.

"I think Veli has been conditioned by fear and pain." Luna smiled at her spunky friend, feeling some of the heaviness lift from her spirit at Barb's heated defense. "I don't think it's my skills she doubts, but our ability to best her husband. She fears him personally because of his deviousness." Luna frowned for a moment. "Evil is a word she associates with her ex-husband. I've had some frightened clients in my time, but I don't think I've ever had one so . . . so downright intimidated as Veli. Some of the things she intimated about her marriage made my blood boil. It must be horrible to be married to a callous man."

Barb shrugged. "I guess it would be hard to imagine it unless you've experienced it."

Luna nodded. "I think you're right. See you later. You and Uel are having dinner at my place Friday night. Right?"

"Wouldn't miss it. I love that crab casserole you make."

All the way to the courthouse Luna tried to blank from her mind anything that didn't pertain to the hearing she faced that morning. That Dray Lodge clouded her mind and that it took all her control not to let her mind dissolve with thoughts of him disgusted her.

Habits of hard work and concentration took over at last and she was able to run the salient points of the case through her brain, playing devil's advocate to her own brief so that she could hammer away at the weaknesses that Skinner's attorney might find. The law firm of Maloni, Telbert and Ward was well known in D.C., and its members were known to be very powerful and clever lawyers. Up the rebels!

Parking the car was the usual chore because D.C. was a sea of autos, and though it was a gray, misty day with a chill that caused tourists to hunch down in their jackets, there were still a great many vehicles making their way through the capital.

Once in the giant building that housed the courthouses, Luna had to hurry. She was almost running when she rounded a corner and cannoned into someone. "Uh . . . pardon me." She fumbled, struggling not to lose her grip on her briefcase.

"I know you." The young man gripped her upper arms, effectively preventing her walking away. "You're the bimbo that tried to railroad me in Germany. Lady JAG!"

"Hetty!" Luna wrenched herself free, her skin shivering in disgust. "Get out of my way." Luna glared at him, wanting to strike out at him, knowing him to be a vicious assaulter and rapist. Scum! She'd had him dead to rights before the evidence had disappeared and she had ended up defending herself against charges of destroying her own case.

After a moment, he shrugged and stepped to one side, his lips curled in a hard smile. "I always wondered if there was a woman under that uniform. I guess not. You still wear the same lousy clothes." Hetty flipped his hand at her navy blue suit and white silk blouse with its own tie, and sauntered past her.

"Creep!" Luna felt the frustrating anger she always felt when she thought of the Hetty case.

God, what a tangle! First Dray Lodge and now Airman Hetty. No, he wasn't in the Air Force anymore. He was a civilian now, just as she was. What in hell was he doing in D.C.? Wasn't his home in New York somewhere? Why had he turned up here? At this courthouse? This morning? To hell with him! Who cared what he was doing as long as he stayed out of her way.

Pressing her hand to her forehead, she forced her mind to the work at hand. Find Veli Skinner and get to court. She glanced at her watch. *Ten minutes!*

When the judge entered the chambers scant minutes after Luna and called the hearing to order, Dray Lodge and Airman Hetty evaporated from her mind.

"Your honor, we will show that despite repeated warnings Charles Skinner has been grossly negligent in his fiscal and emotional responsibilities to our client, though he had ample —no, excessive—amounts of monies and properties with which to do so—"

"Objection, your honor . . ."

Repeatedly the judge's gavel hit the wood as both Luna and the other lawyer spoke heatedly. "Counselors, this is a court of law, not a boxing arena. Tone down your animosity, if you please. Proceed, Miss McAfee."

"Your honor, I maintain that Charles Skinner has not only abrogated his duties but in doing so has managed to intimidate my client into fearing to testify in her own behalf. And I intend to present evidence to prove the allegations."

The courtroom erupted with shouting and gesticulating, the judge pounding his gavel over and over again.

And so it went until finally the judge adjourned, saying that he wanted summations on Fridays and that he would give his decision the following week. "I do not enjoy these long-drawn-out hearings. This is a courtroom, not a circus. There will be no further delays or histrionics. Do counsels understand that?"

"Yes, your honor," both lawyers responded.

Wrung out, but buoyed by the way the judge had played close attention to all the evidence she presented, Luna put her arm around her client. "I think it looks good, Veli."

"Don't count on it . . . yet. Chuck is a very underhanded man and very much into power and money. He won't like any of his money going into my pocket. We married when he didn't have two pins. Now he's married to a wealthy widow who had two children he's adopted. That's the only family he wants now. It's as though his own children and I don't exist. I'm a zero he wants to erase." She drew in a quavery breath, her lopsided smile disappearing, her eyes looking fearful. "He won't give anything away easily."

"Neither will we." Luna smiled reassuringly at her client, liking the pretty woman with the streaks of gray in her brown hair. They left the courtroom side by side.

Luna accompanied Veli Skinner to the dented Chevy with the rusted left fender that the woman had parked near the courthouse.

"Thank you, Luna. I never thought we'd get this far." Veli got behind the wheel and rolled down the window.

"And we've got miles to go before we sleep, to paraphrase a famous poet." Luna leaned down, putting her forearms on the door. "Stop looking so worried, Veli. We'll win, and then you and the kids can take up your lives again and you'll have the finances, which are rightly yours, to do it. You can take that teaching job and maybe do a little traveling."

Veli Skinner swiped at her eyes. "You make it all seem so possible, Luna."

"It will be, and soon."

Veli put her hand on Luna's, where it rested on her car door. "I know you're right and that I'm a fool to let him loom over us, but I don't want him trying to get at me or the children. I think I'd rather have no money at all than that."

"He won't get to you, and you will get your fair share of the money." Luna stepped back from the car, waving to the slightly built woman with frightened eyes until she was out of sight.

Shivering a little in the damp early afternoon air, she hurried to her car and unlocked it. Damn Skinner and all men like him who put such fear into good women like that. It made her remember Stenzi Heilmann, Airman Hetty's girlfriend, who had been trying to get away from Hetty and who'd moved from the apartment she'd shared with him. One day Hetty had found Stenzi again and had beaten her so badly that she almost died. When she'd left the hospital she had told Luna that she would testify against Hetty, but then on the day of the trial she'd been a no-show. Luna had never heard of or seen the woman again. Luna hoped that Stenzi had found happiness somewhere. She deserved some joy after the horror of living with Hetty.

Luna sighed. It would be a banner day when she could settle this thing for Veli Skinner. It would somehow mitigate Luna's frustration and anger at not having been able to help Stenzi. Glancing at her watch, Luna knew that she had to hurry, she had another court appointment several miles away in Baltimore.

The day passed with Luna's rushing and scurrying around, dashing from pillar to post, seeing clients, going to court. It was a merry-go-round, but one that she loved. Storefront law had become her great career ideal, and she blessed the day that Uel Lopez had invited her into the firm.

When she had finally finished her caseload for the day, the gray sky was turning to dusky night and she felt bone-tired. She decided that she would go for a swim. There was a community college not too far from her apartment house and she would jog there for a swim.

Bypassing the office, she called in when she reached her apartment. "Barb? Tell Uel I completed what we discussed this morning and that I'll be in at eight tomorrow to work on the Walker case if he would like to sleep in for a change."

"I'll tell him. Are you going for a swim?"

"Yes. Don't worry. I always jog in well-lighted areas."

"Even so, I wish you'd drive there. Uel and I worry about you."

Luna laughed at her friend, who was just a year older than she and two years younger than her husband. "At almost twenty-seven I think I'm safe. See you tomorrow, Barb."

Donning soft cotton sweats in pale blue that magnified the sapphire hue of her eyes, she pushed on white running shoes and put her swim things in a knapsack.

When she passed her neighbor's door, it opened.

"I thought that was you, Luna. I wanted to tell you that the roses are still beautiful and my whole apartment smells so wonderful."

"I'm glad, Mrs. Finnerty. See you later. I'm going for a swim."

"Be careful, dear."

Taking the elevator from the fourth floor to the ground, she went out the main entrance, checking to see that she had her key; then she jogged across the parking lot to the street, up the sidewalk, where the streetlights had already been switched on, and across two thoroughfares, where some other joggers waved to her. People who were out finishing up some cleanup on their lawns called out to her in recognition. She had begun to feel very much at home in Silver Spring.

Dray had been watching Luna as she came out of the parking lot of the apartment building and started down the sidewalk, and he was about to get out of his car and join her. He paused when he saw someone come out of the bushes flanking the drive and begin following her. Closing his car door silently again, he waited a few moments, ascertaining that the shadowy figure was indeed trailing Luna. He switched on the engine of the Ferrari but didn't turn on the headlights, cruising slowly down the street, keeping the two figures in sight.

Luna felt comfortable jogging along at a steady pace, with the brisk breeze in her face blowing away the cares of the day. It wasn't until she was on the campus of Montgomery Community College that she had a sense of being followed. Not even turning around to check, she increased her speed, survival making her feet begin to fly over the tarmac. She had never had any problem with being accosted in this neighborhood, but caution was the better part of valor.

The entrance to the gym and sports area of the college was but a hundred yards ahead and she homed in on the weak light beside the door. She lengthened her stride as she heard the pounding footsteps at her rear.

When she was sure whoever it was was going to reach out and grab her, car lights focused on her, stopping the person behind her.

With a final kick she was at the door, wrenching it open and throwing herself inside, air rasping from her throat as she leaned against the wall of the corridor leading to the pool area, the warm, damp surface seeming so welcoming to her.

"Are you all right, miss?" a young man asked.

"I think so," Luna gasped. "But I think someone was following me."

Chapter 6

Dray saw the figure following Luna veer off when the head-lights picked him out, as though becoming aware of being pursued. The dark shape fled over the campus, showing an agility and speed that spoke of athletic prowess.

Dray pulled on the parking brake and jumped out of the still-running car. "Hey, come back here." He saw the runner redouble his efforts and in seconds disappear. Grinding his teeth in frustration, he wished that he'd tried to intercept the person back on the road where there might have been a better chance of apprehending him.

Dray got back into his car and drove it over to the parking area. Pulling the lever that released the trunk so that he could get his sport bag, he then got out of the car and locked it.

Inside the college athletic complex Dray stopped at the front desk, where a uniformed security guard asked to see his ID.

Dray held out his wallet with his driver's license. "By the way, I noticed a suspicious-looking man following a woman who entered this building. Will you inform the grounds security?"

"I'll do that."

"Thank you. I don't have a membership here, but I would be glad to pay whatever annual fee there is, up front."

"That will be fine, sir. I'll take your name and a card will be issued to you in about a week. Here, take this temporary ID that you can use until then. Men's locker room to the left."

Dray entered the steamy atmosphere of the locker room and donned his Speedo swimsuit, removing his goggles and earplugs from the bag. Then he secured the rest of his things in the metal locker with his own lock, which he always carried with him.

The chlorinated heaviness of the pool atmosphere was a familiar scent to him because he swam every day, but it also always reminded him of the times he and Luna had cavorted and swum in the *Schwimmbad* in the little town where she had lived in Germany. His teeth came together with a crack, cramping his jaws as he thought of all they had become to each other in a matter of days. No one in the world had ever invaded the core of him as Luna had done. He had been totally in love. And she had felt the same way! Damn her for not listening to him, for trying to deny it now! They belonged together.

He stared at the pool, finding her at once; the strong crawl she did up and down the lane was as familiar a stroke to him as his own. Perhaps they hadn't known each other more than three weeks, but in that time they had learned a lifetime's worth of intimate details about each other.

Dray took note of the sign that said no diving and jumped into the pool, beginning his slow, easy crawl alongside Luna, increasing his speed when she attempted to pull ahead of him, so that stroke for stroke they were side by side. He was aware that she could see him as easily as he could see her through the goggles, but he couldn't be sure if she'd recognized him.

Luna had been swimming for some time, her heartbeats slowing down into normal rhythm after the scare of someone following her. It wouldn't be too frightening going home, because most of the people who worked out at night in the sports complex walked in her direction, and one couple even lived in her building. She would make sure she had company on the way home.

All at once her musings and stroke counting were interrupted by the presence on her left of another swimmer, whom she was quite sure she had never seen in the water when she had been swimming. That didn't mean much. The pool was open at various times and there was a goodly number of people who used it.

That stroke! There was something so familiar about it. So easy, fluid, eating up the meters in the pool . . . yet restrained, as though the swimmer were pacing her.

Irked by a sense of being patronized, Luna forgot her scare, stopped counting her strokes, and concentrated on getting past the person on her left. Digging in, she increased her speed; instead of an easy open turn at the end of the pool, she flip-turned and shot back the way she'd come, feeling an inordinate elation when she passed him.

At about the middle of the pool, when she was still pulling hard, she sensed rather than saw her nemesis of the water pull alongside, then stay shoulder to shoulder with her again.

Her temper made her almost swallow water as she dug in again, flipping at the end, but now she wasn't able to shake the swimmer.

Up and down the pool they went, staying head to head, throwing up waves over the other swimmers as the power of their stroke drove them through the water like seals.

Luna swam until she thought her lungs would burst, but she was unable to best the other swimmer. After they had completed a mile or what she guessed was at least seventy-two lengths, she flung herself at the end of the pool, clutching at the tile surround, air heaving from her body, one hand tearing the soft cap from her head. Turning her head, she eyed the swimmer, who had stopped also, not breathing nearly as hard as she was. *"You!"*

"Hello, darling. You are a wonderful swimmer."

"You . . . cheat."

"No, I don't. You just hate to lose."

"Leave me alone," she muttered, bracing her hands to heave her body up on the tile deck of the pool. Before she could move, Dray had ducked under the lane line, taken hold of her waist, and hoisted her upward in one smooth stroke, his hands sliding to her hips to give her that extra shove. Damn him! Those were his hands that feathered over her bottom. Did he think for one moment she didn't know that? She turned to glare at him even as he thrust himself upward to stand next to her. "I'm warning you, Senator, stay away from me."

"You still have the sweetest backside on two continents." He smiled down at her. There was sapphire magic in her eyes!

"And you've felt every one of them, no doubt." Luna wanted to bite him, tear at him with her hands and teeth, because of the sleepless nights he'd put her through, the bitter memories.

"Not all, but enough to make an accurate assessment." Dray grinned down into her eyes.

"Lecher."

"Darling, did you know that your breasts move in the most delightful way when you're angry or out of breath . . . and that that diamond-shaped mole on the front of your thigh shows most delightfully in that suit?"

Luna inhaled, her skin prickling with heightened awareness of him. "Someday," she told him in measured tones, "someone is going to punch your lights out, and I want to be there to see it."

"Bloodthirsty little thing, aren't you? Red in tooth and claw." Dray watched appreciatively as she whirled and stalked away from him. Even in her anger, the graceful sway of her body couldn't be masked. His blood seemed to pump faster, his body hardening in response to her lissome beauty. The soft swell of hip and buttocks, the intriguing indentation of her waist, made his pulse race, but it was the spirit of her that made him feel white heat.

All at once she stopped and swung to face him, retracing her steps until she was face-to-face with him, glaring up at him. "Are you the one who followed me tonight?"

"I followed the person following you. I had every intention of coming with you tonight until I saw that someone was on your tail. So I went after him." Dray could see the uncertainty flash across her face. "You couldn't have thought that I would try to accost you."

Fury seemed to limn his features in lightning. Luna inhaled shakily. "What do you want? A character reference? You run with a pretty tough crowd, Perrin Draper Lodge. Who says that you're not capable of emulating your chums?"

"You damn well know better than that," he said angrily.

Luna lifted her chin and spun away from him.

"I don't know who the hell was following you, Luna, but I didn't like it and I don't want you coming over here again unless I'm with you," Dray called after her, raising his voice over the pool sounds.

"What?" She faced him again, almost sputtering in indignation.

"You heard me. Now, get dressed." He strode across to the door marked MEN and disappeared.

"Arrogant bastard," Luna muttered under her breath before going into the other locker room. Standing under a hot shower, then under a cold one for a long period, helped alleviate some of her ire. Dressing quickly, she rolled her wet suit into her towel and then put everything into her knapsack before leaving the locker room.

Leaning against the wall outside the door, Dray watched her face change, her eyes flash, before she masked her irritation. "I broke a few speed records for dressing." He cocked his head at her. "You kept me waiting, Luna."

"Tough."

Dray bowed, then followed her to the exit. "We can either jog back to your apartment and I'll come back for my car, or you can let me drive you," Dray ventured amiably.

Luna wasn't fooled by his easy tone. His face looked carved from granite.

"Yes, I would be willing to toss you over my shoulder if you balk at this." He read the myriad expressions that flashed over her countenance.

"Terrorist." Luna smiled stiffly at the security guard and, chin high, went out the door, heading for the parking lot, spotting the Ferrari at once and going to the passenger side. The quicker she got rid of him the better.

Dray exhaled inaudibly. For once she was going to be reasonable. He unlocked her side, taking her bag from her and tossing it in the back. Then he went around and got under the wheel, pressing the switch that locked the passenger door.

"I don't intend to throw myself into traffic, so there was no need to lock my door." Luna glared at him.

"I'm glad you're not foolhardy." Dray didn't unlock her door.

Luna leaned forward and pressed the button that activated the compact-disc player, letting the strains of Barbra Streisand waft through the auto. Then she was sorry she'd done it. It was Luna who had introduced Dray to Streisand's music. Before that he hadn't cared one way or the other about pop music, being more interested in the classics. He had become as addicted to her music as Luna, but it hurt to hear the wild love song being sung by Barbra and Barry Gibb. It was such poignant music.

The song ended as they turned into the driveway of the parking lot, and Luna turned off the player before any more of the memory music could be played.

"Thank you for the ride." Luna stared out the windshield, wishing he would unlock the door.

Dray turned to her and placed his hand along the back of the seat. "I understand that you're very anxious to contact Haddon March." At her tight, questioning look he shrugged. "He heard me call your name the other day, so he asked how I knew you, and when I mentioned your full name he told me that a person by that name had been barraging his office with calls and visits."

"I don't see how that could concern you."

"I think it's more your concern. I can arrange for you to see March in very amenable surroundings."

"How?"

He could hear the tension in her voice. "There's an embassy dinner tomorrow night, very exclusive, and you could accompany me. It would get you close to March. Will you go with me? One of the Middle Eastern emirates is hosting it. All very lavish and opulent. Exotic food and even more exotic entertainment. You'll fit right in, no alcohol will be served at all."

Luna didn't miss his salty tone. "That should make the streets of Washington safer." Luna looked at him. "I don't think . . ."

Dray put one of his fingers on her lips, stopping her words, feeling irked with her when she jerked back from him. "Whatever it is you want to discuss with March will be easier to broach when you meet him on the no-man's-land of a Washington party." He moved his hand expressively. "It will be very casual between us, just as if we were strangers meeting for the first time, but it's up to you."

Luna felt as though she were backstroking in quicksand. It was such a golden opportunity to talk to Haddon March. He was a very important person on the Hill, a former congressman from Maryland, he was a close friend of lawmakers and lobbyists alike. It seemed as though he had no enemies. Haddon March knew all about business deals in Washington. Even though Uel had told her that March wouldn't answer any of her questions, she had to try to make the man see how important it would be to her client.

"I don't know what you want to ask him, Luna, but you'll have to admit it's a golden opportunity."

"What?" Luna stared at him, coming out of her reverie.

Dray smiled grimly. "You'll never get a better chance to meet with the man, something it might take months to achieve if you wait for an office appointment." He took a deep breath. "And neither Hetty nor Skinner will be at this party, Luna."

"Trying to keep out the riffraff, are they?"

"I can't be totally sorry I know Hetty. If it hadn't been for him, I might not have met you for a long time."

"If ever." Her skin prickled with menace at the personal turn the conversation had taken.

"Not true, Luna. I would have met you, it just would have taken a little longer." He touched her shoulder lightly. "I can't do much about what happened to you in Germany, Luna, but I don't intend that my constituents ever regret they voted for me because my name is hooked to questionable people." His face hardened.

"Be glad you know about them before they can tarnish your reputation," she replied flatly.

"Will you go to the reception, Luna?"

Luna heard the hardness in his voice, but she ignored it. It was true what Dray had said. Months might go by before she could contact March, and then it could be too late for Veli.

Be stalwart! Shun the carrot that Dray was dangling in front of her. Did he think her a fool after what he'd done to her in Germany . . . even if he had denied it? No! She would not go with him. Yet, could she turn her back on a prime opportunity to aid her client? "It would be just a casual date with no commitments on either side . . . or even any implication that we might do it again." What made her say such a thing? She was caving in like an underdone cake. Luna struggled with herself, running all the reasons she should stay away from him around her brain. Giving him a flat no was the only way to handle it.

"If that's what you want."

"Huh? Yes, of course that's what I want." It was stupid, but all at once she felt such an overwhelming desire to dress formally, to be pampered, even if just for a short evening, despite the business she would try to transact. "Would it be easier if I met you at the embassy? Then you wouldn't have to drive out here to Silver Spring."

"No. I'll come here and get you. Can you arrange to be out of the shower so that you can buzz me into the building when I arrive?"

"What time will you be here?"

"Seven."

"I'll be ready and waiting in the lobby."

"Efficient of you." Dray pressed the button and unlocked her door. "See you."

"Ah, all right."

* * *

Dray waited until she'd unlocked the outer door, stepped through, and walked to the elevator without once looking back before he fired the powerful car and screeched away from the entrance.

Why the hell was he bothering with her? There were more beautiful women . . . maybe. Certainly he'd had his share of gorgeous creatures who had everything and were willing to give it. Why in hell should he bother with a female who begrudged him a smile most of the time? He'd never hurt her, and if she weren't as stubborn as a mule, she would listen to him. What the hell was the magnet that drew him back to her?

He shot down the wide avenue leading to Georgetown, where he owned a town house with a cornerstone that was dated during the time of the Revolutionary War. The house was filled with priceless antiques, some of which had belonged to his grandmother, who'd been a collector in the grand tradition.

Dray had a career he loved with a zealot's passion. Law had always interested him and he'd enjoyed trial work very much, but it hadn't been until, cajoled and urged by friends, he'd run for the Senate and won, that he'd found a way of life that absorbed him. In many ways it had mitigated the loss he'd experienced when Luna told him to get out of her life and never see her again. But nothing had really wiped her from his mind. She was there in everything he did, both as a spur and an irritant.

When he'd returned to the States from Germany, despite Luna's adjurations to him, he'd tried to find her, searching Pennsylvania and New York and the other surrounding states with no luck. It was as though she'd dropped out of sight. He'd called all the McAfees in any phone book he could get his hands on, even plowing through the Manhattan directory one gloomy afternoon.

Perhaps it was as well that he hadn't found her then. Because his friends did a great deal to get him out of the blue funk he was in and because his law work was suffering from his distracted state, he'd allowed them to coax him into running for the Senate. In that work he'd found solace and a great deal of purpose.

The campaign had been a tough one and it had taken all his mind and heart to win. Eighteen-hour days were common, and hopscotching from city to town to hamlet, meeting the grassroots people from his state, had given him a new perspective. Gradually the desire to serve those people in the best capacity possible allowed him to accept the memory of Luna in his life and still do mountains of work. Nothing completely banished her from his brain.

When he'd won and come to D.C., it had seemed only natural to take over the home that had belonged to his grandfather, who'd been a federal judge, and to his beloved grandmother. They had been close to him and had left the house to him, much to the chagrin of a few aunts and uncles, his sister and his mother and father.

Dray hit the steering wheel with his fist. Damn his family! When they saw Luna tomorrow evening they would know something was up. He hadn't been squiring anyone since he'd returned from Germany, and it hadn't been hard to squelch any desires he might have had. Luna was the woman he wanted. When he had seen her after her catapult down the Capitol steps to serve Skinner with a subpoena, all the desire he'd thought was buried erupted like a flood. He was damn well going to thrash out those feelings with her and dig away at her until he knew her deepest desires too.

Dray's body became hot and cold at the thought of Luna carrying his child . . . only if she was strong enough and able to carry it though. Otherwise they would adopt. Tiny Oriental babies or blond babies . . . or Indian babies. "Jeezus, man, you'd think you'd been drinking," he chided himself, but he couldn't keep his smile from widening at the thought of Luna and himself as parents.

Dray drove through the streets of Georgetown, admiring as he always did the activity of the area, with its underlying

serenity that seemed pervasive no matter what time of day or
night it was.

He steered down the alley and pulled into the garage that
belonged to his town house. His domicile was separated from
the garage area by a small yard with curving brick walks,
asymmetrical flower beds bursting with blooms, a miniature
cherry tree almost in flower, and a high wooden fence,
painted pristine white every spring. The small backyard was
totally enclosed with a door opening off the garage onto a
pathway leading to the back door.

Dray crossed the lawn and entered the back hall of the five-
floor home that led past a laundry room and utility room and
through a butler's pantry into the huge kitchen with every
modern accoutrement it would take to prepare a gourmet
meal. Though he had a full-time houseman who was a fine
chef, he had often cooked for a few friends on very special
occasions. There had been no time in the last year when he'd
been so inclined. He had sought and welcomed his solitary
evenings, which he'd filled with the senatorial work he loved.
It was at night when he was asleep that Luna invariably came
to him in his dreams.

Dray poured himself a glass of milk and put some carrot
sticks on a plate before going through to his study. He had
some proposals to peruse, and Skinner had put more material
in the Senate mail for him to read about the chemical development firm that wanted to open a subsidiary in an upstate New
York town. Dray knew that his recommendations would
carry weight and he was well aware that Skinner knew it too.
Damn the man! He was like a dog with a bone when he
wanted something. Dray had no intention of being stampeded
into anything, and he intended to remind his assistant to be
more diligent in heading off the man. Despite Skinner's affa-
bility, there was something about the man that repelled him.

He'd been in his comfy chair by the fire not more than five
minutes when the phone rang at his elbow. Wilkins, his
houseman, would be asleep by now, so if he let it ring it would
waken him. He cursed himself for switching off the message

machine. "Hello. Yes, Haddon. How are you? Yes, I am going to the party tomorrow night. I look forward to seeing you. Incidentally, I'll have a friend with me who wants to meet you. Right, that's the one. Yes. Good night."

Even as he cradled the phone it rang again. "Marite, it is late, so why don't you hang up. Yes, Marite, I know I'm an ungrateful reprobate. Get to it, will you, Sister. I have some work to do."

"How can you be so abrasive with your own family. Oh, never mind, you'll never change. Bret and I were wondering if you'd want to come and pick us up in your Rolls and the three of us could go to the party together."

"Sorry. I'm escorting someone and I'm driving the Ferrari. Guess you and Bret will have to suffer a ride in your Cadillac."

"Who's your date?"

"You don't know her, but you'll see her tomorrow. Come to think of it, why don't you pick up Mother and Father and bring them."

"Rat. You know how she gets on me about everything."

"So long, Sister."

"Dray, you wretch, I want to meet the woman you're escorting tomorrow. Remember."

"I told you I tried, but someone interfered. How do I know? Some guy in a fancy car, that's all I know. His headlights were right on me. What was I supposed to do? Hang around and get his phone number? No, I'm not sure if it was a man or a woman. . . ."

"I want that done before Friday."

"I read you. It'll be taken care of. I'll try the other side of this problem. It might work better anyway. Right. Sure, I'll get back to you."

"No slipups this time."

"Don't worry."

* * *

"What do you mean, you're not getting a new dress?" Barb scowled at Luna, who gave her a lopsided smile and escaped to her office.

"Luna's crazy," Gretchen offered sagely.

"Well, she isn't getting away with it." Barb shook her fist at Luna's closed door. "We're going to Charine's. It's not that far from the Mayflower Hotel and we can get there easily on our lunch hour. I'll call Diane right now and get the ball rolling."

"Charine's? Wow! I'll drive us there. Luna will be too nervous and you only have your learner's permit, Barb."

Barb rolled her eyes. "I still think I could do better than you," she muttered as she went into her tiny office and began dialing.

If Luna had known that she would have to face her two insistent friends at noon, she would have arranged a court date . . . or something. "I really don't need a dress and I can't afford . . ."

"Bull," Barb said inelegantly as she pushed her friend into the front seat of Uel's secondhand but in very good condition sedan. "And don't suggest we go to Gillian. She knows Charine's back numbers and she says we'll get a good buy."

"Does Uel know Gretchen is driving his car?" Luna asked, not paying attention to what Barb had been saying.

"Luna, I'm a very good driver."

"No, Luna, he doesn't, but this once we'll risk it."

"I have a good mind to pull over and let Luna drive," Gretchen said, careening around a truck and almost going head on into another one.

"God, I could do better than this with my eyes closed," Barb said with a sigh.

"If you keep your eyes closed, you'll feel better," Luna advised, holding her breath when Gretchen cut from the left lane to make a right turn. "Gretchen, did you ever train for Demolition Derby?" Horns blared behind them and pedestrians looked at them askance.

"Don't be silly. I'm far too dignified for that," Gretchen opined, making a left turn in front of two lanes of oncoming traffic.

"Uel will never forgive me if I die on him. He doesn't want to be responsible for my mother." Barb let out a squeak and covered her eyes with one hand.

Luna almost wished that they would have a tiny fender bender, anything to keep from going to the designer shop Barb described as full of bargains. She would be bound to see something that she would fall in love with and couldn't afford, something that would be much more appropriate for an embassy party than the basic black that she was going to wear. She didn't need to feel any more insecure about the evening than she already was.

Arriving at the small, discreet shop just down from the Mayflower Hotel was another shock for Luna. "Charine's! Are you out of your mind, Barb? I can't even afford to finger the material."

"Not to worry. My cousin works here and I told her we were coming."

"I don't care if you own the building, I cannot shop here."

"We aren't looking at the spring line or anything like that. There are some gowns that customers have refused. Charine usually sells them over the counter. Some of these don't go even when they're marked down, so they're around for some time. Those will be the ones we look at to see if we can come up with something."

Luna shook her head, following the other two through the curtained door of the salon to face the smiling dark-skinned woman with flashing brown eyes that were so like Barb's.

"Luna, this is my cousin, Diane Halland. Diane, this is Luna. Do you think that you could find her something to wear to an embassy dinner party?"

"I've been looking and I saw a few things that . . . oh, madame, how . . . how are you? I didn't know you were going to be in D.C. today." Diane's eyes fixed on the woman who had come from a curtained area behind the spacious circular room, tottering on ridiculously high heels, her black hair, which had the sheen of patent leather, cut in a French bob, the ends falling softly against her cheeks.

"What is it, *chérie*? Is something wrong? I know you do not expect me today, but it is very important that I see to my clientele for such an auspicious evening. You wish my help with something, *hein*?"

"No, madame, ah, that is, this is my cousin, Barbara Lopez, and these are her friends. I was going to show them some of the older gowns that have been discarded. . . ."

Charine nodded, her sharp eyes running over each of the women in front of her. "That is good."

Diane gestured to Luna. "My cousin's friend is going to an embassy party this evening."

Charine's quick movements stilled. "Ah, is it the Hashan emirate's fancy do?"

"It might be. I'm not sure," Luna answered, liking the tiny woman, regretting she wouldn't be able to purchase anything.

"It must be that one. *Très important*. It is why I have come to the capital . . . many of my clients will attend." The tiny woman gave a very Gallic shrug. "You must have Charine dress you for such an evening. Come."

"Wait. You don't understand . . ." Luna was talking to the air. The designer had already gone through the curtained area into the rear of the establishment.

"You'd better follow her, Luna. I have to stay up here. Someone might need help." Diane smiled at them weakly.

Luna looked at the other two. "Come on. I'll have to tell her that I won't be buying anything."

"It doesn't hurt to look. Right, Barb?"

"Right, Gretchen."

Charine was waiting for them in a large high-ceilinged room with drawing boards and podiums for pinning. "This way . . . tell me your name again."

"Luna McAfee."

"Ah, the moon lady. Such a romantic first name. Is it not a

shame your surname couldn't have been French? *Quel dommage!* But never mind. Stand up here, please."

"Madame, I cannot wear your creations. I think even your cast-offs would be too expensive to me."

"That is good because we have no cast-offs, mademoiselle. Come along, over here."

Luna opened her mouth to argue, but the tiny woman plucked at her sleeve, inviting her to stand up on the podium. "Madame, I must tell you that I . . ."

"Yes, yes, we will talk of that later. Marie, Marie, *vite, vite.*"

In minutes Luna was being swathed in materials of varying hues and designs, the minuscule designer seeming to have no difficulty in handling the materials while she waited for the unseen Marie.

Charine said nothing but "hmmm" the whole time. Gretchen and Barb sat in straight chairs, enthralled with the proceedings.

A cherubic-looking woman came through a door in the workroom and crossed to stand at respectful attention next to Charine.

"Ah, good. Marie, I want you to get me the Blue Night creation and bring it here at once."

"But, Madame Charine, that belongs to Madame Weatherfield."

"*Non, non,* it did not suit her. I refused to sell it to her. She is wearing the Sunglow model."

Marie nodded once and retraced her steps.

"This is fun, but I think we're running over our time," Barb whispered to Gretchen, who glanced at her watch and nodded.

"Luna's calendar is pretty free this afternoon, though." Gretchen rose to her feet and approached Luna and the designer on tiptoe. "Luna, we have to get back, but you call when you're through here and I'll pick you up."

"Oh, but wait—"

"That is a fine idea," Madame Charine interrupted with a

wave of her hand. "It was charming to meet you. Please do come again."

Luna stood openmouthed as her two friends sidled out to the front of the salon. She could hear them speaking to Diane Halland, and a few moments later there was the distinct tinkle of the bell over the door as it was opened and closed again. Luna sagged, staring at Charine. "Madame, if you knew . . ."

"Do not slouch. It is very bad. Everything in the body is thrown out of balance when you do that. That's better. Shoulders back, tummy tucked. *Vraiment,* you have a fine figure, Mademoiselle Muck-fee. Ah, here is Marie." Charine pointed. "Dress her, then get the shoes we will need. Your hair will need doing this afternoon, of course."

"I do my own hair," Luna told her firmly.

"*Ma foi,* the women today are foolish, are they not?"

Luna suffered through the fitting, rehearsing a refusal speech in her mind. Must visit Mother in Hong Kong . . . or my checkbook is on a suicide mission . . . or . . .

"*Voilà,* mademoiselle, see how you look. You are a goddess. You must wear this creation. I will loan it to you for the evening because I cannot let you wear anything else. It would be anathema to me. My artistic sense could not take the blow of your refusal, so you will leave my presence at once and return the dress in the morning."

Luna felt as though she'd spent time on the planet Venus by the time she left the salon with strict advice from Mme. Charine on where she should buy shoes.

Realizing that it was too late in the day to get anything done at the office, she called from a pay phone to say that she wouldn't be returning to the office.

"Okay, but Veli Skinner called twice and wanted to talk to you."

"Thank you, Gretchen, it's probably about the hearing tomorrow. I'll call her from here. Good-bye."

Luna let the phone ring twelve times but there was no answer at Veli's. Then she redialed, thinking she might have dialed wrong the first time. Still there was no answer. She could call when she got home. Veli might be at the store.

Luna found some shoes, then she took the Metro home to Silver Spring and walked the five blocks to her apartment.

When she reached her place and put down her parcels she called Veli's home but there was still no answer. Sometimes Veli took the children to her mother's house, which was about ten miles out of town.

Luna figured she would call the other woman early in the morning before she left for the courthouse. No doubt Veli needed bolstering.

Showering and shampooing took considerable time because thoughts of Dray that she had managed to keep submerged all day now erupted with a vengeance. She couldn't stop thinking of the times they'd showered together in Germany. What a tempestuous time that had been. There had been nothing in her life to prepare her for the hurricane that was Perrin Draper Lodge. Not only had he swept her away, he'd plumbed depths of feeling in her that had stunned and delighted her then. Now, as she looked back on their brief encounter in Germany, she shuddered. She had given herself completely to a man she'd known less than a week. One week of blistering passion they'd shared. The third week it had all blown up in her face. Her career had been marred, her life blighted, a cynicism born that she'd never even thought she could have. "It's insanity to see him tonight, even if Haddon March will be at the stupid party." Luna wiped a clear round spot in the steamy mirror. "You're a fool, Luna McAfee. Better to face a firing squad than Dray Lodge."

Shaking herself free of her reverie, she finished with her makeup and turned to the midnight-blue dress that was a shade deeper than her eyes, grateful that the zipper for the strapless chiffon swath was under her arm.

Grimacing at the clock, she saw that she had dressed far too early. She whirled in front of the free-standing mirror in her bedroom. "My goodness. This is some dress." The dress wrapped around her body to a length of about eight inches from the floor, where it became a diagonal ruffle that swept the floor behind her in a minuscule train. When she slipped on the the three-inch peau de soie navy slings she stared at herself, amazed.

The doorbell rang and she spun to face it. Dray! Already! What was she doing? Why was she going out with him? Driving a wooden stake through his heart would be the more sensible thing to do. She touched her face with trembling fingers. There were probably a million things she'd forgotten.

Flinging open the door, she stared at her three friends. "What are you doing here?"

"I told them they shouldn't—but you do look gorgeous," Uel told her, following his wife and Gretchen into the apartment. "You'll knock their socks off. I've never seen your hair up that way. It shows off your beautiful neck and shoulders."

"Uel's right. You're absolutely yummy. But shouldn't you have jewelry?"

"Earrings are enough," Gretchen told everyone. "She's dramatic enough with the navy-blue eyes, dress, and shoes, that moonglow hair color, and porcelain skin." Gretchen nodded sagely. "You could be kidnapped into a harem, Luna. Better take a toothbrush."

"Gretchen!" Luna gave a teary laugh. She was so glad they were here she wanted to keep them with her and lock the door against Dray. "It doesn't matter about the jewelry. Besides, these sapphire buttons are the only good ones I have."

Uel kissed her cheek. "You look wonderful." When the doorbell rang, he turned automatically and crossed the room to answer it.

Barb started to giggle. "Maybe he'll think that Uel's your houseboy."

"Very funny." Luna glared at her friend.

Barb stifled another chuckle when Gretchen grinned at her.

"How do you do. You must be Dray Lodge. I'm Uel Lopez, Luna's law partner." Uel stepped back after shaking hands, allowing Dray to enter and face the three women.

Uel seemed to be masking his own mirth at the way Dray

Lodge's eyes flitted politely over his wife and Gretchen, then homed in on Luna, running up and down her body several times. The man's damned dangerous! Uel thought. Luna had better keep her guard up! Those laser eyes of his could cut through steel.

"How do you do." Barb stepped forward, grinning. "So nice to meet you."

"Ah, yes, very nice meeting you, Mrs. Lopez."

"Hello." Gretchen grabbed Dray's right hand, pumping it, forcing his attention off Luna and onto her. "Amazing what a tune-up will do for a woman, isn't it?"

Dray's halfhearted smile broadened, his eyes needle-sharp all at once. "Astonishing."

"Good. He has a sense of humor," Gretchen muttered in Barb and Uel's direction before frowning at Luna again. "I wonder how she was able to afford that dress. It looks to me like it cost a year's salary. I'm going to check my pay stub closely this week."

"We should go," Uel said hurriedly. "Have a good time." There was a run of color up Luna's neck; Dray Lodge's gaze followed its path with great intensity. Did Luna need her law partner to be a chaperon?

"Don't do anything I wouldn't do," Gretchen admonished as Uel took her arm in a firm grip. Then she paused. "That's silly. I never do anything out of whack. Have a good time and do anything you choose . . . don't forget your toothbrush."

"Let's go, Gretchen." Uel grinned at Luna and winked, then shepherded the women out the door and closed it firmly behind him.

Dray looked over at Luna, noting how her chin was up, the high color in her cheeks deepening even more. "Toothbrush?"

"Inside joke." Luna coughed to clear the huskiness from her voice.

Dray nodded. "You do look very exciting. That gown is lovely on you."

"It's borrowed for the evening." Luna ground her teeth, irritated with herself for telling him that. It was stupid to go out with him this evening! She felt like a human sacrifice. After all the agony she'd undergone for this party, Haddon March *had to* speak to her this evening!

"The gown looks as if it had been designed for you. No one else should ever wear it but you."

"Charine would disagree with you, I think."

"Is it hers? I know her. She's a very talented lady, with salons in New York and Boston as well."

Luna bit back the question of how he would know so much about a couturiere. "I just have to get my bag and wrap."

Dray inclined his head, watching as she walked down a short hall that he was sure led to the bedroom or bedrooms, the stately sway of her body pushing his libido into power drive. His eyes didn't leave her as she made her way back to him. *Moon lady, you are lovely even though there are shadows in your eyes.* "Shall we go?"

Luna nodded, going around to check her windows and appliances as she always did before she left her apartment. Then she preceded Dray out the door, letting him lock it for her. The handwoven shawl slung over her shoulders was a remembrance of a trip she'd taken to Portugal when she'd been stationed in Germany.

As Dray and Luna walked down the hall, Mrs. Finnerty's door opened and she peeked out past her chain.

"I thought that was you, Luna. Are you going out?"

"Yes."

"You look so nice and so does your young man. The roses still look good, Luna, and I've pressed a couple in my dictionary. The fragrance is still very much in every room."

"That's nice. Have a good evening, Mrs. Finnerty."

They were silent until they reached the elevator and got into it.

"So that was the recipient of the roses."

"Yes, she loves flowers."

Dray moved and slipped a hard arm around her waist. "Next time I'll send hers directly when I give some to you. That way maybe you'll keep them. Will you, darling?"

Luna couldn't miss the velvet fury in his voice. How Dray hated being thwarted. "I don't need flowers." Luna's heart beat out of sync as she pushed free of his arm.

"Your voice is so husky. Are you coming down with a cold?" His arm tightened again at her waist, and he breathed in the essence of her. "Is that the Joy perfume I bought you in Germany?"

"No. And I don't want to discuss Germany with you. You said this was going to be a casual date."

"So I did." Dray took his arm from her waist, but he didn't move away from her, even when they stepped from the elevator, left the building, and walked to the waiting car.

Dray helped her into the passenger side, then went around and got behind the wheel.

The compact-disc player had Barbra Streisand singing a ballad about why she'd chosen the man she loved.

Luna knew the tune, and the poignancy of the lyrics caused her throat to tighten. She had to say something, anything, to keep from listening to the words of the song. "Charine said that she had come from New York to dress some of her patrons for this party."

"That includes my sister, sister-in-law, and my mother, no doubt." Dray's harsh laughter drifted over her skin, making goose bumps rise from it.

"Will your family be at the party this evening?"

"Being gagged and bound wouldn't keep them away." Dray felt her stiffen in the seat next to him and he lifted his hand from the gearshift and put it on her knee. "Not to worry. I won't let them devour you."

"Oh?" She pushed his hand away. "Do they make a habit of eating people?" Luna tried to keep the quaver from her voice.

"Never more than one a month."

Chapter 7

Luna gasped when they approached the embassy. A magnificent Greek revival mansion was set back from the road with a half-moon drive in front of it and a high cement wall all around the perimeter. Now the high metal gates stood open. "Lord, we'll never get in there. The line must be a mile long."

"Not to worry. The line will move steadily. It's always like this at one of Ahmed's stampedes."

"Oh."

In moments an attendant was at their car, inspecting their invitation and each of them in turn before nodding curtly, then gesturing at them to continue to move forward in the snaillike procession. Shortly they were on the embassy drive and pulling up to a side entrance.

"That wasn't too bad." Dray squeezed her hand, his grip tightening when she attempted to pull free. "Relax, Luna."

Luna didn't answer him. As he helped her out of the Ferrari, she stared up the fan-shaped steps that led to the mansion, whose doors stood wide open.

She stopped dead on the threshold, glad that Dray had his hand at her back, blinking against the glitter that met her eyes. Everywhere there was white and gold. White walls and sirocco trim, gold flatware and plates, gold vases filled with white flowers, sparkling gold and crystal chandeliers overhead.

They were led forward by an attendant, who made the Arabic obeisance and directed them into the receiving line.

They passed several people, some in formal Western dress, others in Eastern, both men and women greeting them.

"Dray, my friend, how are you?"

"Fine, you desert cat. Luna, may I present our host, Ahmed ben Al-Alal. Ahmed, Miss Luna McAfee."

A Middle Eastern man in a djellabah embraced Dray, then pushed back from him to take hold of Luna's hands. "By Allah, she's lovely. Goddess of the moon, where did you get that silver hair? How right that you are named after the goddess."

"Yes."

"I'm Prince Ahmed of Hashan. Come live with me and be my love."

Luna chuckled, relaxing all at once, smiling at the handsome swarthy man.

"By Allah, Dray, if you don't marry her, I will. That smile just turned all the gold in this room to dross."

Luna saw the awareness in his eyes and she wanted to laugh, especially when he looked at Dray, then back at her, and winked. Still smiling, she turned to Dray, the smile freezing in place when she saw the granite hardness, the slate color of his skin. "Dray? Are you ill?"

"Yes, I think he is." Ahmed, prince of Hashan, grinned. "I think he has been bitten by . . . a green-eyed creature." The prince guffawed and slapped him on the back. "Go in and enjoy the party, my friend. Your family have preceded you, so we will not have the wild times we once had at Princeton, *hein?*" The prince laughed again, causing the coterie of secretaries and bodyguards who stood behind him to stare in amazement.

Luna moved down the line, well aware that Dray's hand had tightened at her waist. At the end of the line an attendant appeared from nowhere and proffered a tray of drinks. Luna took what she assumed would be, from Dray's description earlier, sparkling grape juice, sipping some of the ice-cold drink gratefully. "You didn't tell me that you were such an intimate friend of the prince."

"Didn't I?" Dray glared at the glass in his hand and

quaffed it. "You'd think they could have provided some Irish whiskey."

Luna watched him, biting down hard on her lip. "You sound like a little boy."

"Really?" Dray looked haughty for a moment, then his face relaxed in a rueful smile. "I should be grateful to that bastard Ahmed. His digging away at me made you relax and laugh."

"You were amusing."

"And you're too damned beautiful to bring to this cattle run." He grinned at her when her face pinkened. "It's nice to see you disconcerted for a change."

"Rotter," Luna said mildly.

Dray leaned down and kissed the corner of her mouth before she could move back from him, the featherlike caress causing his heart to thud against his breastbone.

"Dray! There you are."

Dray closed his eyes for a moment, then he opened them and grimaced at Luna before turning to face the tall woman at his back, his arm still around Luna's waist. "Hello, Marite. Where's Bret?"

"Right behind me." Marite was looking at Luna, her eyes sweeping from her face down the front of her, the polite smile changing to cool puzzlement. "That dress," she murmured.

"Yes, doesn't she look wonderful. Darling, this is Marite Weatherfield, my sister, and that long-suffering male behind her is her husband, Bret. How are you, man?"

"Great." Bret smothered a yawn with the back of his hand. "I wish Ahmed would stop inviting us to his bashes, and so I told him. Damn him, he is forever telling Marite about some minor peccadillo we were involved in at Princeton."

"Painting Bergdorf Goodman's window green one weekend in Manhattan is hardly minor," Marite said absently. "That dress. I know I've seen it."

Luna was thinking that the name Weatherfield was familiar to her and she was about to say that when it flashed through her mind where she'd heard the name. Charine had mentioned it that afternoon! This was the woman who'd ordered the dress and hadn't been allowed to buy it after Charine had seen it on her. Lord!

"That's my dress," Marite Weatherfield said softly, her eyes traveling back up Luna's form to her face. "How did you get it?"

Bret Weatherfield put his hand on his wife's arm, two small wrinkles of concern appearing on his face. "Don't be foolish, Marite. That dress would never have suited you, and it looks positively stunning on Miss McAfee. That color is smashing with your eyes. Even if my brother-in-law is sizing me up for a punch in the face, I have to say it."

"That's after I toss your wife through a window," Dray said lazily, a muscle jumping at the side of his mouth as he stared at his sister.

"Please. She's right. I went to Charine's because a cousin of one of our partners works there." The words tumbled from Luna's mouth. "I intended to get one of the markdowns that she had, but the designer was there and she said that this dress would be perfect for me. I'm returning it in the morning."

"Damn Charine. She knew you'd see me here tonight . . . and I never forget a dress I covet."

Dray watched the play of emotions on Luna's face and knew what it cost her to make the admission she had. "Not in a million years could anyone wear that dress the way you have, and Charine knows it. You are the best advertisement for her designs in D.C. at the moment because most of the very rich in this area are here this evening."

"Dray's right, you know." Bret smiled at Luna. "And besides, I wouldn't let my wife wear that dress. The color is wrong for her."

"Please don't tell Luna that I have a lousy eye for color."

"But you do," Dray said smoothly.

"Bastard." His sister smiled sweetly at him before turning back to Luna. "You do look wonderful. It's not just because you look like a moon goddess with that hair; there's a haunting quality about you too." Marite shrugged one well-curved shoulder. "I suppose it comes from dating Dray. If I spent more than an hour with him, I'd feel sure I was in the land of the banshees. Come, you'll have to meet Mother and Father and the others. You might as well meet all of us at once."

"Not to worry," Dray whispered to her when he saw her start. "I'm with you."

"I came here to speak with Haddon March and that's all. Remember that." It took all Luna's strength of character not to fly in the face of the fury working its way through his features. "That was the bargain."

"I remember." Each word shot from his mouth like a missile. "Shall we join my family? No doubt he's with them or they have seen him." What he wanted to do was place her across his knees and paddle her until she yowled.

On their slow trek around the perimeter of the gigantic ballroom, they made numerous stops to greet friends of Dray's and the Weatherfields'. Each time he drew her forward to introduce her.

"Dray, darling, is this why I haven't seen you? My goodness, I never thought of you as the faithful type."

"Monica, for heaven's sake." Marite Weatherfield shot a rueful glance at Luna. "This is Monica Daleson and she's terribly spoiled and outspoken."

"It's just that I'm so jealous that Dray didn't bring me to this little gathering." The petite dark-haired Monica looked Luna up and down, a smile touching her lips. "Lovely dress. Very pricey. Did Dray buy it for you?"

Luna stared at the other woman, noting the anger glittering behind her smile. "No, he didn't. Is that usually how you manage a new outfit, Miss Daleson? You mustn't judge others by your, ah, modus operandi."

Bret whistled softly.

"Luna is rather outspoken too, Monica." Dray's satin chuckle had a lacing of arsenic in it. "Shall we go, my pet?" He bent down, still smiling, to kiss Luna's nose. "See you soon, Monica."

Luna shivered at the dry-ice look in those bourbon-colored eyes. He was still furious with her!

Marite looked at Luna, a reluctant smile hovering on her lips. "You dumped on her, Luna. She won't forgive that, but who cares. I wouldn't have wanted her as a sister-in-law anyway."

"No fear of that," Dray drawled.

Bret chuckled. "But Monica won't give up until you're married."

"Save me." Dray drew Luna's hand to his mouth, his tongue touching her palm, making his sister and brother-in-law laugh.

Luna knew that neither of Dray's relatives had noticed how plastic his smile was. "You're very capable." Luna tried to clear the huskiness from her voice. "I don't think you need a marriage to rescue you."

"Oh? How disappointing. Mother and Father will have to wait to be grandparents to my children. Let me know if you change your mind, sweetheart." Dray looked down into her sapphire eyes, seeing the confusion and ire warring there. He was sure they almost mirrored his own tumultous feelings.

"Don't hang by your thumbs."

"I like this lady." Bret grinned at his brother-in-law, who shot a sharp look his way before fixing on Luna again.

"But you wanted children right away, so I think we should get to it." Dray watched the run of color across Luna's face, unsure if it was a flash of pain he saw in her eyes as her well-shaped mouth worked in frustrated anger.

"Children? Get to it?" Marite looked angrily amused, her eyes going from her brother to Luna several times. "Dray, for heaven's sake, this is all news to me. Why haven't you said anything to the family? Mother will be livid. A wedding is not an intimate barbecue for a hundred close friends. It requires a great deal of planning. Luna, what is it? Is something caught in your throat?" At Luna's negative shake of the head Marite stopped patting her on the back, scowling up at her brother, who stared back at her.

Luna looked from one to the other, ready to kick Dray in the shins. "I assure you there are no nuptial plans," she managed huskily.

"Don't be modest. You've pulled off a major coup," Bret said at her side. "I would have bet my best polo pony that my brother-in-law would have stayed single ad infinitum." Bret smiled when she shook her head.

"Could we change the subject?" Luna glanced at Dray and his sister as they exchanged greetings with a small group.

"Of course, though I don't think there's any sense trying to hide things like this. The paparazzi would be bound to ferret it out anyway. Best to be up-front with it." Bret took her arm to steer her clear of a passing waiter, a thoughtful expression on his face. "I could tell something had changed him when he came back from Germany. That's where he met you. Right?" Bret looked pleased with his deduction. "Even during his election campaign he would be miles away at times. Once or twice he mentioned your name to me because he was looking for you. Glad he found you."

"Listen to me. You mustn't think there's anything between Dray and me. . . ."

"All right, I won't think it, but I don't see that changing anyone's mind. It was bound to come out anyway. You'll be written up in all the Washington rags tomorrow because you were with Dray, and because you're one of the prettiest woman in Washington, aside from my Marite," Bret told her cheerfully, patting her on the arm.

"No," Luna said faintly.

"Yes," Bret answered emphatically. "Dray is news. Always has been, even when he crewed for Princeton. Bigger than life! He'll probably be president one day."

"Of Princeton?" Luna struggled to keep on keel.

"The United States." Bret smiled kindly, patting her gently on the back when she began coughing again.

"Good Lord," she wheezed.

"Mustn't get upset. You might turn out to be a great first

lady. You'd bring a little dash to Sixteen Hundred Pennsylvania Avenue."

"Dash? God, this is crazy." What would Bret Weatherfield say if she told him she despised his brother-in-law?

"Everyone says that about the Lodge family, but don't count them out, they usually come out winners." Bret angled her toward a cluster of people standing around a settee. "Ah, there's my mother-in-law. Sterling lady. We all call her Bellemère. She likes that."

Luna stopped dead, letting others drift past and around her, Dray and his sister now having a low-voiced disagreement as they stood apart from the crowd.

Bret followed behind them, exchanging pleasantries with an acquaintance.

"Is something bothering you, Miss McAfee?"

Startled, Luna looked around at the rather rotund but pleasant-faced man who was their host. "I'm sorry, Your Highness, I was daydreaming. I didn't mean to block your way."

"Do not bother yourself about that. Ah, but I do understand about the daydreaming. I enjoy doing that in the desert. That is the best place for any type of contemplation."

"Yes." Luna smiled. "That would be wonderful."

"Perhaps I can persuade you to join me in the desert one day?"

"Thank you for the invitation, but at the moment I would just love the opportunity to speak with Haddon March."

"It shall be done." Ahmed snapped his fingers, whispered into the ear of an attendant, and in minutes the man Luna had come to see was striding toward them. "I shall leave you alone with my guest, Miss McAfee, but I shall reclaim you for a dance."

"Thank you, Your Highness."

The tall, spare, balding man with the sharp-featured face and benign smile bent over her hand. "Miss McAfee, allow me to compliment you on your ingenuity."

"Thank you, Mr. March, but I was willing to go to great lengths to speak to you. I'll get right to the point."

"Please do."

"My client Veli Skinner is trying to get her fair share of a company owned by her former husband. I have traced to him the ownership of a holding company that you were also partner in, Mr. March."

"Yes, Alpha Corporation. I sold out of that some years ago, Miss McAfee, so I don't know how I can help you." Mr. March put out his hand, bracing her arm. "I can see I've disappointed you and I'm sorry."

"Thank you. I did so hope that you might give me some idea of the company's worth."

"I can't do that because there've been so many fiscal fluctuations since I sold out, but I will tell you that I don't think Chuck Skinner is hurting for money. Does that help you at all?"

"Some. It's better than nothing, but it would have been better had you still been tied to the company."

Mr. March's lips tightened. "I got out when I felt that all was not on the up-and-up, I will tell you that."

Luna nodded. "I believe that about Mr. Skinner. Thank you for your help, Mr. March."

"You're very welcome, and if there's anything else you need, call my office. I'll make sure I get back to you."

Luna was still smiling when another guest came up to Haddon March and began speaking with him.

"Ah, now I see that you are free, so would you do me the honor of dancing with me." Prince Ahmed was at Luna's side, his hands raised as though in supplication. "It is not a custom of my people to dance with partners, but I became addicted to the practice when I attended Princeton." He shrugged and grimaced. "The orchestra will not play until I begin the dancing." The prince inclined his head and offered his arm.

"I'd enjoy dancing. Thank you." And it would give her a chance to gather her scattered thoughts. It had been a bitter pill to learn that there was no business link between Skinner and March. She would have to think of another way to attack the holding company and get the information she needed. Luna sighed. What a crazy evening! Being with Dray Lodge, a man she'd had every intention of avoiding, and being on the brink of meeting the rest of his family was much like grasping the tail of a cyclone.

Luna took the prince's arm, aware that Marite was looking at her, mouth slightly agape, and that Dray looked thunderous. What was biting him, for heaven's sake?

The prince was well versed in the steps of the waltz, but he was not a natural dancer. Still, it had been a long while since Luna had done such a frivolous thing and she gave herself up to the enjoyment of it. She smiled at the prince and forgot her many worries for a short time.

Dray watched Luna glide around the floor on the arm of the prince, and his teeth came together with a crack that he felt behind his ears. Damn Luna McAfee! He had a powerful urge to go out on the dance floor and drag her away from the prince and out the door.

Luna had no end of partners after that, mostly men she'd never met but who spoke ingratiatingly to her.

When Dray took her in his arms, after several tunes had been played, he was quivering with fury.

"If you'd like to take me home now, or even send me home in a cab, I'll understand . . . but I honestly can't figure out why you're so bent out of shape. We're not exactly what would be described as a couple."

"Can't you? Charming. You came with me, Luna. Did you forget that?"

"You're talking like a character out of an antebellum novel."

". . . And then you dance the first waltz with the prince, which makes it look as though you're a favorite of his."

"Is that why so many of those men spoke to me in that oily way?" Luna tried to control the laughter that bubbled up in her but she couldn't. It burst out of her, turning heads, eliciting admiring smiles. "Oh, that's so funny."

"I don't see it that way."

"Oh, Dray, stop glaring. You should have heard what some of these men were saying to me. I had no idea why they were talking about contracts and leases." She leaned her head back, mirth getting the better of her. "They think I have access . . . to the prince." She caught the slight relaxation of Dray's features, though there was no appreciable warming of the arctic expression of his eyes. "Admit that it's funny."

"It's Washington social life." Dray shrugged.

Luna lifted her head and chuckled, looking right in his eyes. She didn't guess his intention until his mouth was on hers, teasing her lips gently, parting them, his tongue just touching hers before he lifted his mouth. "Don't do that again . . . ever."

"Why not? That's another aspect of Washington social life, just a harmless flirtation, darling."

Luna staggered, gasping when his hands dug into her. "You're about as harmless as a cobra."

"Yes, moon lady with the shadows in her eyes, you've got that right." Dray stopped dancing, not seeming to notice the curious glances other dancers were shooting his way. "C'mon. It's time to meet my parents."

Luna tried to wriggle out of his hold but she wasn't able to free herself. "Don't you think it must look funny to the other guests the way you're trolling me across this room?"

"Don't exaggerate." Dray led her right to the group of people Bret and Marite were standing with, and an older couple seated on a gold-trimmed settee. Dray stopped in front of his parents. "Mother, Dad, this is Luna McAfee. Luna, this is my mother and my father."

Luna didn't know whether to shake hands with the stately woman and the stern-faced man who looked to be an older version of Dray, or to genuflect. "Hello. It's nice to meet you."

Dray's father rose to his feet. "You are a very beautiful girl, my dear. Are you a model?"

"No, sir. I'm a lawyer."

"A lawyer?" Dray's mother trilled. "Goodness, you are coming up in the world, Perrin Draper. Does this mean you are finished with actresses and fan dancers?"

Luna felt as though she'd stepped through Alice's looking glass. Quiet hysteria manifested itself with a giggle that turned all heads toward her. She tried to cough to cover her lapse, but Dray's mother's needle-sharp eyes fixed on her.

"I saw you dancing with the prince. Ahmed is so entertaining, isn't he?"

"Yes."

"And accommodating. I saw him steering Haddon your way. Did you succeed in wheedling out of him the best bets on the bull market, my dear?"

"Ah, no."

The silence settled like a blanket as several pairs of eyes swerved to Luna expectantly.

"Actually, he wasn't able to help me, but it was nice to meet him." Luna didn't look at Dray, but she felt his gaze on her.

"Haddon said you were bright and determined. Left fifty messages with his secretary." Dray's father observed in general.

"My, that *is* an encomium," Dray's mother murmured, her eyes still assessing Luna.

"I like her," Bret whispered to his wife, who nodded.

"She is certainly a change," Melanie Lodge, Dray's mother, offered silkily.

Luna felt she had suddenly become invisible, the way the Lodge family was making observations.

Dray's father had been standing since Luna had joined the group, and now he moved forward and kissed her cheek. "I love your name, my dear. What romantics your parents are!"

"Yes, they were, sir. My father died when I was a teenager,

and my mother and stepfather were killed in an auto accident some years ago."

Perrin Lodge Senior helped Luna to a chair. "Do you have brothers and sisters?"

Luna shook her head, noting the auburn-haired woman who was sailing up to the group at that moment and who evidently caught Perrin Lodge's question and Luna's silent negative.

"Heavens, how fortunate you are. Hello, I'm Belinda, Dray's younger sister, and I wish I had as little family as you."

"Lin, dear, you're so affectionate." Dray's mother laughed, her eyes on Luna. "We are a large and sometimes rambunctious gaggle."

"I see that."

"So, are we to know how long you and my son have been seeing each other?"

"No," Luna said forcefully. "That is, we haven't. This evening is just a fluke."

"When I have something to tell you, Mother, I'll call." Dray's words superimposed themselves on Luna's negative.

"I don't think she's as enthusiastic for this . . . loose-knit alliance as you are, Dray," his sister Belinda whispered, causing his mother to smile.

"You must be an old friend of Ahmed's too, is that not so, Luna?"

"No, Mrs. Lodge, I just met him this evening."

"No doubt Ahmed was being cute when he decided to open the dancing with her." Dray shot a glance at his mother.

"Ah, then you are not the latest visitor to his desert hideaway?" The older woman's dulcet words seemed to echo for a moment.

"No, but he did invite me there."

"What did you say?" Dray whispered. "I'll tear him apart."

"Think of what you're saying, old boy," Bret whispered. "You don't want to bring down the SWAT team from Hashan on our necks. Marite would be angry if I were drawn and quartered, wouldn't you, dear?"

"Put out a bit, to be sure." His devoted wife patted his arm before turning to her brother. "Bret is right. Don't be an ass, Dray, and make a scene here. You are, after all, a senator from New York."

Every muscle in Dray's face tightened, then relaxed. His head whipped around, focusing on Luna, then he looked back at his sister. "I only needed you to remind me of who and what I am, Marite." His voice was a silky whip that flicked everyone within hearing.

"My, my," his mother whispered. "Another revelation, I do believe."

Reaching out one hand, Dray curled it around Luna's fingers and brought her forcibly against his chest. "I assure you I am aware of my position as a senator from New York." The words shot around the group, ricocheting off each person.

"My, my, our son is getting physical at an embassy party. What should we do with him, Perrin, dear?"

"Nothing, my love." Dray's father leaned down and kissed his wife on the cheek. "Stop baiting him."

"Me?"

"Yes, you, or I'll take you home this instant."

"Dance with me instead and I'll be very good." Dray's mother rose to her feet, touching her son's cheek with one finger as she passed. "Why don't you bring Luna to dinner one evening?"

"I may." Dray didn't smile at either parent, but he inclined his head politely before turning to Luna. "Shall we dance?"

Luna was about to tell him that she felt she should be leaving when she was propelled onto the oak parquet floor and whirled around to face Dray. "For heaven's sake, you almost pushed me into that couple."

"You danced with Ahmed without complaining."

"How do you know that? You weren't there." Luna frowned at him. "This conversation is ridiculous. Ahmed was being a good host and he also introduced me to Haddon March."

"And did it go well?"

"Unfortunately no, but it wasn't Mr. March's fault. I shall have to try another tack."

"Care to tell me about it?"

"I don't think so. I don't want to breach client confidentiality."

"But you didn't mind doing that with March."

"For heaven's sake, Dray, I was discreet, but I had to approach him about something to do with a case. I really can't discuss it."

"Of course."

Luna didn't miss the hard intonation in his voice. Dray Lodge was plenty irked.

The music was pure swing and had a sensual rhythm that seemed to enter the fiber of their beings, drawing them together as their bodies responded.

"When we lived together in Germany we were very good. Maybe we should try it again," Dray whispered in her ear.

Luna stiffened. "I'm not into sadomasochistic experiences, Senator."

"Tough brat, aren't you?"

"Tougher than I was." Luna pushed back from him so that she could look up into his face. Those damned magnetic eyes! "Think of the bad publicity for you, Senator, if your name was ever coupled with a person with a cloud over her background."

"That's bull and you know it. Nothing was ever stated as fact by the military or the private sector that you had anything to do with the so-called missing material or that you made up such evidence. First, Hetty's defense attorney would have, and did, defeat your case without the material, ergo you'd have been a fool to have lost it intentionally. Second, you had and have a reputation for honesty that most people who know you would be glad to verify." He had surprised her, and her mouth opened as she gazed up at him.

"That didn't stop the rumors or innuendos." The words pushed themselves past her lips, the memory of Germany making her freeze up inside.

"Gossipmongers are virtually impossible to control, but even the gossip wasn't as strong as the positive character references you had."

"That's because I had nothing to do with impugning my own witnesses or their testimony, nor did I tamper with any evidence," Luna said stiffly.

"Haven't I been saying that?"

Luna pushed free of him, no longer dancing. "And how about the rumor that I gave my evidence to the man I was sleeping with? How should I have dealt with that when it was on everyone's rumor list?"

Dray pulled her back into his arms. "You should have lifted your chin as you just did and ignored the bastards."

Luna shook her head. "Nothing stopped it." She looked up at him. "I'll tell you something else. Hetty was and is scum, and he should have been put away for what he did to those women in Germany, especially Stenzi Heilmann. There was a very good chance that she would have been an invalid for the rest of her days." Luna shook her head. "Poor Stenzi disappeared. God knows where she is."

Anger flashed across Dray's face. "I have severed my relationship with Hetty, Luna."

"Similar to closing the barn door after the horse is gone?"

"Yes, but it is done."

When she felt his fingers dig in at her waist, she looked up at him once more.

"Hetty contributed to my campaign and was generally helpful when I was seeking election, but even then I was leery of him. I had no proof that he'd been responsible for the underhanded business in Germany, but I suspected it. After my election I had the chance to put a few people on him. There was nothing concrete to bind him to what happened to you in Germany, but I discovered enough to make me want to sever all ties with him. I had my staff repay every nickel he had given me . . . with interest. It doesn't change what was done to you, because the culprits haven't been apprehended, but I needed you to know I never would have wanted you to go through such a painful experience."

Luna stared up at him, her feet moving to the music even though she wasn't paying attention to the tune. Chink by chink Dray Lodge was chipping away at her barriers, and that made her dig in her heels emotionally. No way would she leave herself vulnerable again. He sounded so sincere, but that didn't mean much. A lot of people pretended to be sincere. She was both angry and sad that she couldn't allow herself to believe him.

Dray watched the play of emotions over her face, then he reached up and tapped her nose with his index finger. "It's a start."

The music ended and they strolled toward the sidelines, where Dray's family was congregating with friends. When Dray saw that one of the persons in the group was the prince, he steered Luna away from them and toward a huge buffet table in an adjoining room.

"Won't it look a little strange if we avoid your family?" Luna couldn't stop the chuckle that escaped her when she saw the mulish look on his face. "Actually, I find your family very diverting."

Dray shrugged. "Wonderful. We're going to sample Ahmed's elaborate buffet. We're just being good guests."

The buffet was exotic and overabundant, but Luna stuck to the wonderful array of fruit, having no desire to taste the other rich choices and barely containing a shudder at the animal eye that held a place of honor on the table.

"Goat's eye. Ahmed's people feel that it is the ultimate compliment to offer it to guests."

"I hope the custom doesn't catch on in Washington."

"Not hungry?" Dray proffered a small chunk of pineapple on a skewer, which she took after he seated her at a small side table near a floor-to-ceiling window.

"Not really, but I do like fruit. I'm addicted to it, I think."

She smiled at him. "If you don't mind, I should be going soon. If you'd like to stay, I could get a cab. I have an early court hearing tomorrow and I want to be up for it, and I do have to consult with my partner about a new approach, since Haddon March provided little help."

"Sounds serious. Would it involve that subpoena you served the other day?" Dray grinned at her. "You're quite a runner."

She smiled back at him, feeling some of the tension leave her. "As a matter of fact, it *is* the Skinner hearing. I want it to go well."

"It should. You're a very capable advocate."

"You only saw me in court once . . . and that was rather a fiasco."

"You were strong, sure, and aware of your facts; and even though your written and photographed evidence had disappeared, you were still able to call on some strong arguments to prosecute your case. You didn't bend or break when the pressure was on. I would take you into my law firm anytime."

Luna felt her body heat and freeze at his words. She'd been proud of her talent as an advocate, she'd always loved the law. Hearing words of praise about her work from Dray made her dizzy.

They stared at each other as though they were in a separate room from the rest of the company where none were allowed to intrude.

Luna shook her head to clear it. "You say that because you're not practicing now."

Dray shook his head. "That's not true. I would make no such offer if I didn't want you." Dray leaned over and caught her hand, bringing it to his mouth, his tongue touching the palm. "I wouldn't want you to sue me."

"Thank you," Luna said quietly, her heart thudding so hard she found it difficult to breathe. Freeing her hand, she looked at him. "That was kind of you, but I have no intention of changing my legal direction. I happen to love storefront law and I don't think even the prestigious firm of Lodge, Crimmins, Dell and Lodge could woo me away."

"I can understand that. As long as you accept that the offer was valid I won't quibble about the length of time it takes me to get you."

"I thought we were talking about law," Luna said huskily.

"That too."

Luna sat back in her seat, looking around the elaborate room, barely noticing the gold escutcheoned ceiling and walls. "Dray, people don't go backwards in relationships. It doesn't work that way, and even if it did, I wouldn't want to try. What we had was badly damaged—irreparably, it would seem—"

"Not to me," Dray interrupted roughly.

Luna looked back at him. "It's that way for me. I will never involve myself in that type of entanglement again. It was all too fast, too facile. That will never happen to me again."

"Luna, sometime you will have to take the time to go over this whole affair, step by step, until everything is clear between us. Not even a friendship can survive when so many things are hidden."

Luna put down her fork, her head beginning to buzz with a headache. "It's time for me to go, Dray."

"We're just conversing. Do you like children?"

"Yes, but . . . Dray, this is a silly conversation." Luna rose to her feet, wiping her hands on the fine linen napkin. "I'll call a cab."

"I'm taking you home." Dray rose to his feet, his face determined.

In silence they made their way across the large room toward his family once more.

"Perhaps we should thank our host first." Luna's suggestion was answered by the merest inclination of Dray's head.

Luna couldn't help notice how Dray stiffened when Ahmed turned to her as they approached him.

"Luna has an early call in the morning, Ahmed, so she won't be joining you in your jet to fly to your desert home. If she ever does come, I will be accompanying her," Dray drawled.

"Very direct, my friend, as always." Ahmed chuckled, joining them as they moved toward Dray's family.

Luna eyed the man at Ahmed's heels.

The prince followed her glance. "You must not mind Abdul. He is a bodyguard but also my secretary. He is always with me. Abdul, make your obeisance to Miss McAfee."

"How do you do." Luna thought better of putting out her hand when the tall, dark man bowed from the waist, his own hands remaining in the sleeves of his garment.

"People from my part of the world often have bodyguards, Miss McAfee."

"Yes, I can understand that. There is unrest."

"That is an understatement." For a moment the affable prince's features darkened, then he was smiling again, nodding to members of Dray's family. "Miss McAfee has come to bid you good night, Mrs. Lodge."

"It was nice meeting you, Miss McAfee. You must come to an informal party I'm having next week. Dray will bring you." Dray's mother smiled sweetly.

"It's kind of you to ask me, Mrs. Lodge, but I feel I must decline. My work load is very heavy for the next three months, but I thank you for thinking of me."

The Lodge family was too well bred to stare openmouthed at anyone, but there was polite surprise on their faces.

"Good-bye, everyone." Dray took Luna's arm and stalked across the ballroom toward the entrance.

"Wait, will you." Luna had all she could do to keep her balance, unused as she was to being whisked across a highly waxed floor in high heels.

"You might have considered my mother's invitation and told her you would consult your calendar. Hell-bent to get rid of the Lodges, are you?" Dray raised his arm as they passed through the front door, gesturing to a hovering auto valet. He saw Luna shiver. "Are you cold?"

"Not really, and I wasn't being impolite. I do have a mountain of work to go through, and quite frankly I don't see any need for us to meet socially, Dray."

"You've made that crystal-clear." Dray flexed his hands as they waited for the car.

The good feeling that had been between them, that had seeped into her soul and spirit like a balm, warming and soothing her, dissipated in seconds. She felt a rush of pain because she and Dray were at odds once more.

She stood stiffly apart from him, finding nothing to say, feeling his eyes glance her way more than once.

The attendant drove up to the steps and jumped out of the car, deflecting any chance for speech.

The ride home through the spring night in D.C. was as spectacular as ever. The capital, as always, was aglitter and bustling.

"It's beautiful, isn't it?"

Luna sighed at the sound of his voice. "Yes, I've been happy here in D.C."

"You went to school here, didn't you, Luna?"

"Yes. Law school. Uel, Barb, and I all went to George Washington."

"I went to Harvard."

"I remember."

"Yes, we talked about everything during the short time we were together."

"Do you miss practicing law?" Luna changed the subject.

"Sometimes."

Luna turned to gaze at his profile. "I had the feeling that you loved being a senator."

Dray nodded once. "More than I ever thought I would. I like my constituents and working for them. New York, to me, is the most fascinating state to represent in the entire Union. Putting together laws that can help them challenges me as nothing ever has."

"And I like the legal profession because I'm able to help the ones who sometimes haven't the money to get recourse to the law."

"We both work for the good of the law, Luna. We have a lot in common."

All at once the picture of the two of them together in Germany flashed across her mind and a pain lanced through her. "That isn't always enough," Luna said hoarsely.

Dray's head whipped her way for a moment. "Stop it. Don't concentrate on the bad things, Luna. Can't we put the past behind us? Every relationship has wounds."

"Like falling off a mountain and being battered and bruised all the way to the bottom. Wounds like that leave scars."

"We could take it slower, examine what we have, Luna. There were a lot of good things."

"They were buried by the bad. Plummeting into a torchy affair is no answer. Neither of us had any defense when there was a crisis. It was too thin, with no substance."

"I don't agree with that, Luna, but I'm willing to try to discuss it with you. . . ."

"Let's not talk about it anymore. Do you mind, Dray?"

"Fine."

The car purred into Silver Spring with the unspoken things vibrating between them.

Dray pulled up in front of the apartment building, turning off the ignition before getting out and going around to Luna's door, opening it, and helping her to the pavement. He took the key from her and opened the outer door of the vestibule that housed the mailboxes, then crossed to the other door that opened to the lobby.

Luna faced him. "Good night, Dray."

He took her in his arms, his mouth descending and working over hers, gently giving but taking too, his tongue thrusting into hers. "Good night, Luna. Don't look so shaken. It was a good-night kiss. Give 'em hell tomorrow."

"I intend to do just that." Luna inhaled a shaky breath, feeling as though she'd just been put through a paper shredder. She spun on her heel and went through the glass doors, heaving a sigh of relief when she heard the lock click behind her.

She was sure she wouldn't sleep. Dray was larger than life in her mind, and the Skinner hearing intruded like a dissonant drum on her consciousness. Sleep would definitely be out of the question!

Chapter 8

Early the next morning, Luna was about to leave the apartment when the phone rang. "Yes? Oh, Gretchen, what is it? I have to get to the courthouse. What? When? My God, what hospital? Barb went? Thank God. Call there if you can and tell Barb that I'm on my way as soon as I see the judge. Yes. Thank you." Luna hung up the phone, her shaking hands covering her face.

When the door buzzer rang, signaling that someone was downstairs, she jumped as though a bomb had gone off next to her. Staring at the speaker system next to the door as though it were the enemy, she approached it, pressing the release after a few seconds. "Who is it?"

"It's me, Luna. Open up. I've brought you breakfast."

Luna heard Dray's voice, and a shudder ran through her. Her trembling fingers pressed the release, but she didn't move from the door, the shock of what Gretchen had told her about Veli Skinner going through her in waves.

When there was a rap at the door, she unfastened the bolts and opened the door.

"Hi, I just— What in hell is wrong?" Dray dropped the paper bag he was carrying on a nearby table and gathered her into his arms. "Are you ill? Tell me," Dray ordered huskily.

"God, it's so awful," Luna told him in a reedy voice, her fingers clutching, unconsciously, at the front of his dark gray worsted suit. "Veli Skinner was mugged last night in her home, beaten so badly that she's been hospitalized. Her children are so young that they slept right through it, but they

found her this morning. She was alone . . . God knows how
long. . . ."

"Luna, you're trembling. Sit down. I'm going to give you
some of this hot coffee. . . ."

"I can't, I haven't time." Luna's voice was raw with the
pain she was feeling for her client and friend. "I have to see
the judge before the hearing begins."

"Just a little coffee, and then we'll both go. My meeting
isn't until ten."

Luna didn't try to argue him out of it. When they left a
short time later, it seemed very natural to have him beside
her, to let him do the driving.

Luna blinked at what seemed to be the speed of light that
carried them to the courthouse.

Dray took her briefcase from her, his eyes narrowing on the
slight trembling of her lower lip.

In a blue fog, Luna shot a hazy smile his way before she
strode purposefully up the steps to the courthouse, not speaking, but aware that Dray was matching her step for step, and
that many passersby spoke to him. Every time she thought of
Veli, the juice and coffee she'd had for breakfast seemed to rise
in her throat.

When she tried to explain to the bailiff that it was impera-
tive she see the judge, he shook his head.

"Let her in at once. She has court business," Dray answered the man curtly.

The man's face worked for a moment, then he shrugged
and opened the door to the chambers.

After Luna had explained Veli's situation the judge nodded,
looking pressed. "All right, all right, Miss McAfee, I see your
point and I assure you the court is understanding. I will speak
to you and Mr. Ward when the case is called to order."

"Thank you, your honor."

The moment court convened, Luna leapt to her feet and
demanded a continuance. "My client was to be the first witness here. Since she can't be heard because she is in critical

condition in the hospital, I request that the court grant a continuance in the name of humanity and justice."

The judge looked over his half-glasses. "Your defense of your client is duly noted, Counselor." The judge cleared his throat and gestured. "Counselors will approach the bench."

The judge tapped his fingers for a moment, looking first at one lawyer then at the other. "Miss McAfee says that her client was going to be her first witness at this hearing, Mr. Ward, but that her client was the victim of a robbery and mugging and is in the hospital."

"Your honor, we sympathize with the plight of Miss McAfee's client, but we are prepared for this hearing, and, I respectfully remind your honor, you said that there would be no more dragging of feet on this case. My client has undergone a great deal of emotional pain and discomfort because of this case. Expediting this situation is the most humane way to handle it for my client; ergo, we do not see the need for a continuance."

"What your client has gone through is nothing compared to what Veli Skinner has experienced with no money, limited job prospects, and house payments that haven't been met by your client as promised per the first divorce agreement," Luna shot back angrily.

"Now, wait a minute . . ."

"Counselors, you will return to your seats. I'll have no more outbursts in my courtroom."

Luna was shaking when she sat down again. Her eye happened to catch a movement, and when she looked up, Dray was rising to his feet. He mouthed good-bye and gave a small nod and a thumbs-up sign, then he left. She hadn't realized he had been in the courtroom all that time. To her surprise, just that small gesture buoyed her flagging spirit and she sat straighter in her seat, looking up at the judge.

"Counselors, in light of the unfortunate accident that befell the plaintiff in this case, this court will adjourn until three weeks from today." The judge looked sternly at Mr. Ward, who was representing Skinner. "If there is any inconvenience

to your client, we are sorry, Mr. Ward, but I do think that
justice must be served first in these courts, don't you? And I
feel that the plaintiff deserves her day in court."

Mr. Ward nodded once unsmilingly, drumming the eraser
of his pencil on the desk in front of him.

The judge used his gavel and adjourned the court. The
courtroom rose and the judge retired.

"Nice move, Miss McAfee. My name is Jason Ward. I don't
think we've met." Mr. Ward put out his hand.

Luna shook hands with him, then turned back to her briefcase.

"Of course I have heard of you." Mr. Ward smiled when
Luna looked back at him. "Germany, wasn't it?"

Luna rose to her feet, facing Ward, who was not much
taller than she. "If you have something to say, get it out in the
open, Mr. Ward. Intimidation won't work with me. I'll go
right back to the judge and repeat everything that you say to
me . . . if you are trying to coerce me."

Jason Ward's face reddened. "I've been practicing many
years, Miss McAfee, and no one has ever accused me of coer-
cion."

"Then you'd better not start now. You might also have
heard that I don't back down from a fight, in court or out,
Mr. Ward. That part about me is true, but there is no truth to
the accusations made about me. However, there again, they
were made by a rather nefarious group of people. I would hate
to think that you were connected with them. Now, get out of
my way." Luna stared at the other lawyer until he stepped
aside, then, chin up, she strode past him. She would have
laughed at his livid face if she hadn't been exercising every bit
of strength she had not to crack apart.

Fury lent speed to the things she had to do at the courthouse, checking a court date and any messages there might
have been for her. Was she never to live down that time in
Germany? Would it dog her steps forever? Even if she shouted
her innocence to the heavens, would there still be voices who
berated her, accused her falsely?

"Hi, Luna. Are you daydreaming or what?"

"Hello, Elmo." She spoke to another law-school peer who was about to pass her. "Wait, Elmo. Are you still working with the Witness Protection Program?"

"Yes. I like it. How are you doing?"

"Sometimes it gets tough."

Elmo Behrens grinned at her. "Yeah, I heard you told old Ward to take a hike. You do like to tackle the Titans, don't you?"

"Lord, the rumor mill around here is incredible."

"Right. See you. Give my best to Uel and Barb. Watch it in the clinches. I would hate to see you get clawed by the vultures." Elmo sauntered down the hall.

"Thanks." Luna gazed after him, smiling.

Having finished the last of her chores at the courthouse, she sprinted along the marble corridor toward the exit.

When someone stepped away from the wall and stood in front of her, Luna skidded to a halt. *"You!* Get out of my way, Hetty. Are you in trouble with the law again? Is that why you're hanging around the courthouse? I have a sensitive nose, and when I'm around you I get nauseated from the odor. So stay away from me."

"You have a smart mouth, lady JAG. Make sure it doesn't get you into trouble."

"It looks like you were already there, Hetty. Somebody's scratched up your face rather badly. Too bad they didn't take your head clean off." Luna saw the way his teeth cracked together, and she strode around him without another word. There was something primal and nasty about Hetty, and it had always made her shiver. It did so now.

Luna had a little trouble hailing a cab because it was primetime use in D.C. Damn! She wished she had taken her car, but, preoccupied as she had been with Veli's trouble, she had found it so much easier to ride with Dray. At last a cab stopped and she was on her way to the hospital in Silver Spring, where Veli Skinner was on the critical list.

At the hospital, she encountered Gretchen. "Hi. How is Veli?"

"She's stable. The doctors are very optimistic about her complete recovery." Gretchen slid over on the plastic-uphol-stered couch so that Luna could sit next to her. "I came down here to wait because Barb had the Wilson trial this morning."

"I had forgotten about that. Tell me what happened to Veli."

"Well, as you know, she was pretty badly beaten . . . they think it was a rape attempt and a robbery." Gretchen tried to smile. "Barb and I looked at her through the window. God!" Gretchen shook her head. "It's so terrible. She was always so nice when she came to the office."

"Yes." Luna stared at the other woman. "Someone tried to rape her as well as rob her?" Horror washed over Luna.

Gretchen nodded and sighed. "That's what they think. They haven't been able to give her a complete examination yet because she's been so traumatized, but they'll know more in a while. I wish I could take her two kids for her. The neighbor who has them has to work the night shift and she hasn't been able to get someone to care for them yet."

Luna patted her friend on the shoulder. "We'll work some-thing out, but the solution won't involve your house. You have your hands full now with your children, and your par-ents. Don't worry, Gretchen, we'll take care of it."

Gretchen looked relieved and nodded, looking at her watch. "I should get back to work. Are you going to be here for a while?"

"Yes. I'll call in before I leave." After Gretchen had left, Luna picked up a tattered copy of *Sports Illustrated* with a woman on the cover who was barely covered by her swimsuit.

When a nurse came into the waiting room and looked puz-zled, Luna stood. "Ms. Taylor had to leave. I'm Miss Mc-Afee, Mrs. Skinner's lawyer. Could I see her, please?"

"All right, but I'll have to ask you to vacate the room if the police come. . . ."

"Not really. As I said, I'm her lawyer."

The nurse smiled vaguely and told Luna to follow her.

Luna thought she had prepared herself to see Veli. After all, she'd seen people who had been shot, and had once seen the mangled remains of an airman who'd run afoul of the Auto-bahn on his motorcycle. But when she looked down at the multicolored swollen-faced woman in the bed, with her head shaved and her arm in a sling, Luna's midday apple and glass of skim milk were in danger of rising up in her throat. "Oh, Veli, Veli, who did this to you?" Luna leaned over the other woman, feeling her eyes sting.

As though she'd recognized Luna's voice, Veli moaned and turned her head a little. Her mouth moved several times and finally a word came through.

"Did she say something about a check?" The nurse queried Luna as she adjusted the I.V. in Veli's arm.

"I'm not sure. It was something like that," Luna muttered, almost to herself. What was Veli saying? Could she have known the perpetrator? God! How could any human have done this to another?

Luna stayed a while longer, but Veli didn't say any more. In fact she seemed to slip into a deep slumber. Luna glanced worriedly at the nurse.

"She's sleeping peacefully. That's a good sign," the nurse reassured her.

When Luna left the hospital she took a cab to her apart-ment, then picked up her car and drove right to Veli's home, which was just outside of Silver Spring.

The house was not in the best shape, but when Luna en-tered it she noticed that though it was untidy, it was very clean.

"Are you the baby-sitter for tonight? I'm the neighbor, Mrs. Scheller. I have to go to work and . . ."

Luna looked past the agitated Mrs. Scheller to the boy and girl who were standing close to each other just behind the heavyset neighbor. "I'm Luna McAfee, Mrs. Skinner's law-yer, and I will be taking the children home with me. I'll keep them until we can work something out."

Mrs. Scheller beamed. "Thank you so much. Veli is my friend, and her kids are very good. Right now they're very worried about their mother, of course, but . . ."

"I just came from the hospital and your mother spoke to me." Luna looked past the woman to the youngsters. "The nurse who takes care of her told me that the doctor is very pleased with the way your mother is responding." Luna saw the infinitesimal relaxing of the small bodies. "Let's get some things together, shall we? I'm your mother's lawyer and I'm taking you to my house for a few days."

"We have school."

"We can't go with strangers."

Both children spoke at the same time.

"It's all right, Tommy and Amy. I remember this lady now," Mrs. Scheller interjected. "I took your mother to see her a couple of times. Now, be good and call me in the morning." Mrs. Scheller kissed each child, told Luna where their clean clothes were, and left in a flurry.

Luna didn't know what to say to the children so she just helped them pack and gather their schoolbooks, and then she ushered them out the door, her eyes stinging as she watched the solemn way they made sure the house door was locked and how carefully Tommy put the key into his zippered pocket. "Ready?" As Luna said this a great hulking bear of a dog whose paws looked like Eskimo mukluks bounded up to the children. Their faces lit up and they hugged and patted the clumsy animal.

"Who is this?" Luna asked faintly.

"We call him Lance," Amy said softly. "After Sir Lancelot."

"Mrs. Scheller can't keep animals. She has allergies," Tommy informed Luna.

"Of course." Luna thought about the fifty dollars a month extra rent it would cost her to have an animal in her apartment. What the hell! "Okay. Put him in the back of the car. I hope we all fit in the Bug." Luna put the luggage in the front trunk of the car, then unlocked the door. Maybe the dog would be afraid to ride in the car. After all, Veli didn't own one.

Lance leapt into the front seat.

"We don't mind riding in the back," Tommy told Luna graciously.

Luna shot a look at the panting creature sitting in her passenger seat, his furry head taller than hers, his large pansy-brown eyes peeking through the hair that fell forward on his face. "He looks like a Walt Disney reject."

"What does *reject* mean?" Amy piped up from the back.

"I should have said . . . performer," Luna amended.

Flustered by the nearness of the large canine, Luna tried to start the car and flooded it, necessitating a short wait until she could try again.

Tommy Skinner leaned forward from the backseat and patted the dog. "We know he isn't pretty or anything, but he doesn't bite."

"That's a big plus in his favor." The car turned over with a muted roar and Luna pulled into the traffic.

The ride through town both irritated and amused Luna. She noticed more than one double take and much laughter directed at the huge dog riding in the passenger seat of the VW.

When she pulled into the parking lot of her apartment, maneuvering the car as close to the door as she could, she decided she would get the children settled before she called the super and explained her canine visitor.

To Luna's relief Lance was walked along the flower bed, did what he had to do, and followed Tommy back without any need to chase after him. She had forgotten to tell the children to bring a leash for the dog.

Lance had to be coaxed into the elevator, but finally they were all on the fourth floor and approaching her apartment, each of them loaded down with clothes, the dog cavorting about them.

Mrs. Finnerty opened her door a crack and peered out. "Luna, dear, I—my goodness—I didn't know you had a dog.

Nice doggy." Mrs. Finnerty paused, frowning, for a moment. "What was I going to tell you? Ah, that's it. The meter man. I don't know why he had to go into your place, but I told him not to be stupid, that our meters were read on the first floor . . . but he went in anyway. Oh, dear, nice doggy, mustn't kiss my mouth." Mrs. Finnerty smiled at the children when they called the dog.

"Thank you, Mrs. Finnerty." Luna felt cold sweat trickle down under her arm as she approached her door, turned the handle, and found it unlocked. There had been break-ins in their area, and posing as a meter man seemed as good a way as any for gaining entry.

Staying where she was, Luna looked inside the living room. It looked as if someone had gone through it with a giant eggbeater. Everything was upended, tipped, and some things were broken.

Luna looked around at the children, then at her neighbor, who was still peeping out her door. "Mrs. Finnerty, would you take the children into your place, please, and would you call the police."

Luna heard the elevator doors open as Mrs. Finnerty unhooked her chain and flung back her door fully, saying "oh, dear, oh, dear" all the while.

"That's what happened to our house." Amy pressed close to Luna, who put an arm around her shoulder.

"And they hurt Mommy," Tommy said shakily.

"What's wrong, Luna? Why are you standing out in the hall?" Dray strode toward them, seeing the chalky cast to Luna's face. Without a second thought he enveloped her and the little girl at her side in his arms. "It's all right. I'm here. Tell me what happened."

"She doesn't know," Mrs. Finnerty chirped. "Her apartment has been burgled, I think." The older woman pointed at the door. "I think the meter man did it."

"Wait here. Have you called the police? Do so at once."

At Dray's command Mrs. Finnerty scurried back into her own place, shepherding the children in front of her.

Dray entered Luna's apartment, searching thoroughly but being careful not to touch anything that might interest the police. Then he returned to the hallway and Luna.

"We'll stay long enough to give a police report, then you'll come to my place. What's this?" Dray laughed when the big dog jumped up the front of him. One firm command had the animal back on its haunches and looking up at Dray expectantly.

"That's Lance. Please teach me how to do that, since he is my houseguest for the time being . . . and we are not going to your place. I have the responsibility of Veli's children and . . ."

"So? Now they'll be mine for a while." Dray held her by her upper arms, scanning her features. "Veli? Isn't that the client who was mugged?"

"Yes. And I took the children because there was no one else who could care for them. And now this." Luna shook her head. "Those kids have been through enough."

Dray nodded. "Don't worry about anything."

"It's a little hard at this point not to." Luna's knees threatened to give way on her, but she felt buttressed by Dray's presence.

In short order the authorities were at the apartment. Dray dealt with the police, then he hushed Luna when she wanted to argue with him about going to his house. "It's the only logical thing to do. Do your friends have room for you?"

Luna pictured Gretchen's overcrowded house and Uel and Barb's small apartment.

At her silence, Dray nodded. "My place is the only solution at the moment. Later you can work out something else if you choose, but you did say that these kids have had enough."

"They have."

"All right, then. It'll work out fine. Don't make a fuss, Luna. There's room at my house for the children and the dog."

On the drive to Georgetown and Dray's row house, Tommy and the dog managed to squeeze into the small area behind the front seat of the Ferrari, and Luna rode up front with Amy on her lap.

Dray shot a quick look at her. "What's worrying you, Luna?"

"I don't know. It's just too coincidental having two break-ins so alike in such a short time." Then she proceeded to explain in low, veiled terms what had happened to the children's mother.

Dray ground his teeth together as he noted the way she hugged Amy to her, computing what was running through her mind, anger growing inside him. "We'll talk later, after we settle the children."

"This is a long way from my school," Tommy said worriedly as they drove across Washington.

"Not to worry. I have a houseman by the name of Wilkins who will drive you to school and pick you up. You'll like the big car he drives."

"Lance and I are pretty squinched in this one." Tommy's tone was reproachful.

"Your Ferrari has not made the right impression in all quarters." Luna chuckled, feeling a little better.

"That's life. You win some, you lose some." Dray was grateful for the smile on her face. There was still a lacing of tension there, but not the tight grayness that had been on it when he'd first seen her at her apartment door.

They drove into Georgetown and down the narrow streets until they came to the alley behind Dray's home.

"It's pretty." Amy sat up on Luna's lap and looked around her as they drove down the narrow alley in back of the row houses and into the three-car garage.

The children took charge of walking Lance around the small enclosed yard. When he sprinkled on the rose garden, Luna grimaced at Dray. "You'll be sorry you were landed with us."

Dray shrugged. "Maybe. We'll have to see, won't we. It's Wilkins who may get a little out of sorts with Lance. You can deal with him. When Wilkins gets his English back up, he's downright formidable."

"I have no intention of duking it out with your houseman. I'll walk Lance in that small park we passed."

Dray grinned. "Fine, but the rules are, you bring your own cleanup bag. Nothing naughty left behind in the park."

"Very amusing, Senator."

Dray swept her into his arms, giving her a hard kiss, his mouth bruising hers. "Just so that you know I'm more than amusing."

Luna swiped at her mouth. "If you do that again, I will walk out of here, children and dog."

Dray spread his hands. "Understood."

Looking more formal and more distant than she had all afternoon, Luna asked, "May I use your phone, please?"

Dray inclined his head. "Use the phone in my study. It's the second door on the right side of the main hall as you approach the front entrance. I'll take the children upstairs and show them their rooms." Dray shepherded them all through the back door, smiling at Tommy and Amy when they oohed and aahed over the large kitchen.

Luna followed them through to the main gallery of the house, which was an extra-wide corridor that bisected the large five-story home. The pale-lemon wainscoted walls with the lemon-and-crimson-striped wallpaper provided a striking backdrop for the original paintings hung there. She had known that Dray was wealthy, but she realized as she looked around her that she hadn't been aware just how richly endowed he was with the world's goods. Luna felt a frisson of wary discomfort. She was in the home of the enemy, on the point of accepting his hospitality. Had she gone mad? "Escape!" she advised herself.

Luna caught a glimpse of Dray's sudden twisted smile, as though he'd read her mind.

Without breaking off his conversation with the children, he indicated the study door, his ironic bow in her direction causing her blood to congeal in her veins. "Perhaps I should consider a hotel." Luna hoped he couldn't hear the tremor in her tone.

"Tommy and Amy, you go right up the stairs and follow them around until you come to more stairs, then go right into the sitting room there. Each of the bedrooms has its own bathroom. So you choose which rooms you want to the left of the stairs. Can you do that?"

At their nods he smiled at them, watching until they disappeared around the landing of the second floor before turning to Luna. "If you don't choose to stay here, that has to be your decision, but can you afford to risk that boy and girl if what happened at your apartment is tied to the attack on their mother?"

"You do manage to position events your way, don't you, Senator?"

"Let's say I'm being realistic, Counselor."

"Is that what it is?" Luna resented his cynical tone. "I'll just use the phone."

"Do that. I'll see to the youngsters." He swiveled away from her, going up the stairs two at a time and disappearing around the corner.

Luna sagged, feeling as though she'd just tap-danced through a cyclone. On unsteady legs she turned the handle of the heavy oak door to the study and pushed inward. She was awestruck by the two-story room with a three-sided balcony that gave access to the floor-to-ceiling books on the second level. There were sliding ladders for use on the two book-lined walls of the first floor. The third side was a communications center complete with compact-disc player and ham-radio set. The fourth was a window wall that looked out on a quiet cul-de-sac and provided a view of the closed-in yard and garden as well.

Luna called Uel and explained the situation.

"Are you sure you'll be all right staying there?"

"Yes. If I have any trouble, I'll take the kids and run."

"Senator Lodge has a very good reputation, Luna."

"Not everyone knows him as I do."

"Then get out of there."

"Pay no attention to me, Uel. I'm sure the children and I will be fine here. I'll keep in touch."

Luna was still holding the phone after the connection was broken when Dray walked into the room. She turned to face him, the instrument held in front of her like a weapon.

His eyes touched the phone, his lip curling, then he looked at her. "All set?"

Luna nodded, feeling as though she'd just finished a marathon.

"Good. You're safe and so are the children. I'm sure that will be a consolation to their mother."

"Yes, it will."

Dray saw the way her eyes narrowed on him, her chin lifting. "But you hate taking aid from me. Right?"

"Yes."

Black lightning flashed across his face. "So? For now it's 'better the devil you know,' isn't it, Luna?" The anger that quivered in her face mirrored his own feelings.

Chapter 9

"I assure you it's no bother, Wilkins. I always drive myself to work."

"I'm sure you do, miss, but the senator is concerned about what happened at your apartment. He wants you to take extra precautions."

"That's fine, but I travel all over the area in the course of a day's work, going from my office to the different courthouses. I put miles on my car every day."

"Then perhaps it's time you gave it a rest, miss." Wilkins's stoical features twitched once. "You might look at it from my point of view, miss. If I don't drive you, the senator will send me packing and just get someone else."

"Oh, I'm sure he wouldn't do that, Wilkins."

"He was adamant, miss."

"Couldn't you just follow me and—"

"It would be better if I drove you."

Luna sighed and nodded. It was like shadow-boxing a brick wall. "Have the children finished their breakfasts?"

"Oh, yes. I was just going to walk Lancelot while they brush their teeth."

"I'll hurry them along." Luna paused. "On second thought, you see to the children, I'll walk Lance." It didn't seem fair to saddle the houseman with the dog.

"Oh, but, Miss McAfee . . ."

"Never mind, Wilkins, I need the fresh air." Wilkins couldn't have his way all the time!

Going down the long hall to the kitchen, where Lance could usually be found, Luna ignored the fading sounds of

Wilkins's protests. "Ah-ha, you marauder you. Lance, get down from there."

The hairy canine was standing on his hind legs trying to reach the basket of homemade bagels that sat on the kitchen counter. Not looking a bit sheepish or guilty, he dropped back to all fours, his tail thumping the tile floor.

"Let's go, we're going for a walk." Luna led the animal to the back hall, where the leather lead that Dray had bought him was hanging from a hook.

Slipping the choke chain over his head, Luna checked that she had her keys, then urged him back along the hall toward the front door.

Once past the wrought-iron grillwork that fronted Dray's property, Luna closed the gate behind her and walked to the corner so that she could cross to the park.

Congratulating herself on the ease with which she was able to handle the dog, she took a deep breath of cool, sweet morning air, admiring the myriad collections of flora.

Breathing deeply, she gazed at the bright-blue spring sky. The cherry blossoms were in bloom but the air was brisk with a winter bite to it. When she felt the tug on her hand she was too startled to react. "No! Lance! Stay!"

The squirrel was too much temptation for the dog, and he bolted after it, almost pulling Luna's arm from its socket. "Lance! Stop." Not hesitating, Luna plunged after the galloping canine as he bent to his task, no tree or bush deterring him from his intended objective.

Luna considered herself in good shape, but the dog soon outdistanced her. It surprised her to discover that the park had more depth to it than she had at first supposed. Soon she was lost in a labyrinth of shrubbery and trees. Pausing to catch her breath, she looked around her at the surrounding greenery. "Lance! Come! Lance, you come here this—" The words died in her throat when she saw the black-garbed man come through a break in a hedge.

Perhaps it was the hands flexing at his sides or the masklike purpose of his face that first alarmed her. Backing away, she shot glances right and left, and spotted an opening. "Lance, come! Help! Lance!"

Turning, she jumped through a thatch of bushes, their branches scratching her face, but it didn't deter her. Danger was behind her and she could hear over the thudding of her footsteps and her heart the sounds of pursuit. "Lance!" The shout burst from her.

When someone gripped her shoulder she screamed, but turned and twisted to free herself. Forced back against a tree by the superior weight, she continued to struggle.

All at once she was free, the hands that had been throttling her now trying to flail at the mixed-breed dog that jumped onto his back.

Stunned, Luna listened to the snarling, growling Lance. The sweet, easygoing dog had metamorphosed into an angry fighting machine bent on tearing his enemy apart.

With a heave the man was free and on his feet, running in the same motion.

"No! Lance, stay." Luna dropped to her knees, sobbing her thanks into the neck of the hairy, panting canine.

"Dammit, John, I thought you were going to keep him off my back." Dray glared at his assistant, then at the phone.

"I tried, Senator, but he insists that this is something personal that you should find interesting." John gave him a deprecating smile. "After all, he is a constituent from New York."

"True." Dray's hard smile was mirthless. "Hetty, what do you want?"

"That's pretty abrupt, Dray."

"Yes, it is. I'll give you three minutes, starting now." Dray didn't know what made him push the small recording button on his phone.

"Senator, I think your constituents would be better pleased with your accepting the chemical plant on the Hudson than they would with your carrying on with a woman who is under suspicion of evidence tampering. Senator, are you there?"

"I am."

"McAfee's reputation for smirching names has reached Washington now."

"I assume you mean the Skinner case that's pending because the plaintiff is in the hospital with injuries from an assault that almost killed her?"

"You don't know that the accident Mrs. Skinner had had anything to do with the case." A wariness had entered Hetty's voice.

"Don't I? Well, I do know that you've tried to blackmail me on the phone, and since I've recorded our conversation and intend to have it copied and sent to party headquarters, I think we've just about ended the conversation." Dray slammed down the phone, his hand going at once to the recorder and removing the disc. Pressing the buzzer on the console on his desk, he waited until his assistant had entered the room. "John, get me four copies of this disc. Make out a letter to party headquarters and send one to my office vault in New York. Put one away in this vault and send another to my father. I want it done yesterday."

"Right away, Senator."

When Dray was alone he sat down in his swivel chair, gazing out the window. A frisson of dread ran up his spine. Hetty was threatening Luna even more directly than he was threatening him. There was too much he didn't know about the back-street politics of Washington. Reaching for the phone, he dialed. "Father? Yes, it's Dray. I was wondering if you and Mother would be at home this evening. No? Tomorrow evening sounds fine. Haddon March will be there? I don't want to intrude. No problem. Yes, I could bring Luna and the children, but I'll have to ask her first. I would like some time to talk with you, privately. Right. Thank you."

Breaking the connection, Dray dialed again. "Hello, Gretchen, is Luna there? Which courthouse, do you know? Thank you." Dray replaced the receiver and stared at the instrument. Gretchen had sounded a little reticent. Shrugging off the conversation, he scanned his calendar and looked at the clock. He was free until two. It was twelve now. The court would be breaking for lunch.

Snatching his suit jacket off the hook, he went out to John's office, catching him packaging the discs. "You've finished copying that already?"

"The new disc copiers are very efficient, Senator. These are going out in the afternoon mail."

"Thanks, John. I'll be back at one forty-five."

Washington was cool, but after so many days of rain the sun was shining. The cherry blossoms were in bloom and the city was dressed in its Easter best.

Dray walked briskly, wishing he had his jogging clothes on so that he could take advantage of being in the fresh air. When people called out to him, he turned and smiled but he didn't stop to talk.

He was almost at the courthouse when he saw Luna come down the wide steps, talking and laughing with a man he didn't know.

Pausing at the roadside where she would be crossing, he watched her. Her chin was up, showing her long, lovely neck. The breeze blew her suit skirt against those strong curvaceous legs that looked almost delicate in their perfection but which he knew were beautifully muscled. Though she was balancing a purse and briefcase, her stride was smooth and rhythmic, as though she danced for a living instead of practicing law.

What made Dray glance up the wide avenue lined with cherry trees, he didn't know, but he fixed on it when he saw the large vehicle moving slowly toward Luna and her companion as they stepped onto the crosswalk.

His skin crawling with awareness, he moved across the road toward Luna, his eyes shooting toward the black car.

"Dray! What are you doing here?" Luna's mouth dropped open when the senator from New York took hold of her arm and that of her companion and hurried them back the way they'd come. "Wait, what are you doing?"

"Never mind, just keep moving, both of you." Dray didn't

stop until he had the two bewildered people inside the court-house again.

"Now, will you tell me what's going on? Elmo has a luncheon date and I was going to . . ."

Dray put his finger to her lips and stretched until he could see the black car, which all at once did a one-eighty and sped away. "Maybe it was nothing, but I didn't like the way a car seemed to be waiting for you to cross the street. I don't think I was being paranoid." Dray put out his hand. "I'm Dray Lodge. How are you?"

"Nice to meet you, Senator, and I don't think you're being paranoid. In my line of work, caution is a byword."

"Elmo works with the Witness Protection Program." Luna stood on tiptoe to look past Dray. "I don't see any car."

"It's gone, darling."

Elmo looked from Dray to Luna. "Is Luna in danger?"

Luna shook her head. Dray shrugged.

"Tell me. I went to school with her. Maybe I can help."

Dray walked between the two as they made their way out of the courthouse again. This time, the three were watching their surroundings and not each other. "I don't have any concrete proof, but I think that Luna is in danger. However, I don't know the whys of any of it."

Crossing the street hurriedly, the three of them paused on the lee side of a tree, still scanning the street.

"As Luna told you, I work for the WPP and I have a few contacts. I'll put out some feelers to see if I can discover anything, Senator."

"Thank you." Dray shook Elmo's hand, and he and Luna watched her friend saunter down the avenue. Then Dray gazed down at the woman beside him.

"Don't look like that, Dray."

"How do I look?" His bitten-off words seemed to telegraph the strain that had gripped him.

"Like you want to duke it out with the Senate and House, single-handedly."

"Very close." He pulled her into the circle of his arms. "No matter where we're headed, Luna, I'm telling you now that I won't allow harm to come to you, that I want you to use every precaution in your job."

"I do." It was such a temptation to remain there, held by Dray. Pushing back from him, she took a deep breath. "I may be in danger from you."

"Only in danger of marrying me, my sweet."

"That's what you say." Stars seemed to explode behind her eyes.

"We won't talk about it now. Come along, we'll go home for lunch."

"Dray, I don't have time."

"We'll hurry."

Arguing with him seemed fruitless, so Luna went with him to the parking area where his Ferrari was kept, glad to be out of the breeze, which had grown sharper. "What do your constituents say about your driving a foreign car?"

"This was a gift from my parents. I keep it in Washington because here there isn't the salt problem there is in New York. I also drive an Allante, and that's made by Cadillac. The tractor and jeep that I use on the farm are American-made."

Luna chuckled. "You sound defensive, Senator. Has someone else remarked on this?"

"Yes, you, my sister, and my mother. Speaking of them, we're invited to dinner there tomorrow night. We'll bring the children."

"I don't think so. It's a school night. Wilkins will be with them."

"Not to mention Lance." Dray shot a smiling look her way, all at once wondering at the amount of makeup she was wearing.

"Lance is a wonderful dog."

"I like him myself, so I'm glad to hear you say that. When did you become his champion?"

"Oh, he grows on you, I guess."

Dray heard the hesitation in her voice and wondered what she wasn't telling him.

Pulling into the garage behind the town house, he turned off the ignition and went around to help her from the car. When she put her hand in his he saw the marks on the back of her hand. "What are these, Luna? Did you have an accident?"

"Yes. It's fine. I put disinfectant on it."

Luna didn't look at him as she hurried in the kitchen door.

"How are you feeling, Miss McAfee? Better, I hope." Wilkins saw the frantic hand signal she gave him.

"What are you talking about, Wilkins? I won't stand for being put off. Speak up."

"Of course, Senator. Miss McAfee had a run-in with a mugger this morning when she was walking Lance in the park. Lance intervened and ran the fellow off."

"Why the bloody hell didn't anyone tell me?" Dray's face turned scarlet. "Damn you, Luna."

"I haven't seen you since it happened."

"Don't give me that crap about my leaving early. I have phones in my office. Were you going to tell me at all?"

"It was nothing, Dray. Just a fool of a mugger. Lance chased him away."

"Speaking of the dog . . ." Wilkins frowned and strode from the room.

Luna watched him go, wincing when she heard the butler say, "Ah-ha, just as I thought," quite sure that Lance was up to no good. "I hope Lance hasn't been sleeping on the brocade couch in the front room again. It was covered with hairs yesterday."

"I'll give him the whole damned front room," Dray muttered, reaching out and pulling Luna into his arms. "Don't ever keep anything like that from me again."

"I'm all right, but I do have to eat and run. I have a court date in Maryland this afternoon. Would you mind driving me to my car?"

Dray shook his head, his eyes on her mouth. Even if she punched him in the eye, he had to kiss her. "I will keep you safe, Luna," he whispered against her lips even as Wilkins returned to the kitchen with the dog in tow.

"He was on the brocade settee again," Wilkins said tightly. "I have just given him a severe tongue-lashing."

Dray eyed the tail-wagging dog, who first greeted Luna, who hugged him. Then he turned to try to jump on Dray. "No! Stay, you mangy beast." Dray patted his head. "I wonder if you shouldn't put him on some of that high-protein dog food, Wilkins."

"The commercial garbage they sell is very inferior, Senator. I go to the pet store on K Street. They understand the canine diet." Wilkins's nostrils flared. "He also has his first appointment with the veterinarian and the groomer, sir."

"Good. He is a little gamey."

"Dray, I expect you to submit whatever bills Lance incurs to me." Luna put on hold the idea of having the dents removed from her car and having it repainted. She looked at the kitchen clock. "Gadfrey, I'll be late."

"I have some lovely salad prepared, miss, with my special Caesar dressing, and there are fresh rolls, and with milk to drink your energy level will be up all day, miss. I am very careful with the children's lunches and I have noticed a difference."

"Oh." Luna also noticed that Wilkins gave Lance a very large dog biscuit. "Should he be rewarded for sitting on the brocade?" she whispered to Dray.

"No, but he should be given a box of those for rescuing you."

Luna smiled. "I think your house will need a thorough cleaning once we all leave."

"Don't talk about that now. Eat your lunch." Dray almost lifted her into her chair.

By the time Luna had finished in court and got back to the storefront offices, everyone had left and she had to use her key and then dash to the wall console and press the buttons to turn off the alarms.

She wasn't there very long when she heard a noise at the back door. Taking a grip on the paperweight in the shape of law books that sat on her desk, she opened her office door cautiously.

A man had his back to her and he was rifling through the files, tossing them every which way. What made her skin crawl was the can of kerosene he had with him and the long tail of rags that he'd put on the desk.

Closing her door quietly, she went to the window overlooking the driveway and unfastened it, praying it wouldn't squeak when she raised it. To her surprise it went up silently. She blessed Manuel and Consuela Torres and their habit of cleaning, waxing, and maintaining everything, even the windows.

Luna figured she had a few seconds before he came into her office, assuming that he would go through everything before torching the place.

Dialing 911, she held the receiver to her mouth and whispered into it. She gave the location and stated that there was a robbery and possible arson in progress. "Yes, I'm getting out now. . . ." The door crashed open and the stocking-masked intruder stared at her. His contorted face was angry as he stared from the phone to her. "I've called the police. They'll be here in seconds."

"You won't be so lucky next time." The intruder turned and ran.

Without thinking, Luna followed the running man out the door. There was something familiar about him. Did she know him? The stocking had effectively blurred his face and voice.

Still keeping herself as inconspicuous as possible, she peered out the front window, watching as the man sprinted across the avenue, then hopped into a limousine with black windows. Limousine?

In seconds the limo disappeared. Two police cars drove up moments later.

"Did you touch anything, ma'am?" Another patrol car had stopped at the offices and an officer approached her.

"No, Officer, I'm an attorney, I'm aware how valuable a fingerprint can be."

After interminable questions the police cautioned her against coming into the building, turning off the alarm system, and leaving it that way.

"He might even have followed you, ma'am."

Luna nodded slowly. "I suppose, but I got the feeling he was surprised to see me."

Finally she was able to lock up and leave. As she put the alarm into operation and closed the door, the phone began to ring. "No, I'm not going to answer it. Let the machine get it."

The relatively short trip to Georgetown, which took twenty minutes longer than it should have because of heavy traffic, was an irritant rather than a lovely distraction.

At a stoplight Luna tried to decide what she would wear when she took the children to visit their mother . . . something cool. The spring day had turned warm. Since it was a school night, they wouldn't be able to stay long at the convalescent home where Dray had arranged to move Veli.

Then tomorrow night she and Dray were going out to Virginia to Dray's parents' home. Why was she doing it?

Finally the light changed and she made her way to the lovely old section where Dray lived.

She parked her car in front of the town house, but before she could turn off the key, the front door opened and Dray was down the steps, two at a time. Openmouthed, she stared at him when he wrenched open her door and slid into the passenger seat. "Is something wrong? The children?"

"It's bloody hell in there, but that's not why I'm here. Where have you been? I expected you an hour ago. When you didn't arrive I called, but your damned machine answered." Dray was dizzy with anger and relief.

Luna opened her mouth to respond when the front door flew open again and Lance flung himself down the front steps at the car, Wilkins at his heels. "Heavens, he looks clean!" Luna exclaimed.

"Down, you mongrel." Dray tried to push the heavy dog off the car door. With one powerful heave he was able to force the door open and the animal back to a sitting position, Wilkins taking a firm grip on the collar.

Luna forgot what she was going to say as Dray helped her from the car. Her attention was on Lance. "He looks like a giant powder puff with four legs. This is the first time I've ever seen his eyes. Did you know he was white?"

"Under that charcoal coat he'd been wearing? Never!"

The front door shot open again. "Hold him, Luna. He might run away." Tommy ran toward them.

"Fat chance," Dray muttered, eliciting a laugh from her.

"I have him, Master Tommy," Wilkins assured the panting boy.

"What do you think, Luna? Isn't Lance handsome?"

"Wonderful, darling. Are you ready? I'm going to take you to the convalescent home so that you can see your mother."

"We're ready. Should we take Lance?"

"No," Dray answered before Luna could speak. "Dogs aren't allowed in the home, and it would be too hot for Lance in the car."

Both children nodded solemnly.

Wilkins coughed and looked at his watch. "You should go now, sir, since the children have to get to bed by nine. The car is parked in back of Miss McAfee's, sir."

"Ready, Luna?" Dray saw how quickly she masked a sigh. "Tough day?"

"Yes." Luna was glad to get into the roomy Rolls with the children in the back.

"Mommy will be surprised." Amy leaned over from the backseat.

"Yes, she will, darling, but you must refasten your seat belt now. You'll be safer."

"Okay."

The children played a word game with Dray during the trip and Luna leaned back and closed her eyes, listening to the soft music on the disc player. It took all her strength to force herself to relax.

Merry Hill Convalescent Hospital was situated on a knoll

in the rolling country of Maryland. Though it smacked of countryside charm, it was only a short ride from D.C., which made visiting Veli very simple.

"This is not for poor folks," Luna murmured, eyeing the low-slung brick building modeled after Monticello, Jefferson's home.

"I didn't think you would want her to be too far removed from the children," Dray ventured dryly. "Stop shooting those suspicious glances at me. Veli can remain here as long as it takes her to recuperate. I've also arranged a teaching fellowship for her so that she can continue her schooling and have enough money to take care of her children and herself."

"That's some fellowship," Luna muttered as she watched him come around the car to open her door.

"What's a fellow's ship, Luna? Is it big?"

"Fellowship, Tommy. It means your mommy will have enough money to take care of things."

"That's good. Sometimes Mommy cries."

Luna got out of the car and watched the children alight, noting that Tommy's lip quivered for a moment. She took his hand and smiled down at the boy.

Walking through the wallpapered corridors was like traversing a glitzy hotel corridor.

Luna sucked in a surprised breath when she saw the suite of rooms with the canopied bed, all done in roses and pinks with pale rose carpeting throughout.

Veli hugged and kissed her children, chattering and laughing, hungry for news of their doings.

When Dray caught the quick looks the Skinner woman kept shooting at Luna, he turned to the children. "Why don't we go and look at the swing set out on the playground?"

"And leave Mommy?" Amy's thumb went to her mouth.

"We'll come back in a few minutes, and next week when Auntie Luna and I are in New York, your mommy will be coming to stay with you at my house. You can show her the park."

Tommy blinked. "Is that really true?"

"Yes." Dray nodded, looking as solemn as Amy.

"All right. I guess we could look at the swings." Tommy beamed.

Both children hugged their mother before they left with Dray.

"Luna, he introduced himself as Dray Lodge, but isn't he Senator Lodge?" At Luna's nod, Veli whitened.

"Don't look like that, Veli. He's cut his connection to Chuck Skinner."

Veli nodded slowly. "I suppose I'm getting paranoid, but Chuck's arm is long."

"So is Dray's. He'll make sure that Skinner stays away from you." Luna could have laughed out loud. Here she was telling Veli not to be frightened, to trust Dray, and she meant it. How could that be, when she was still wary of him? Shaking away the uncomfortable paradox, she concentrated on the woman in the bed. "You do look one hundred percent better."

"I feel a thousand percent better, I can eat, and there are no more tubes in me." Veli frowned. "Luna, I've received excellent care, first at the hospital and now at this elegant convalescent home. How will I pay for it? Please don't put me off. The staff keeps saying it's all taken care of by a special insurance."

Luna shrugged. "That would be great, but I'll ask anyway. The most important thing is not to worry. Life is getting better for you, Veli. Your job is to get well." Luna laughed out loud. "At least you don't have to worry about your dog, Lance. He's getting the best of care, even grooming and all his shots."

"Lance? That big dog in the neighborhood? That isn't ours, Luna. The children just play with him."

Luna stared at her for long minutes. "You mean that I have been keeping someone else's dog all this time? God, I'll be arrested."

Veli shook her head. "He doesn't belong to anyone. A few of us in the neighborhood have been feeding him. A couple of times during a sleet storm he slept in our garage; but he isn't ours, he's a stray."

Luna put her hand over her mouth, but she couldn't contain her mirth. "How will I break this to the illustrious senator?"

"My children should have told him," Veli said worriedly.

"Don't be silly. None of us asked. I just assumed it was theirs." Luna laughed harder.

Veli smiled. "He is awfully big."

"A monster. And he shed all over a Queen Anne settee covered in brocade."

"Luna, how can you laugh? It's awful."

When the visit ended and they were returning to the capital, the children were subdued.

"Before you know it, your mother will be with you and Wilkins will cook all her favorite foods."

"That's nice. Mommy has to do the cooking in our house because we don't have a Wilkins." Tommy was very matter-of-fact.

"That's why it will be fun for your mommy to be waited on during her stay. Right?"

"Right," Tommy and Amy chorused, then settled back on their seats, belts fastened.

"They're asleep," Luna whispered to Dray some minutes later.

"It's been a full day for them. Why are you smiling that way?" Dray glanced at her a few times, managing to keep most of his attention on driving in the fast-paced traffic.

"Lance is a stray. Veli and the children don't own him. No one does, it would seem."

Dray's lips twisted into a smile as the laughter bubbled out of her. "Very amusing. I've inherited a nondescript hairy elephant, it would seem."

"No, I won't do that to you. I'll take him with me when I leave and—"

"No!" Dray's peremptory tone awakened the children.

"Where are we?"

"Are we home?"

"See! The children think of my house as their home. They're not in a hurry to leave," Dray pointed out.

Luna stared at his hard profile, at the lean, strong hands gripping the steering wheel. "We can't stay forever," she said.

"We'll see about that."

Chapter 10

The following day rocketed by as most of the days had since Luna had begun her practice. Running between courthouses had become a way of life for her. Two of the cases that she'd been handling were adjudicated in her clients' favor. That more than made up for the dizzying pace.

It wasn't until she was almost back in Georgetown that she gave any thought to what she would wear to Dray's parents' dinner. Uel and Barb's Christmas gift! It had been a total extravagance to give her the silk sarong that they'd brought back from a business trip to New York.

Luna could still hear Barb's voice when they presented her with it on Christmas morning.

"We found this marvelous Korean family who own a place on Third Avenue not much bigger than a walk-in closet, but they had wonderful clothes."

Luna had been agog when she saw the kaleidoscope of peachy hues in the no-seam wraparound garment that was like a gossamer dawn.

Luna parked her beat-up car in front of Dray's house, shaking herself from her reverie. Would the silk be too dressy? Opening the front door with her own key, she smiled when Wilkins came down the center hall to greet her.

"The children are visiting friends for dinner, miss, and the senator is showering. No need to worry about Tommy and Amy. I've arranged to pick them up well before their bedtime."

"Thank you, Wilkins, I appreciate all you do." Luna looked beyond him and saw Lance, who had broken into a gallop when he saw her. "Easy now." Luna laughed as the dog skidded around Wilkins and caromed into her, his whole body quivering in welcome.

"I thought he was still eating his kibble and liver, miss," Wilkins said primly. Then he issued a sharp command. "Sit at once, you miscreant."

"He doesn't bark, he whuffs." Luna chuckled, patting the dog's head. "I hope he doesn't lounge on the brocade anymore."

"I've put another, less precious piece of furniture under the window, but I've had to purchase some special seat covers for the back of the Rolls. He does so enjoy riding in the car with the children. Excuse me, miss, I'll take him to the kitchen."

Luna stared after Dray's retainer, who was towing Lance into the kitchen. "He likes to ride in the Rolls? Good Lord, Lance is a capitalist." Still smiling, she strolled up the curving staircase to the second floor.

Dray's home was so attractive. Luna never tired of admiring it.

"Hi." Dray leaned over the balustrade that ran along the second-floor hallway. "Going to change?"

Luna nodded. Was there ever such a handsome man with so much magnetic pull?

Dray met her on the top step and pulled her into his arms. "You work too hard," he told her gruffly, leading her into his suite of rooms.

"I have to get ready."

"You will. Sit for a minute and unwind."

Unwind when he was walking around in nothing but a terry-cloth hip wrap? Not bloody likely, she thought.

"Here. Have a little of this." Dray handed her the goblet of brown liquid and watched her sip. Instead of pulling up another chair, he kneeled in front of her, his arms resting on her chair and pressed against each side of her hips. "There, isn't that better?"

"Better." Luna coughed hoarsely, every nerve end on red alert because he was touching her. "I should get ready."

"All right. What would you say to an evening stroll by the reflecting pool and a reacquaintance with Mr. Lincoln?" His face was even with hers. Never had she seemed more beautiful or more desirable, he thought. When his finger touched the vee at her blouse opening, he felt the tremor run through her. "You are still the most sensuous woman I've ever known."

"And you've known a few."

"Some. Would you marry me and have my child, Luna McAfee?"

Luna stood so abruptly that Dray had to fall back or knock her over, his sensuous sprawl revealing much more of his masculine body. That he was aroused was no mystery to her, that she was aroused was a personal fury. "That isn't funny, Senator."

"I wasn't making a joke, darling." Dray hadn't moved from the floor, his eyes gazing at her warmly.

"Stop looking at me as though I were on the auction block, Dray."

"If you were, my love, I would mortgage my soul to get you," he told her lazily.

"Twaddle!" Luna strode from his suite with as much composure as she could muster, his low, sexy chuckle burning her ears.

"Luna, come back, you didn't finish your cognac."

"Damned high-flying predator." Luna stormed up to the third floor, muttering dire threats against any and all lawmakers. Her diatribe lasted all the while she showered and dressed, which she did by instinct rather than design as ire fueled her movements.

When at last she was ready, she left her room and descended to the second floor.

"Beautiful!" Dray was frowning, not smiling, when he complimented her. "That peach sari is a sexy innuendo, darling."

Luna lifted her chin, aware that even with the three-inch heels she was wearing she had to look up at him.

Dray reached out and lifted her left hand, sliding a marquise-shaped blue diamond on her lax finger. "There. That was my grandmother's. It's almost as beautiful as your blue eyes. One day I'll get you a sapphire the same color. No, don't pull back, and stop sputtering. Maybe if people find out you're engaged to be married to me, these threatening things that are happening to you will stop. It might provide a measure of security."

"Dray, this is insane," Luna managed when she found her voice. "I don't want to wear this." Pretending to be engaged to him! She could never pull it off. How had he managed to insert himself into her life again?

Pain put steel in the hands that closed over hers when she tried to remove the ring. "Stow the histrionics, Luna. Wear the ring, it's just to protect you." Damn her for rebelling against being engaged to him!

"Now, listen, Dray . . . Histrionics! Me! Don't accuse me of such a thing. I happen to be a responsible member of the D.C. and Maryland bars and . . ."

"Then act like it. Shall we go? Should you wear your hair twisted on the top of your head like that? Won't that give you a headache?"

"You do that." Stung, Luna shrugged off his hand as she descended to the foyer just as Wilkins came from the back of the house to open the front door.

"The Ferrari is out front, Senator. Are you sure you wouldn't like me to drive you?"

"No, thank you, Wilkins. Just see to the children," Dray answered stiffly.

"Of course, Senator. Good evening, Miss McAfee."

"Good evening, Wilkins."

Silence was heavy between them as they drove through Georgetown toward the highway that would take them to Virginia.

Dray put in a compact disc and Barbra Streisand's strong but sultry voice filled the confined area.

Germany was like a nettle in Luna's mind, stinging throughout her system. How often they'd held each other and listened to the famous songstress.

"You're thinking of Germany."

"Yes."

Dray sighed. "I'm aware that you still suspect me of colluding with Hetty's people. . . ."

"No! That is, I don't think you would do that, because you love the law and live within it, but I can't say that I trust you fully." Luna watched those strong features contort, that tough mouth turn granite-hard. The desire to reassure him, to take away that expression, tore at her, but she fought it back.

"No one can say that you're not frank, my dear."

"I think I've learned to be up-front, Dray."

"Like an avalanche, maybe?"

Luna swallowed, her throat tight. "I can go back to my apartment with the children tomorrow."

"What? And pay fifty dollars extra in rent for a dog? I would be failing in my duty as a servant of the people," he ventured acidly.

"I'm not a New Yorker. Don't fret yourself."

"Ah, that nippy tongue of yours! You must be quite a sight in court, Counselor."

"You saw me work."

"So I did."

Silence descended like a steel coat, weighing them down, pressing them into their private worlds.

When Dray turned into the long, inclined drive leading to the house, Luna exhaled shakily. "It must be one of the most beautiful farms in the area. The house is like a very large Mount Vernon and the view is breathtaking."

"It's a wonderful place. We used to come here in the spring and fall for the horse shows." Dray chuckled. "Once Mother gave permission for a hunt across the property, then she and my uncle found the fox and hid it."

"You're making that up."

"No. Wait until you meet my mother's brother, Darius Mallory, paleontologist and all-around student of mankind. That's my dear uncle."

By the time the Ferrari was parked under the white portico,

the front door of the redbrick home was open and a tall dark-skinned man with high, wide cheekbones ambled toward them.

"Is that man an American Indian?"

"Yes, my uncle introduced us to Timeo. Then he insisted that my mother hire the man because he was out of work. That was thirty-five years ago. By the way, Timeo is also black, white, and maybe a touch Oriental."

"A paleontologist's dream?" Luna's heart flipped over when Dray laughed.

Timeo opened Luna's door and leaned down to help her alight, earning a twisted smile from Dray. "The senator doesn't want anyone touching you but himself. Welcome to Mayhill, Miss McAfee."

"Thank you, Timeo. Are you really black and Indian?"

"Yes, ma'am. My mother was full-blooded Cree, my father was a mulatto from Louisiana. They met in Chicago and still live there with the rest of the family. I've been around this family for many a moon, so ask me anything you want about him."

"I will." Luna had an idea that Timeo was very important in the Lodge family, but since she didn't want to pry, she asked no more questions.

"He runs this house and is the general nuisance value in Lodge Enterprises." Dray elbowed his friend aside and put his arm around Luna. "He handles land purchase and development in the company."

"Senator Lodge, I do believe you're a bit shaken up by this lady." Timeo's grin split his face when Dray shot a sharp look at him.

"What do you say to a couple of rounds in the barn later?" Dray inquired lazily.

"An hour after dinner should suit," Timeo answered quickly, his grin widening.

Luna knew they were referring to the well-equipped building beyond the house that Dray had told her held every sort of workout accoutrement imaginable. "Shouldn't we go into the house?"

"Don't you approve of my method of working off aggression, Luna, my love?"

"Pummeling someone because you're irritated with him? Ridiculous."

"Timeo was digging at me, darling," Dray told her silkily. "And I'm going to knock his block off."

"Barbarian." Luna sailed up the steps and into the foyer, blinking against the sudden gloom after coming from the sunlight of a spring evening.

"Ah, there you are, Luna," Mrs. Lodge said in greeting. "I'm delighted you're here. I do so want you to meet my brother, Darius. Darry, this is Luna."

"The moon lady. Lovely. So you're going to marry my nephew. Interesting." Darius Mallory blinked at her. "Thought he was involved with a woman in Germany. Looked like a sick calf when he came back from there. How are you?" He grabbed her hand and shook it.

"Fine," Luna answered limply, her arm feeling numb after the vigorous handshake.

"Uncle Darius, how are you?"

"You look mad enough to tear the house down, brick by brick. What's eating at you, Dray?" The slightly built man stared up at his nephew. "What happened to the German gal?"

"Luna is the 'German gal,' as you call her," Dray said abruptly.

Darius whistled softly. "So you tracked her down, did you? Must have stuck in your craw to do the chasing for a change." Darius's smile at his fuming nephew moved over to Luna. In a courtly gesture he offered his arm. "Let me escort you into the solarium, my dear. We have some friends you would like to meet, I know. Ellen, you can escort your son."

Luna assumed Darius meant that Dray's family were the people waiting for her and went along with him.

Ellen Lodge put her hand on Dray's arm. "Your father would like to speak with you in the library, dear."

Dray was watching Luna as she walked along the wide corridor leading to the back of the house. At his mother's tone, he turned to look at her. "Oh? Something in the wind?"

"He seems to have come to a series of dead ends on his search." His mother saw his hesitation. "Don't worry about Luna, she can handle herself with the family . . . even with Darius."

Dray's smile twisted. "She's been hurt badly, Mother. I won't let anyone do that to her again."

Ellen Mallory Lodge watched her son stride toward his father's library, then she turned to look at Timeo, who had been studying Dray too. "She's bowled him over, Tim."

Timeo nodded. "He's going to bloody my face for me."

Ellen smiled. "Try not to break any bones."

"Will do, Ellen."

Dray threw open the door to his father's library. "Father?"

The older Lodge nodded at a chair in front of his desk. "Sit down. This won't take long, or so I promised your mother."

"Is it about Luna?"

"In a way. I had no trouble dredging up her records, but when I searched through the Hetty record, I almost came up blank."

"Almost?"

"Yes, the record has been whitewashed, I'd swear to it. If the man had only one infraction on his sheet, I would have accepted it, but there's nothing to indicate that this man ever was charged with anything, that he ever even had a speeding ticket."

Dray sat back in the swivel chair, facing his father. "That's not right. When I saw his record in Germany he had a list of infractions that led me to believe that he was not a good soldier and, if most of them were correct, that the man had a nasty streak." Dray stared into space. "This might be the very key we need to start things moving. It's inconsistencies like this that lead to other facts. Putting enough of these together might be what we need to clear Luna. I would be willing to swear to what I saw in Germany on Hetty's record."

His father nodded. "That could help, but we'll need more, much more, before we show our hand."

Dray looked at his father. "I have the feeling that we're dealing with more than a JAG trial on assault."

His father frowned. "There has to be power in order to expunge a record illegally in such a way. I can't imagine who would do it; but yes, we have more than a case of perjury, and illegally tampering with military records . . . but what?"

"I don't know yet, but I will find out." Dray slapped a fist into the palm of his hand. "Luna was assaulted in the park when she was walking the dog. Fortunately Lance was able to scare off the attacker."

"The dog must be living like a king now." His father grinned when Dray looked at him quizzically. "It doesn't take a soothsayer to see that you're smitten. Your uncle was in here before you arrived, telling us the same thing. He saw you and Luna together going into the courthouse."

As if on cue the door to the library opened and Darius Mallory pushed around it, his face bemused as he stared at his nephew. "Saw Ahmed yesterday, Dray. Said that you were hooked right through the jaw."

"Thanks, Darius. Just tell Ahmed to stand clear. I won't brook any of his nonsense with Luna."

"He knows that, boy. He's already beefed up his palace guard in case you make a run at him." Darius blinked myopically, seeming not to notice his brother-in-law's mirth or his nephew's irritation. "By the by, what do any of you know about Abdul?"

"Abdul? You mean Ahmed's personal assistant?"

"The very one. He asked me far too many questions about your Miss McAfee and the cases she was dealing with at the present time. Seemed strange. It helps when people think you're daft. They become more daring with their questions." Darius took the chair that Dray had brought forward to the desk.

Dray leaned forward, his hands on the desk. "That bothers me. I wonder what Luna would say if I invited her to Hashan with me?"

"Might be the best thing, but I understand her caseload is heavy."

"How would you know that, Darius?"

"When Abdul asked me about her I decided to do a little checking on the lady. Boy, stop looking at me as though you'd like to break my neck."

"I would."

"The lady leading you a dance, is she?"

"You could say that," Dray answered tightly.

"I think I see the shadow of a ring in your nose already." Darius cackled, in high gig when his nephew ground his teeth.

"Actually I gave her Grandmother's ring this evening to wear for protection."

"Protection? Ha!"

"Could we get on with this?"

"Yes, we can." Dray's father's mouth quivered but he didn't smile.

"Should we inform Ahmed of your suspicions, Darius?"

"I shouldn't think so, Father," Dray intervened. "Ahmed is the best of good fellows but he has a trigger temper. If there was even a hint that someone near him was colluding against him there would be hell to pay, loud and clear. I wouldn't want whoever is running this operation to go to ground."

Darius Mallory sat back in his chair. "Not to denigrate your lovely, my boy, I don't think they would be taking this much time with a woman who was a lawyer or a JAG. She doesn't have anything salable that I can see. I don't think you need worry about her as much as you do." Darius coughed. "I think the attitude would be somewhat different if she were important to them."

"Your uncle's right, Dray. Why would anyone in power bother with Luna McAfee? What is it that makes her important?"

"She began to be important to this—this faction or group

when she was prosecuting Hetty," Dray said slowly, staring at his uncle, narrow-eyed. "What are you getting at, Darius? What are you really saying?"

"Well, it seems to me if she has posed some sort of threat to them, they would not be trying to scare her, but . . ." Darius didn't finish but he shrugged eloquently.

"Kill her," Dray finished, his face slate-gray.

Chapter 11

Luna couldn't help but notice that Dray was distracted. He barely joined in the dinner conversation. When people spoke to him, they had to repeat themselves, and then he replied with only the barest of answers.

After dinner he was no better, and when his sister played the piano and everyone sang, he sat slumped in a chair, a cognac goblet hanging loose in his hands.

By the time they'd left Mayhill, Luna was convinced that he had a headache or was ill in some way.

So when he spoke to her in the car, she jumped. "What did you say?"

"I said, let's walk near the reflecting pool."

"At the Lincoln Memorial?"

Dray nodded, reaching out and taking her hand.

"All right." She was relieved that he seemed more normal now. "Did you and your father have an argument? Is that why you were so gloomy during dinner?"

"What? Oh, no, it was just business talk." He shot a quick look her way and caught her frown. "All right, I'll tell you. My uncle, who is not just a paleontologist but a former member of the CIA in his younger days, feels that what happened to you in Germany was part of a larger picture."

Luna's head whipped toward him. She tried to loosen her fingers from his but to no avail. "I don't like being discussed over cigars, like the price of wool on the open market."

"No? Well, I don't like your being threatened, possibly hurt, by whatever or whoever is making the attempt."

Luna was rendered silent by the menace in his voice. Dray

had always been easy with her. The rare times she'd heard that tone in his voice it had caused her to be wary. That Dray was tough she had no doubt, that he was dangerous shook her.

When Dray parked the car and went around it to help her alight, she stared up at him and he leaned down and kissed her on the mouth.

The reflecting pool was still, not one ripple despoiled its mirror surface.

"Like to go wading, darling?"

Luna looked up sharply, then nodded. "You read my mind again."

"Lovers can do that with one another," he told her, leaning over and kissing her on the nose.

More shaken by the casual caress than she would have thought, she clutched at him, more to steady herself than anything else. "Am I getting your blessing to wade?" She couldn't seem to control the quaver in her voice.

"No, because I'm not sure you wouldn't cut your foot. That was just a peck. This is a kiss." Dray gathered her close to him, his mouth descending slowly.

Pull back, pull back, Luna ordered her body. Then her hands came up to clasp behind his neck.

The kiss went on and on, their bodies swaying as if they were caught in a gentle storm. Though the whirling passion was immediate and powerful, it kept building and swelling until there was no world but theirs, no person anywhere but them.

"I think we can move along now, if you please."

Dray looked at the security guards in the passing car. "All right, Officer." His words were rough and uneven. "It's a beautiful night, isn't it?"

"It is." The laughter in the guard's voice was barely concealed.

"We should go." Luna's hands couldn't push Dray away. Point of fact, she needed him to anchor her. She had no strength, no weight. A slight breeze could have carried her to Venus.

"Yes." Dray kissed the corner of her mouth. "I want you very much, but you will always call the signals, Luna."

Held close to his side, she shuddered with déjà vu. It was as if there had been no time lapse in their lives since they'd been together in Germany.

She didn't want to run from him. Holding him was the reality of her life at that moment. The sense of danger that seemed to have stalked her faded when his strong arms held her to his side.

They walked silently back to the car.

The power of the Ferrari took them through the capital toward Georgetown.

"Would you like to stop for a nightcap?"

"Not unless you would."

Dray accelerated, needing to get her into his home.

When he parked the car in the garage behind the house, he went around to her door and lifted her from the seat. "I need to hold you, beautiful moon lady."

Again there was no need for words as they walked slowly to the house. The night was warm but fresh, the stars were like diamonds thrown on velvet, the beacon moon smiled on them.

The house was silent. They walked through the kitchen and along the hall to the stairs.

At the landing leading to Dray's room, he released her, turning her to face him.

"I've never seen your room." Luna stared up at him.

Shock waves rippled through him. Dray was stunned at the reverberations of joy that shook his body. "No one has ever knocked me out, Luna mine, but at this moment I feel like you haymakered me. I'm weak as a kitten. Carry me."

"Fool." Eyes shining with tears, she led the way into the huge bedroom with the modern king-size bed. "There's one large clip at the back. Can you undo it?"

"If my hands stop shaking, I can."

When she faced him again with the dress loosened about

her, she didn't lift her arms to pull it away. Instead, she moved in slow, sinuous fashion, letting the garment slide down her body.

Dray swallowed, closing his eyes for an instant. "Darling, please, you're too beautiful." Kneeling in front of her, he pressed his mouth against her middle, his lips moving over her in a kneading fashion, as though he would brand every inch of her as his own.

Threading her hands through his thick, crisp hair, Luna swayed in the grip of the ecstasy building within her. It had been so long! How she'd missed him. To hold him like this was to come alive, to sew back the part of herself that had fallen off when she'd parted from him. Her heart was stinging with renewed vigor as Dray's life force flowed into her.

Dray moved up her body, his mouth touching her in the most intimate way, eliciting a shuddering sigh from her that kicked his own libido into overdrive. Rising in a rush, he lifted her up, holding her so that his eyes were even with hers. "You're mine, Luna, and I'll never let you go again, my darling."

"Dray," she whispered dreamily as she gazed at him, no sensible thoughts of retreating coming to the fore.

"Kiss me, Luna McAfee." Easily balancing her in the air, he watched her trembling lips come closer, his own body tremoring with the passion so long held in check.

When she opened her mouth on his and her tongue touched his tentatively, Dray thought that his chest would burst with the pressure of feeling.

Tenderly he lowered her to the giant bed and followed her down so that their bodies never lost contact. "Do you mind if I don't turn off the lights? I want to look at you."

"I want to look at you, Dray." Luna threw all her inhibitions out at once. If this was all there would be, if this one time of loving would be the last, then she wanted it all.

In a fierce, intense exploration she let her hands rove his flesh, taking hold of his aroused body in sublime sexual satisfaction. She had come to life again. "Dray."

"Luna, my moon lady." Was it true? Was he holding the woman who'd captured his imagination and his dreams from almost the first moment he'd met her? It had been hell being without her. Now he was holding her. That was the fantasy. Somehow he had come to accept that Luna McAfee was out of his life forever, that he would never find her, never convince her that they belonged together. Luna!

The world erupted around them; they were the only haven, the only residents on the planet as the passion between them, so long suppressed, mushroomed around them. They rocketed to the moon and back.

Quivering in the aftermath, Luna opened her eyes, gazing right into Dray's. What she saw there, the passion and the gentleness, made her dizzy. There was no way she could doubt the love and commitment of the man who'd resided in her dreams for so long.

"I want to marry you, as soon as possible, Luna. I love you."

"Dray." His name was a sob as she pressed closer to him. "There are so many complications right now. . . ."

"You're not saying no, are you?"

"I should."

Dray pressed his mouth to hers, his tongue jousting with hers. "Say maybe."

"Maybe." The squeaky voice didn't even sound like hers.

"Go to sleep, darling. I'm going to hold you."

"But I should go to my room. When Amy and Tommy wake up they come to my room." Luna tried without success to smother a yawn.

"Shh, I'll waken both of us in plenty of time, then you can join me in the hot tub."

Eyes closed, Luna nodded, smiling. "Sounds wonderful."

"It will be, precious."

After she'd slept for a few hours she woke to find Dray leaning over her, smiling. "Have you been watching me while I slept?"

"Yes, and it was wonderful."

They made love again as if they couldn't get enough of each other, as if they could never be too close.

In an explosion of passion that pulled them apart, then knitted them as one, they came together, groans and sighs issuing from their lips.

The hot tub was wonderful the next morning, and Luna luxuriated in the double warmth, hot water and a very torrid Dray. Making love in a hot tub was a delight.

"I wasn't sure we could do this. Whoops, we're splashing." The words dribbled from her lips as Dray caressed her feverishly. Clutching him, she let her hands rove over his water-slick form.

It was erotic in the extreme to be astride him in the rumbling hot water, but soon all thoughts left her as their pulsating rhythm became one with the whirlpool of water.

They came together in a mini tidal wave that rocked them both and sloshed water over the sides.

"Darling! I've needed you, Luna. Will you like being a senator's wife?"

"Dray, you're going too fast."

Dray shook his head. "Not fast enough. We should have been married by now, with maybe a child or two."

"That's putting things in high gear."

"What is it? You looked as though you just had a spasm of pain."

"Just a stitch in my side."

"Sweetheart! Where? Let me massage it."

"Ah, no, I'm fine. I should go upstairs." Luna surged to her feet, her face averted from him. What would Dray say if she told him that she hadn't taken precautions last night, that it had never entered her head. Keeping birth-control pills on her return from Germany had seemed ridiculous, since she'd had no intention of ever getting involved with anyone sexually again. There was no one in the world to whom she could give her love. Now . . . she could be pregnant with Dray's child. "Have to hurry," Luna gasped, reaching for Dray's terry-cloth bathrobe. "I'll return this later."

"Luna? Wait."

Before he had a chance to reach for her, she'd scampered from the room. Then, still moving at a run, she crossed the bedroom and flung open the door. Wilkins stood there, his hand poised to knock.

"Forgive me, miss. I was just bringing the senator the morning newspapers. I can come back later."

"No! Wilkins, don't make me a breakfast. I haven't time for anything but a quick hello for the children. I'll dress at the office."

"Oh, but, miss, the senator has instructed me to see that you always have a—"

"Not today." Luna galloped up the stairs two at a time to the third floor. When she saw Tommy and Amy in the central hall, she sighed with relief. "Hi, you two. I have to hurry this morning. Give me a kiss. When I come home tonight we'll walk Lance in the park. 'Bye."

"Good-bye, Luna," the children chorused, watching goggle-eyed as she grabbed at her sweats, then changed in her bathroom in milliseconds. Then she gathered up her shoes, clothing, and gym bag before blowing them a kiss and flying past them again.

"Wow," Tommy breathed as he leaned over the banister. "Luna can really move."

"If we slid across the front hall like that, we would get a scolding from Wilkins, I'll bet."

"Naw. Lance does it all the time, Amy, and Wilkins just tells him he won't get his special liver kibble." Tommy shrugged. "You wouldn't like Lance's kibble anyway."

"I s'pose."

Luna was almost to Silver Spring before her muscles relaxed. Was history going to repeat itself? Would she be stupid enough to let it happen?

"No, no," she said through clenched teeth as she waited at a red light, her one fist drumming on the steering wheel.

"Whazza matter, lady? You gotta gripe with your old

man?" The taxi driver behind her shouted and tooted his horn. "Forget the problems and drive. The light's green."

"In your ear," said the proper attorney from Silver Spring as the irate driver pulled around her with a roar.

Life was a jumble, and it wouldn't get untangled if she was in an accident with her car. Sweeping her myriad thoughts into a dustbin of her mind, she drove into Silver Spring and parked in front of the storefront law office.

Unlocking the front door with her key, Luna was surprised to see a coalition of her confreres facing her after she shut the door behind her. "I know it's not my birthday." Luna smiled at Uel, Barbara, and Gretchen.

"It might be your waterloo," Gretchen muttered. "Ouch, Barb, you know I hate to be pinched."

"Has something happened to Veli?"

"No, no, she's just fine," Uel assured her. "Barb talked to her last evening. Do you want to come into my office?"

"Uel, by the look on your face you're going to tell me something I won't like, and since the office hasn't opened and Barb and Gretchen will be in on it, why don't we stay out here where there's more room." Luna had tried to speak lightly, but her insides felt like jelly.

Uel took her arm and led her to the couch. The springs were threatening to rip through the upholstery, but it wasn't uncomfortable. "Look at this . . . and stay calm." He took the newspaper he'd been holding and opened it up and placed it on the walnut-veneer coffee table.

"Since when do you buy the tabloids . . . Good Lord." Luna snatched up the paper, staring at the bold-print headlines on the front page.

SENATOR TAKES UP WITH SHADY LAWYER. There was a picture of her and Dray as though they were together, but Luna knew it was a composite. The article presented a slanted view of what had happened in the Hetty trial.

Luna crumpled the paper in her hands and stared unseeingly out the window at the traffic passing by.

"Luna? Honey, don't take this to heart. This rag lambastes anyone and everyone."

"I'm all right, Barb," Luna told her, her voice hoarse. "I worry what this will do to my case for Veli and . . ."

"Now it's hit the fan," Gretchen observed gloomily, staring at the Ferrari that had just screeched up to the curb, fixing on the grim-faced senator, who got out, slammed his door, and approached the office. "I'm opening the door before he rips it off the hinges." Gretchen unlocked it and stepped back.

Dray barreled through, his gaze raking the room until he spotted Luna. "Don't get any damned ideas about ducking out because of this crap, Luna." He smacked the paper he had in one hand with his other fist. "It won't work. Our engagement will be in the evening papers, and tonight we'll be celebrating at Chez Robert. And if anyone tries to come between us, I'll break his damn neck for him. Do you hear me?"

"All of Silver Spring can hear you, you're drawing a crowd." Luna glared at him.

"I think it's great," Uel exclaimed. "If you decide to punch this columnist in the nose, I'll help you."

"Uel! Stop that." Luna turned her frown on her friend.

"And I'll help." Gretchen rubbed her hands together. "I'll rabbit-punch the sucker."

"I'll kick him in the whatsis." Barb lifted her foot experimentally.

"Well, at least we have an army." A calmer senator's smile beamed at Luna's stalwarts.

Luna stared at her friends, then at Dray, fighting back tears. "There's no defense against this, Dray. It will ruin you with your constituents."

"Our engagement announcement will put this article right into perspective, love. Here. Wear this when you go to court today." He put the blue diamond back on her finger. "And stop taking it off. I have to run, Luna." Dray lifted her from the chair and kissed her hard and thoroughly. "Not to worry. We'll win. Next week I'm taking you to New York and we'll make a flying tour of the state so that my constituents can meet you. There are no people in the world more open-minded and fair than my constituents. You'll see. Have a nice day." Dray kissed her again, slowly and deeply. When he lifted his head, he looked at Uel. "Thanks for the offer. You, your wife, and Gretchen will be coming to our engagement party, and I look forward to getting to know you better."

One minute Dray was there, then he was gone, firing up his powerful car and disappearing.

"Able to leap tall buildings in a single bound. Up, up, and away," Gretchen murmured. "If you ever clone him, Luna, I'm first in line."

"He certainly moves fast." Barb sighed. "I feel much better now."

"He has that effect on people." Luna looked at Uel. "What do you think about the court appearance this morning? Will this nasty article about me prejudice Veli's case?"

"Go in there like the professional you are and bash 'em," Uel told her, shaking his fist. "They wouldn't have pulled this crap if they weren't worried. Go for the throat. Use the pictures you have of the disrepair of the house, produce those letters Skinner sent to Veli telling her that she was out of his life and that he had no intention of supporting either her or the children. Introduce the fact that she'd been beaten and threatened about pursuing her support suit. Drag it all out, don't let them get in a word. Blast them with everything you've got. Fight like the lawyer you are. Nobody beat you in Germany even when they criminally stole from you; no one is going to get you here."

"Rah, rah!" Barb clapped her hands, then kissed her husband.

"I'll go with you if you like, Luna."

"Thanks, Uel, but I can handle it, especially after that pep talk."

"Go get 'em, tiger." Gretchen smiled at her.

Luna did feel better; anger had replaced the immobility of shock she'd sustained when she'd seen the newspaper. Confidence born of the knowledge that she had the facts and evidence to win the case bolstered her when she entered the courthouse.

"You'd better think twice, lady JAG." Hetty was in front of her as she rounded the corner in the corridor leading to Courtroom C.

Luna stared up at him, his close-set eyes having a feral look that repelled her. She glanced past him at the uniformed attendant. "Officer, would you come here. This man is threatening me," Luna said in a loud voice, making heads turn.

Hetty stared at her openmouthed as she backed away and pointed a finger at him. "Hey! What the hell you doin'?"

"Officer, I want this man detained for questioning."

Hetty started for her, then shot a look at the security man, who'd loosened his nightstick. Quick as a cornered fox, he ran toward the exit.

"Watch yourself, Officer. The man is dangerous."

The officer nodded as he sped past her, his walkie-talkie to his mouth.

Luna hoped security would apprehend Hetty and turn him over to the district attorney's office.

All thoughts of her bête noire left her when the judge banged his gavel to signal the opening statement.

Remembering what Uel had told her, Luna leapt into the fray, trotting out damaging evidentiary material that was blackening to Skinner. This elicited constant objections from his attorney, but Luna was making points. She kept rolling, hitting fast and hard, barely drawing a breath, overriding every objection with a countermove.

Luna could tell when the balance changed, when the sharp-eyed looks of the judge settled more and more on Skinner's attorney.

In the end, the judge found for Veli Skinner and for the monetary judgment that Luna had put forth in her arguments.

"This court is adjourned."

Like Peter Pan, Luna wanted to crow with joy, spread her wings, and fly.

"Well done, McAfee," Skinner's lawyer told her grudgingly. "Of course we'll appeal."

"Your case won't hold up in appeal. When I charge that there is chicanery on the part of your client in order to avoid his legal responsibilities, it will go against you, and we should be able to get even more money and a good property settlement as well." Luna stared at the other lawyer.

"When you play hard ball, Counselor, you can get hurt."

"Are you threatening me?"

"Not at all. Just making a statement," Skinner's lawyer said acidly.

"Then watch your mouth, Counselor. I like playing hard ball, and I do it well." Head up, Luna marched past him, hoping no one could tell that her knees were shaking.

It was almost five o'clock when Luna left the courthouse. Instead of returning to the office, she decided to call in, since her present location put her closer to Georgetown. "Yes, we got everything, Gretchen. Tell Uel that I followed his instructions and went for the jugular."

"Good for you, Luna. I'm going to be a tough lawyer too."

"I know that. Oh, Gretchen, tell Uel that security chased Hetty from the courthouse this morning. I don't know if they caught him; but if they did, I'm going to accuse him of harassment and press charges."

Gretchen was silent for a moment. "Wasn't that the man who hassled you one other time at the courthouse?"

"Yes."

"Gee, Luna, I'd be careful. He sounds borderline to me."

"I'll be careful."

The return trip to Georgetown was accomplished in no time. Luna wasn't perturbed by the many times she had to stop for traffic lights. They gave her opportunities to gaze at the beautiful blue-and-violet-hued diamond that Dray had put on her finger that morning. It was his grandmother's ring, the one he'd given her a couple of weeks ago. She wouldn't think of the future, or envision a time when the ring might come off for good. The present was too wonderful to fear the future. Being tied to Dray by the wonderful stone gave her joy.

Parking in front of the house instead of going around to the garage, she was about to use her key to open the door when it opened in front of her. "Good evening, Wilkins. Thank you."

"My sincerest felicitations, Miss McAfee. I know that you and the senator will be very happy." He handed her a newspaper. "Perhaps you would like to see the picture and write-up, miss."

Luna hesitated, remembering what she'd seen at the office that morning, but at Wilkins's urging she read the article, extolling her and Dray. Gazing at the picture of them taken at his folks' home gave her a thrill. It was a *fait accompli.* The *Washington Post* said so.

"I thought you might have enjoyed this more, miss."

"Thank you, Wilkins. Where are the children?"

"I'll be picking them up in half an hour, miss. They went to the museum. The senator will be home at about the same time."

Luna was halfway up the stairs to the second landing when Wilkins spoke again.

"The senator says that the reservation is for seven-thirty, miss."

"Thank you, Wilkins."

She would have time to soak in a hot bath and try to figure what she should wear. Not that she had many choices. Luna hadn't been so flush financially that she had been able to build more than a professional wardrobe of suits and tailored dresses suitable for court. Putting aside money for something frivolous was not so easy to do when every nickel had to be accounted for, day by day. Though the firm was building equity and the volume of clients they handled increased the income every day, none of the partners took home a fat salary.

As she luxuriated in the bubbly tub, which could comfortably have fitted three more people, she decided she would wear the silk skirt and blouse that she'd bought on sale a few months back. . . .

"Hello, darling. Are you wearing your ring?"

"Yes . . . Dray! What are you doing in here? What if the children come upstairs and find you in here with me?"

Dray knelt down on one knee next to the tub, leaning down to kiss her. "What if they do? We're engaged."

"Are we, now?" What gremlin had gotten into her, Luna didn't know, but all at once she reached up two soapy hands and latched them around his neck, pulling at him.

Dray was too strong to have been moved ordinarily, but he was off-balance. "What the hell . . . ? Luna! Damn you." Dray laughed as he tumbled into the perfumed water. Blowing bubbles from his mouth, he grinned at her. "You'll make *some* senator's lady."

Luna caught her breath at the satanic sensuousness of the man. "I should say I'm sorry."

"Why? You're not."

Laughter burst from her. "Your suit must weigh a hundred pounds about now." Mirth faded when she fixed on the fine material. "You're wearing a silk suit and I pulled you into a bubble bath," she ventured weakly. "It's ruined."

Dray had been so glad to hear her unrestrained laughter that he didn't give a damn if she doused his entire wardrobe. "I'll tell you what: You leave me one dry shirt and suit for this evening, and you can do your damnedest with my closet." Rising to his feet, sloshing water everywhere, he began stripping off his sodden clothes and piling them on the floor.

Horror and humor warred in Luna as she gazed at him.

"Your lip is trembling, darling. Don't hold back your laughter on my account."

Luna covered her mouth for a second, then looked all the way up that naked aroused body. "Would you accept ten dollars a week in payment of the suit?"

"Sounds fair. I agree to the terms as long as you wear my ring. How does that sound?"

"Why do I have the feeling I'm being blackmailed?"

"Beats me." Dray stepped down into the tub, sloshing more water over the sides. Settling down next to her, he pulled her close to him, rubbing his chin on the top of her head as he positioned her on his lap.

Luna stared into his eyes, her face reddening.

"Darling, are you blushing because I'm aroused? I'm afraid you're in for a permanent red face, because I'll always be in the mood for love when you're around me."

"I'd better stay out of the Senate chamber, then."

Dray laughed. "You're a source of constant entertainment to me, Luna love. I think our marriage is going to be very eventful. Let's set a date."

"What?" Luna tried to straighten up, but Dray wouldn't release her. "I don't think I have time for anything like that this year. . . ."

"How about in a month? We'll have a small wedding in New York in the Little Church Around the Corner. Doesn't that sound nice?"

"I've always wanted to see that church," Luna answered, momentarily diverted. "Dray, we can't . . ."

"We can and will. Would you like children? I would."

"So would I but . . ."

"How many, do you think?"

"How many? Like how many apples or something? Why not start with one and see how that goes?"

"Fine. We'll try right away. Maybe we'll have a baby this time next year."

"A baby?" Luna leaned against him, the vision of a sturdy little boy with silvery blond hair and bourbon-colored eyes rose up before her. She wriggled with a kind of wonder and joy.

Dray gasped. "Darling, you're too potent, we may have that baby sooner than we planned." Dray lifted her in his strong arms until she was astride him, feeling the shudder in her body when he penetrated her. "Ummm, that is so good, isn't it?" All the memories of their times together in Germany came back to him like a rosy tide. The pain of being parted from Luna had lodged in him like an ice log. Luna's passion battered it, melted it, wiped it out. Love that had been dammed broke free and flooded him.

Luna felt wild, unfettered. She expected a rough, out-of-control response because she felt that way. Dray's kiss was like no other, but it had a timeless familiarity that had her heart beating out of rhythm. The ineffable gentleness bound her to him with a thousand silk threads. She was no longer a separate woman. Now she was part of him. Passion enveloped her, making her giddy, powerful, helpless, on fire. She would love him for all time. "Yes." Luna sighed, closing her eyes, answering his query, every movement of the hot water abrading their bodies, moving them in sensuous rhythm so that further talk was impossible.

The love power was there. It opened his mind and heart. He could read her feelings, sense her responses so clearly. Dray felt her moment of hesitancy, the dragging potency of it making her tremble as want and wariness warred in her being. "Darling, I'm yours," Dray whispered into her body.

"And I'm yours." How strange! She could hear Dray speaking, but all other sounds were smothered in the thunderous flash flood of passion.

Dray tightened his hold, bringing her into him.

Reserve crumbled and Luna lifted her legs to bind him more tightly to her. For all her life she had wanted this, for a millennium she'd wanted Dray to love her.

When he kissed her behind the knee, she muttered "Wonderful." Nipping her rounded buttocks with his teeth elicited a groan of delight. "Dray," she moaned, "I need you." The words were clarion-clear; the commitment was total. Maybe the fears would come back, but for now there was nothing between them but love.

"You're my life," he whispered.

"Don't ever leave me," she begged.

As they panted into each other's mouth, heat built between them.

"Luna, my darling, you set me on fire."

"Dray, Dray!" Gripping him with all her strength, she felt the elemental tremor of love shake her from her head to her toes.

"With all of me I want you, Luna mine," Dray told her shakily many minutes later when they were still holding each other.

Rising from the tub carefully with Luna in his arms, he stepped onto the wet tile.

"I hope the water doesn't leak down to the main floor. Wilkins might figure out what we're doing."

"So he might." Dray kissed her nose. "I don't care. If it worries you, I'll have someone check the floor. I don't want to damage your home, darling."

"It's your home." Luna kept her eyes closed as he doused her with a fragrant oil, then began drying her in slow, sweet strokes.

"In a month it will be yours, all yours, to do with as you wish. There's a farm in New York State that you'll like, I'm sure, and a town house in the Eighties in Manhattan."

"I don't need much." Luna rubbed her hand over his face.

"Don't look so worried, Luna mine. We'll have each other, that's what's important." He kissed her nose. "But we'll have to hurry if we're going to make our reservation."

Luna's voice turned to a squeal when she looked at the clock Dray showed her, then she hotfooted it into her bedroom, only to bounce back to the bathroom again. "What should I do with your wet things?"

"I'll take care of them."

"What will you wear?"

Dray shrugged, his eyes running up and down her nude form. "I do love your body."

"Dray."

Luna's protest elicited another shrug from him. "A towel. See you in less than thirty minutes, love."

"Get out of here, Dray," Luna urged him weakly.

"I guess you're right, or we'll be in your bed."

* * *

Luna could barely put in the gold earrings she'd chosen to wear with the pale aqua skirt with cream horizontal stripes and the cream double-breasted shirtwaist blouse. The skirt billowed around her at the least movement, the silky sheen repeated in the blouse giving her skin a peach-blossom finish that was very enticing. Her gold watch and engagement ring were her only other adornments.

Engagement ring! Luna stared at the precious stone and wished that it were welded to her finger.

Snatching a peach silk topper that Gillian Roth had made her for a very small fee, she left the room and walked down to the first landing.

"Hello, I've been waiting." Dray pushed away from the wall where he'd been waiting in the shadow of the stairs. "I was tempted to come up and help you dress."

"That might have made me even later." His warm chuckle ran over her skin like soft kisses, goose-bumping her body.

"True, my sweet, and I certainly couldn't have done a better job than you've already done. You look luscious."

"I think you must be hungry, we should hurry." Luna felt out of breath and helium-light.

Dray took hold of her upper arms. "I'm always hungry for you. I have been since the moment we met. Didn't you know that?"

Luna reached up and touched his lips with her finger. "Is this real? Are we?"

"Very." Dray turned his head, pressing his lips into her palm, then kissing the ring on her third finger. "We have to hurry if we're going to say good night to the children. They're in the kitchen with Wilkins, melting marshmallows for their hot chocolate."

"Made from scratch from imported Dutch chocolate, I know. Amy delighted in telling me all the things that Wilkins was going to bring to their house when their mother was better and back where she belonged." Luna looked up at him as they left the front foyer and went down the wide center corridor leading to the kitchen. "I won today, Dray."

"I know, darling. One of my staff observed and said you were a fire-eater. I'm damned proud of you, and hope you won't give up your practice when we're married."

"Thank you." She smiled mistily at him. "I think we've been an imposition."

"You've been wonderful, and you know it." Dray pushed open the door, the laughing greetings of the children putting aside their conversation.

"Look, isn't it wonderful?" Amy pointed to the glass mugs that sat on the breakfast bar and were now frothing over with chocolate. "We're to do our studies while we drink it, Wilkins says."

"Good idea," Dray concurred, kissing Amy on the top of the head. "Studies aren't painful if done with sips of hot chocolate."

"No! Is that right?" Amy beamed up at Dray. "I'll probably get A's now."

After a few minutes Dray and Luna went out the back door to the garage, where Dray's car was parked.

"If you're looking for yours tomorrow, check the garage next to this. My neighbor is on sabbatical in Africa and I put your car in there. I'm sure Wilkins will have it around front for you in the morning, but I didn't want you to look out a window and think someone had lifted it."

"Thank you, but there was no need to put it under cover, and no one would lift it," Luna told him dryly.

"You're right about that. As soon as we're married you'll have a safer one, and don't tell me I can't buy my wife a car, please."

Luna looked down and saw his hand resting on the wheel, and she reached up and touched it with her own. "I wouldn't think of doing that, Senator."

Dray threaded his hands with hers at once. "Good. I think you'll enjoy Chez Robert." He shrugged. "I would have preferred someplace less crowded, but it will serve our purposes if we're seen by Washington this evening after that rag piece this morning."

Even after they'd driven the few miles to Chez Robert, Dray's mouth was tight, as though he were still dwelling on the unpalatable thought.

Luna had expected Chez Robert to be posh and glitzy, and she wasn't disappointed. As Dray shepherded her across the floor she saw many high-level Capital dignitaries.

"Good evening, Judge. I'd like you to meet my fiancée. Darling, this is Judge Damon.

"Good evening, Congresswoman, may I introduce Luna McAfee, my fiancée. Good evening, Senator." All across the room, Dray went out of his way to introduce Luna as his intended wife.

At last they were seated in what Luna was sure was one of the best tables in the house, if not *the* best. They were screened from any would-be oglers, yet they had a good view of any or all of the inhabitants of the room.

"You look a little taken aback, darling. Are you?" Dray's smooth voice accompanied a lingering kiss on her mouth. "I hope that's kiss-proof lip gloss."

"So do I," Luna answered him breathlessly, reeling from his touch. Were there shots to protect her from Dray's power? "Would that be Lola Martan heading this way?"

Without turning his head, Dray nodded. "No doubt. She can smell a story a mile away. Count to ten and she'll be here."

"She is coming to our table. Lord, Dray, I've read that she's ruined more than one person."

"A few hundred would be closer to the mark. Smile, darling, and look into my eyes. You have nothing to fear from that soignée harridan, and you can count on that." Dray lifted her left hand and kissed the ring on her finger. "I wish we were back in the tub so that I could lave your body with my tongue."

Luna had a sensation of losing consciousness as Dray

seemed to draw her into him. "Shh, stop, for heaven's sake. Oh, dear."

"Senator Lodge, I am angry with you. How is it you didn't call me with the news of your engagement? I had to hear it from the person I'm dining with this evening. How naughty of you, Perrin Draper Lodge."

Dray uncoiled his length from the chair, the electric charm of his smile touching the Washington gossip columnist. He managed a quick wink in Luna's direction before he raised Lola Martan's hand to his lips. "There must have been a snafu, Lola. I gave explicit instructions to my people to call you. You might check with your staff. I'd be very surprised if they didn't have a memo from my office."

"You're a smooth devil, Dray. You could give Beelzebub lessons on conquering Paradise."

"Ah, we're doing Milton, are we? A favorite of mine, Lola." Dray beamed at the columnist.

Luna stared at him. Didn't he see Lola Martan's hard look? Those eyes were agates.

"Let me introduce you to my fiancée, Lola. This is Luna McAfee. Darling, this is Lola Martan."

"How do you do, Ms. Martan."

"I'm just fine. I'm surprised to find that Dray would marry a woman with a past, Ms. McAfee," Lola simpered, her eyes watchful.

Luna opened her eyes as wide as she could. "Oh, really? You have no past, Ms. Martan? Were you born yesterday?" Her saccharine questions touched the atmosphere.

"I don't think you understand me, Ms. McAfee. You see . . ."

"Oh, I understand you very well, Ms. Martan. As a lawyer, I'm fully aware of the laws on scandal and libel and am fully capable of using every facet of the law at my disposal, Ms. Martan." Luna smiled brightly. "I'm sure you wish us well, Ms. Martan."

"Ah, yes, of course I do. When is the wedding?"

"In about a month or so," Dray interjected smoothly. "Won't you join us for a drink, Lola?"

The columnist blinked as though she'd suddenly stepped into quicksand. "No, I think I'll go back to my table, but I reserve the right to print all about your engagement and I'll want to know the specifics on the wedding, Dray."

"No problem. I'll have my staff send you any pertinent information. Won't we, darling?"

"Of course." Luna was sure all her teeth were showing as she said good-bye to the columnist.

"Now you can explode, love." Dray leaned forward, his mouth a centimeter from hers. "Into my mouth, please."

Luna's anger melted in reaction to Dray's heat. "Damn the woman," she mumbled, her lips feathering his. "I think this is illegal, Senator."

"It feels wonderful. I think we'll go to the farm and hibernate after the wedding. We'll stay in bed for a month."

"You might miss a roll call," Luna observed weakly, her mind fading in delight as she pictured them wrapped in each other's arms. "We should order."

"Hungry?"

"I suppose so. It should be safer than the conversation we've been having."

Dray chuckled, an infinitesimal movement bringing the waiter on the run. "Will you let me order for you, darling? Or are you too independent for that?"

"Order for both of us, by all means, but I insist on French, please."

"Was that a lacing of vinegar in your voice, love?"

"Maybe *ein Tropfen.*"

"A drop?" Dray translated from the German silkily. "I would say a cupful. Why don't you order for us, darling? You've been itching for a fight since Lola's appearance, and I won't oblige."

"Ogre." Luna lifted the two-foot-high menu, seeing the flash of shock on the waiter's face as he heard her comment, before it turned masklike again.

In a rough Parisian accent Luna ordered the meal of *soupe à l'oignon, truite en coleur, salade Niçoise, fruits et fromage, et café.*

"Thank you, Nico. That will be all," Dray told the waiter after the man bowed to Luna several times and complimented her on her French. "Damn you, Luna," Dray told her lazily. "You've made another conquest. I don't relish a future of battling your swains, my treasure."

Luna watched him uneasily. "You're angry."

"Yes, at you, for having so much power over me, and any man with more than a hat-size IQ. You're a dynamite challenge to any man who can think." Dray leaned forward and took her hand, nipping the tip of her little finger with his teeth. "I didn't relish giving over my life to you in Germany. I find it's no easier with the passage of time."

Luna gasped. "You're a United States senator. You give over only to your constituents."

"True . . . but you own me in a way that astounds and appalls me, Luna McAfee. Walking through fire to get to you does not seem out of the ordinary, swimming backwards across the Atlantic doesn't seem too big a task. Getting the picture, my own."

"Too fast." Luna was going down for the third time. "That's what happened last time, and look what happened."

Dray leaned forward so fast the table rocked. "Nothing happened, my sweet, except that you forgot to trust me."

Luna was openmouthed as Dray's face turned ugly, menacing.

"You ran from me, Luna, when you should have turned to me. That won't happen again."

Luna's voice was stuck, her mouth paralyzed. She was caught between shock and anger. When she finally had the breath to retort, the soup course was being served.

Sipping the steaming onion brew, Luna tried to reassemble her disordered mind. "Dray, if Lola Martan ever dredged up all that happened in Germany, she could milk it for all it's worth and it could cost you a great deal. You're not up for reelection for a few years, but mud sticks, and she could sling a lot of it."

"Let her try. If she makes any allegations against my wife, she'll think a brick building was falling on her. My family has shares in the international news service that syndicates her. If she attacks you, she'll never have a media job as long as she lives, and she knows I will do just that. Lola Martan would dare many things, but she'd never endanger her own backside."

Luna didn't know the ruthless man with the vitriol spilling from his mouth. "You sound like you'd kill her."

"I might. Here, have some cheese and then we'll leave. I'm taking you dancing."

The Chilton stuck in her throat as she watched the sophisticated mask of the man facing her fall into place again. Who was Perrin Draper Lodge? Hoodlum? Senator? Gentleman? Destroyer? Marriage to him could be like tap-dancing with a cyclone.

"Don't daydream, darling. I have a hankering to hold you in my arms to music."

Luna had the sensation of being in the company of a stranger as they left the posh eatery. Strip by strip the veneer of civility had been peeled away from Dray and she was beginning to see beneath it. The bon vivant was the shell, the man was a determined, sometimes ruthless, strong, killing personality that would brook no interference. He would ride roughshod over adversity.

"Well?" Dray questioned in the car as they made their way through the corkscrew of streets in old Washington. "What are you plotting now? My murder?"

"Do you think I could get away with it?"

"I hope not. Here we are."

"Danilo's? How did you arrange that? I understand it's a three-week wait to get in here."

"Could be." Dray got out of the car, smiled at the valet, and helped Luna from the car himself. "Let's dance, lady."

Luna stepped from reality to fantasy. The red-and-black

decor was cleverly scrolled to give the impression of hell. The devilish waiters were smiling and friendly and the music was pure hot jazz with a lacing of thirties swing and forties jive. Everything was torrid and rhythmic.

The maître d' smiled at them and led them right to a secluded table that was screened with palms but allowed a view of the dancers and band.

"Did you sell stock to get this table?"

"Not every share." Dray was inordinately pleased when she looked around her with a delighted smile. "Shall we dance, darling? I have a hankering to celebrate our engagement."

Luna rose, preceding him to the large dance floor, aware of the eyes that warmed her back.

At the edge of the floor he turned her and they began the throbbing dance steps that matched the beat of the band.

When Dray let her flow free of his body, Luna felt unfettered, her body gyrating with an abandon born of happiness. No one had ever danced like Dray. He was athletic in all he did, and no less so when he exercised to music.

When they finally stopped, Luna was panting slightly. "That was wonderful."

"Why don't we have a cool drink, and then we can dance some more?"

"Okay," Luna replied with a laugh, the low, vibrant sound bringing smiles to the faces that turned toward them.

Sipping a long, cool Sunburst—seltzer water and orange juice with lime—Luna couldn't stop the smile that she knew was on her face. It had been so long since she'd just cut loose and had a good time.

Again Dray sought out other acquaintances, seeming to pull them to their table. "And this is Muriel Deepwater, darling. Her family is from Oklahoma."

"We're one of the still rich Indians. Not too many of us left."

"How do you do." Luna liked the dark-skinned woman immediately.

Over and over again she greeted people, waiting while they

gazed at her ring; listened while Dray told them they would
be getting married in a month.

"A month from now is not that far off. You'll have to re-
tract that much sooner."

"I'm not retracting. We're getting married in a month. It's
all set."

"I don't have a dress," Luna said inanely, rosy visions of
being his wife dancing in her head.

Dray shrugged. "Let Charine worry about that."

"Of course."

They danced again, neither seeming to want to leave.

When the band began to put away their instruments, Dray
looked at his watch and shook his head. "You're going to be
tired tomorrow, Counselor."

"So are you." Luna masked a yawn as she walked out the
exit, glad she was cuddled to his side.

Luna saw the man come at them on the run, his masked
face registering in her mind just as he made a dive at Dray.
She saw the flash of steel and threw out her arm, feeling a
sickening wrench and then pain. Then she was falling and the
man was running away.

"Luna! Luna, darling."

"I'm here." Luna closed her eyes as the world spun too
rapidly on its axis. Blackness came over her like a warm blanket.

Chapter 12

"Senator, I understand your anxiety, but it would have been better if you waited outside the examining room." The nurse tugged at his arm, but he didn't budge.

"I'm staying, and I would like a phone, please."

The words hammered out of his mouth, making the nurse take one step back, release his arm, then scamper away as though stung by a hornet.

Without taking his eyes from Luna, he dialed when the instrument was handed to him. "Chad? Let me speak to Father, but hook into this line. Another incident. This time, unless I'm being paranoid, the target was me. Hello, sir. You heard. I'm fine, but Luna is . . ." Dray paused to clear the hoarseness from his throat. "I think she'll be fine. She deflected what looked like a knife with her purse, and then he struck her before I could get to him. He got away. Yes. I'll be talking to the police as soon as I talk to Luna. Good-bye." Dray handed the phone to an attendant, his gaze still fixed on Luna.

When she groaned he was at her side at once, ignoring the protests of the attending physician and his assistants. "Dray." Her voice was thready.

"I'm here, darling, right beside you."

Without opening her eyes, her hand came up as though in search, and he clasped it, kissing the fingers. "You're all right, Dray?"

"Fine, and so will you be, darling."

"That's if I ever get to taking care of her," the young doctor said crossly, pushing his glasses back up his nose with one finger.

After a while Dray did leave the room when he'd been assured that he could take her home that night, that she had a sprained arm, a few bruises, and maybe a mild concussion.

Dray went right to the public phone. "Uel? Dray Lodge. There's been an accident." In short, terse sentences he told him what had happened to Luna.

The muttered curses and imprecations from Uel were laced with concern. "And you have no idea who it could be, Senator?"

"Call me Dray, please. No, I don't, but I did have the feeling that the perpetrator was after me, not Luna."

"Damn! What a tangle. Listen, don't worry about the office, we'll handle her caseload. Since the Skinner case is on hold for three weeks, we can manage the rest."

"Good, because in two days I'm taking her to New York with me. Veli Skinner's children will remain with Wilkins and he will keep a close watch over them and make sure they visit their mother regularly."

"I saw Veli today. She's looks so much better. That convalescent hospital was just what she needed."

"She's had a rough time."

"I'd like to come to the hospital to see Luna, Dray, if you don't think it would be too much for her."

"It's late. I'm going to take her home and put her to bed. Why don't you, your wife, and Gretchen come over in the morning and have breakfast with her? Say about eight?"

"Thanks, that would be great, and thanks for calling."

Dray made a few other calls, and by the time he was off the phone, his brother and brother-in-law had arrived at the hospital.

"So how do we handle this, Dray?" Chad's normally cheerful expression was grim.

"It's war and we don't know the enemy, so we use anything that will give us an edge. How about those fraternity chums of yours that were so good at war games on campus? You think they would be interested in this?"

Chad nodded slowly, looking thoughtful. "I could put them on it here in D.C. and in New York." Chad hesitated. "Darius was at the house. Father told him. He called some of his cronies."

"Retired CIA?"

Bret nodded. "Don't frown, Dray. He could be damned helpful."

"I know that, but I don't particularly relish involving my aging uncle in something dangerous."

"I'm so glad you don't mind sacrificing us," his brother-in-law ventured dryly.

Dray relaxed for the first time in hours. "Not at all."

"What are you doing about the media, Dray? They're already pawing at the doors of this place."

"I called John. He's coming down here to take care of it."

"The long-suffering Talbot is an asset to you, old boy," Bret observed.

"Yes, he is."

"I'd be a flunky, too, for what Dray pays him," Chad said.

The three men whirled when the swinging doors to the emergency examining rooms opened and the doctor appeared. "Easy, Senator Lodge, your fiancée will be right out." The doctor frowned. "Perhaps it would be better if you left her overnight and—"

"No! Unless she needs some kind of treatment I can't provide, she's coming home with me."

Bret and Chad were openmouthed at the thunderous words.

"Easy, old man, she'd be fine here," Bret whispered.

"Would she? What if the man who tried tonight paid a visit here? The security here is not as tight as what I can muster up at my home and which has already been put into operation."

The doctor shrugged. "As you say, Senator. I'll sign the release, but if there is any—"

"I won't hesitate to return her here, and since I'll be with her all night, I would notice any change."

Chad's mouth twisted in a smile, and he moved closer to his brother-in-law. "Admit that you've never seen him like this."

Bret nodded. "Never. I think it might kill him to lose her." Bret stared at his friend and relative, an awed look on his face. "No one has ever gotten to Dray like this."

Dray caught the looks coming his way and smiled grimly. "I damn near had a stroke when I saw her go down and thought the bastard had stabbed her."

In minutes Luna was wheeled out by an attendant.

Dray was at her side at once. "How are you, darling?"

"Fine, but I think you've permanently rattled the emergency team. You acted like a Tartar in there." She touched the face so close to her own. "I'm fine, truly I am." When she saw the sheen of tears in his eyes, she pulled his face close to hers and pressed her mouth to his, that tongue touching her tongue making her heart slam out of rhythm. "We'll be banned from this hospital, Senator."

"Marry me tonight."

"Too worn-out."

"I'll make sure you get your rest."

"Marrying you and getting rest? That's a contradiction in terms."

Chad chuckled, looking across Dray's back as he leaned over Luna to Bret. "She's got him figured."

"To the last dotted *i.*" Bret grinned when Dray looked his way.

"We have to get her out of here. Chad, did you ride with Bret? Good. Drive the Ferrari, I called a limo service for us." Dray stared at each one in turn. "You know what you have to do."

The two men nodded solemnly.

"What do you mean, you missed him? How the hell did that happen? I can't tell him that."

"Who is this that you can't tell? You make him sound like God."

"Watch your mouth. Not even your father will protect you if you cross the Man. Remember that." It angered him to see the sullen look cross the younger man's face. Damn, he hated to use amateurs. He was going to talk to the Man about eliminating the entire group of green heads from the operation. The punk in front of him could blow the whole deal. Didn't he have enough to take care of without dogging the fool's trail all the time? So far he'd blown every assignment they'd given him. That had to stop.

"If I got to meet the Man, maybe I could explain and that would take care of it."

"Huh? Oh, sure. I'll talk to him about that very thing."

"Well? What happened?"

"He blew it. The lawyer ended up in the hospital, but from what I've been able to discover, she only had bumps and bruises."

"Didn't I say that the senator was the target now?"

"You did, but that punk we've been using is a real ringer. Too rough, impulsive, not accurate."

"I don't want to hear things like that from you. Smooth it out for me, no more wrinkles."

"All right. I'll try to come up with something."

"Do that. Try thinking along the lines of the other source I mentioned."

"Isn't that chancy? You even said that might not be a reliable way. What if he balks?"

"Then he'll have to go. Right now it looks the better of our two options. Try it."

The phone clicked in his ear and he grimaced at it. It seemed to him that though he was in the middle, he was the more visible one, the one who could get nailed if any of this backfired.

"Covering my buns is going to be the first priority," he told the ornate mirror in his rosewood-paneled study. He'd come too far to falter. Another thought intruded, making him scowl at his image. "Damn that woman lawyer. We should have gotten rid of her in Germany, and that's what I told the Man at the time. Now look what we have!"

Ahmed stared at the man long and hard when the servant grabbed the dish of eggs from his hand. "Speak, fool!"

"If Your Highness kills me, that is my fate, but I could not let you eat that dish. I am of the hill people, of your father's people. We know the secret herbs of the mountains and deserts, Your Highness. It is the odor of what we call 'the quiet lady' that emanates from your soup."

Ahmed stared at the man, then glanced quickly around him. None of his bodyguards were in sight, just this man Tabul, who had come that morning to serve him breakfast at the embassy. "And you are not the one to kill me, is that it?" Ahmed watched the blood run into the servant's face.

"My family have been servants and soldiers to your family, Highness. I have forfeited my life to you. If you believe that I betray you, then you must kill me."

When the man drew the curved dress scimitar from its scabbard, Ahmed blinked until he realized it had been offered handle first. "No, no. Put away your weapon. You have saved my life, Tabul. You will be my special guard. Under no circumstances will you leave my side."

"Only my death will separate us, Highness." Tabul leaned down and lifted the plate, holding it close to his nose and nodding. "Yes, it is in there. Would you have me take it, lord?"

"No." Ahmed smiled. "I had forgotten that the Yahdi can track like a hunting dog."

"Better than any tracking animal, lord. It is our pride." He stared at the prince for long moments. "My people have worried that you would be in danger. It is said that there is an outsider who is dangerous to you, lord."

Ahmed nodded. "So it is true. Tabul, you will get in touch

with your elders. Have them send the most trusted of your people to the capital. There they will contact Gamal."

"He is of our people, lord, and cousin to you."

Ahmed nodded, scribbling rapidly in a notebook. "This is for your eyes only. *You* will send this to Gamal from the home of Senator Lodge. He is to see this and if possible hear your conversation. Then you will get back to me at once."

"I do not like to leave you, lord."

Ahmed smiled. "I will prepare my food from a storage area in my apartment. On your return you will come there."

"As soon as possible, lord."

When the man had gone, Ahmed left the dining room, plate in hand, going directly to a butler's pantry, where he sniffed it, then dumped the dish, shaking his head. He could detect no unusual odor.

Wilkins stared at the inscrutable expression of the obviously Middle Eastern person who faced him after bowing and giving his name. "All right. You may come in, but you will have to wait, Tabul."

"I wait."

Wilkins's long experience with persons trying to get to Perrin Draper Lodge had honed his instincts razor-sharp. He stared at the man for long minutes. "From Prince Ahmed, you say?"

"My lord says I must make the call from this home."

Wilkins nodded. The senator had the house screened periodically for bugs since an aborted attempt at kidnapping when he'd been a law student. Since the most sophisticated systems on the continent had been fashioned by another classmate of the senator's undergraduate years, it had been easy to have expert advice on the question.

Many of the senator's closest confidants knew this and used his home for the purpose of secrecy from time to time.

Dray was upstairs in his room eating breakfast along with Luna, the children, Gretchen, Uel, and Barbara.

"I like doing this," Amy told Gretchen solemnly. "And we get hot soup for lunch every day."

"I think I'll move in with you," Gretchen told the little girl.

"Fine, but you'll have to sleep with me. Senator Dray is sleeping in Luna's room." The little girl frowned. "Most of the time he's there, when he's not here." She beamed at the wide-eyed adults who were watching her in varying degrees of emotion.

"I hate to use clichés, but . . ."

"Then don't, Uel," Luna told him grumpily, knowing her face was red.

"But, 'out of the mouths of babes' and all that rot." Uel beamed at his partner. "And stop throwing those killing looks at me, Luna love. You'll be seeing a lot of us. Dray said we should use this house as our office while you're recuperating."

"Recuperating? I don't need any such thing. I'll be back to work tomorrow." Luna stared at Dray. "I still don't know why you deposited me in your room."

"Convenience?" Gretchen offered, reaching for the tray of fresh fruits and selecting a strawberry the size of a tangerine. "I'm in favor of moving the office here. I love the food."

"You're fired," Luna gasped.

"Again?" Gretchen looked pained. "Luna, you fire me once a month."

The door opened and Wilkins stood there with a pot of coffee. "Senator, may I speak with you, sir? It's important."

Dray heard the note of urgency, though the voice was smooth and quietly efficient; he also noted the quick look Uel gave Wilkins. "I'll be right back, darling." He smiled at Luna when she shot an inquiring look at Wilkins.

"What is it?" Dray closed the bedroom door behind him before asking.

In short, terse sentences, Wilkins sketched what Tabul had told him.

Dray nodded. "Get him hooked into Gamal in Hashan at once. I'll join you in the library." Dray turned and opened the door again, not surprised to see Uel looking his way. He gestured to the dark-skinned man to join him.

"Dray? What is it?"

The tinge of alarm in Luna's voice brought a smile to his face. "Nothing, darling. I promise I'll tell you everything shortly."

The two men went down the curving stairway side by side.

"You have good instincts," Dray told Uel dryly.

"It comes from years of bobbing and weaving through life. This is something about Luna, isn't it?"

"I don't know for sure, but it could be. Let's go into the library. I have the house swept periodically for bugs, but that room is checked every day."

Uel whistled soundlessly. "Sounds like you've a few enemies."

"Haven't we all."

"True."

In the library, Tabul looked at Dray, then at a picture he held in his hand, then his grim expression rested on Uel and remained there.

"It's all right." Dray looked at the message from Ahmed he held in his hand. "Tabul, this man can be trusted."

"The call is through to Hashan, Senator." Wilkins held out the phone. "Gamal al Alal is on the line."

Dray gestured to Tabul to take the call. "Speak English, Tabul. I understand the patois but the others do not."

"I will do as you say, lord." Tabul took the phone, read the message that he took from Dray, then recounted what had happened at Ahmed's breakfast table.

Uel bit his lip, his eyes sliding toward Dray. "Then you really think this is an international ring, and that it involves Luna in some way."

Dray shrugged. "I'd like to be proven wrong, but there are too many tie-ins and discrepancies. Much of it is a muddle right now, but I've been getting the feeling, and my family sees it that way, that there's a network centered right here in the capital of international-business mercenaries. They not

only run an underground bank, financing all sorts of take-
overs of countries and companies, they kill and rob for personal gain and vendetta."

Uel inhaled deeply. "I appreciate your trust, Senator. It
isn't misplaced." Uel caught the lopsided grin.

"You wouldn't be within ten miles of this house if I didn't
think you were solid. I trust Luna's judgment."

"And I trust you'll make her happy. If not, I'll come gun-
ning for you."

Dray nodded, seeing the determination behind Uel's smile.
"Understood."

Tabul coughed and handed the phone to Dray, who immediately began speaking in the heavy dialect of Hashan. "We
understand each other, Gamal." Dray switched to English.
"I'm glad the hill people will be coming here as well as to
Hashan City. Ahmed will be safer. Thank you." Dray replaced the receiver and looked at Tabul. "You will go back to
your master the same way you reached here: no main thoroughfares, and as inconspicuously as possible."

Tabul made the Arab obeisance.

"Tabul, if we're going to beat our enemies, we must be as
crafty as the hill people whence you sprang. If we make a
mistake, much could be lost."

"I will do as you say, lord." Tabul moved after Wilkins
toward the back door.

Uel looked at Dray, drumming his fingers on the desk he
was leaning on. "We don't know the enemy, or the numbers."

Dray sat behind his desk and gestured to Uel to take a seat
across the desk from him. "I have a feeling that starting with
Skinner and Hetty wouldn't be such a bad idea. I'm taking
Luna with me to New York, a fact-finding tour of the state
and a rest cure for her. Gil Hetty's headquarters are in New
York."

Uel steepled his hands in front of him. "I know a few people who might be able to get me some underground information on Skinner."

"If it borders on the illegal, have a care, Counselor."

"I will."

The two men stared at each other in grim agreement.

The afternoon passed slowly for Luna. She wasn't used to so much inactivity. Since the children were going to visit their mother, she wouldn't have the benefit of their company or Wilkins's.

The briefs she needed to go over danced in front of her eyes. Even Lance, who was keeping her company, seemed more intent on sleeping.

Irritated with herself, she flipped from channel to channel on the television, bored with it all.

"Need entertaining?"

"Dray! What are you doing here? Lance, stop that. Dray, he'll get hair all over your suit."

"Too late. Down, fool. Come with me." Dray spun around, the dog at his heels, leaving the bedroom and closing the door behind him.

There wasn't a sound. Even Lance's snoring would seem appealing at the moment. Luna glowered at the book on the bed next to her. She should be delighted to have such an assortment of best sellers, but she wasn't pleased. Boring! When the door opened again, her eyes flew to it.

"Sorry, darling, did I take too long? I gave him a short run in the park," Dray told her, yanking off his tie.

"Can't you brush your clothes a little so that you don't have to make a complete change?"

"Haven't got time." Dray grinned at her.

Luna felt as though someone had started a grass fire at her feet and it was slowly burning its way up her frame. She read the hot message in those bourbon-colored eyes. "You'll be late," Luna told him faintly, moving over on the bed as he climbed in beside her, clad only in briefs.

"No, I won't," Dray whispered in her ear as he pulled her close to him. "Do you know how I feel getting you into my bed at last?"

"I've been here since yesterday," she said weakly.

"Not with me here beside you," Dray said, his lips moving over the silk nightgown she was wearing.

"I didn't need such expensive lingerie," Luna told him, apropos of nothing.

"Maybe, but your breasts feel so wonderful covered in silk."

"There's that, of course." Luna felt feverish, her hands going up to hold his head as he moved slowly down her body. "What did you say?"

Dray lifted his head, his eyes glazed, his silver-blond hair mussed from her clutching hands. "I said that I would always need you, darling, and I can't wait to marry you."

"Oh." Luna was on fire. She needed to retaliate with a sexual assault similar to the one she was receiving.

"Darling, no, I don't want you to exert yourself," Dray protested when she began her exploration of his body. "Luna, darling, stop. Darling, it will be too fast for you."

"Not fast enough," Luna muttered, feeling detached from the woman who was taking so many liberties with Dray. Then, throwing caution to the winds, she held him to her, beginning to move down his body as he had moved down hers, her hands questing over him, exciting every inch of him. When her tongue touched and clung to him in the intimate abrasion that fired her, his body shuddered over and over again.

"No more!" Dray gasped an expletive. "I think it's illegal to pull a senator apart, lady," Dray told her shakily, moving over her, entering her gently, and beginning a slow rhythm. "I want it to last, but it's well nigh impossible with you, my sweet."

In thunderous quiet, with only the explosions of their chaotic breathing, they crested in ultimate joy.

Dray held her, soothing her, whispering to her, "I want you, Luna."

"You've just had me . . . and I want you too."

"Don't sound so aggrieved, pet."

She stared up at him, running her fingers over his chest.

"Things happen to people, to what they have, that sunder them apart."

"That's already happened to us, Luna. We know what to guard against."

"Yes." Deep down she wondered if that was true. It was almost painful for her to admit that she wanted and needed Dray in her life, because she wasn't sure it could be for a lifetime. Pushing the unwelcome thoughts from her mind, she turned to face him, relishing the freshness of his breath, the ability to see the very faint beginnings of a beard on his face, the all but invisible scar that tipped up one corner of his mouth. Putting up her hand, she traced that tough mouth.

"What were Uel and you discussing when you left the room this morning?" Luna knew that Dray was well aware of what she was referring to.

Dray shot out his arm and glanced at his watch. "I don't have time to go into it now, sweetheart. Let's talk tonight on the plane to New York. All right?"

"You're putting me off," Luna accused, watching him stride toward the bathroom, his naked body well muscled and tanned. "When do you tan in the nude?" she blurted out.

Stopping at the bathroom door, he spun to face her, grinning. "All the time, and we'll be doing it together from now on, Luna." Dray frowned all at once. "But I think you'll be under a canopy. I don't want the ultraviolet rays damaging your wonderful skin."

"What if I want to protect your skin in the same way?"

Dray propped himself against the doorjamb, his smile widening sensuously. "Whatever you say, my own, since my entire body is yours." Blowing her a kiss, he disappeared into the bathroom.

Luna touched her pulse with her first three fingers. Lord, it was racing out of control. Damn the man! He was like a puppeteer. Could blood boil through the veins and scorch the flesh? Luna looked at herself. What did she expect when she'd just a shared a caldron of passion with the world's most beautiful man?

Luna leaned back against the pillows and stared at the door. He was her greatest menace, yet she felt safer with him than she'd ever felt with anybody. Love was a tangled skein.

When Dray came out of the bathroom not long after, he noticed that she was dozing. Maybe he shouldn't have made love to her. No! It had been as wonderful for her as it had been for him. He ground his teeth in frustration at all that had happened to her. She could have been killed. Losing her was something he couldn't contemplate. His mind couldn't stretch around the horror.

Pulling clean clothes from his drawers and closets, he never took his eyes off her as he dressed. Years of wearing the best clothes had given him a casual elegance that was an integral part of him. Dressing had become automatic; his well-groomed, tasteful look was not something he even noticed anymore.

"I will keep you safe, my own darling, I promise you that," Dray whispered to her, kissing her forehead.

He hurried from the room. There was no way he was going to miss the afternoon vote; he'd worked too hard for the high-way bill. It was a matter of pride to him to be in any roll call where the bill had his backing or where the bill was one he strongly opposed. Even with the smaller matters that had less significance, he didn't miss the roll call except for a good reason.

Meeting Wilkins in the downstairs hall, he paused. "Miss McAfee is sleeping, and I would like her to stay that way as long as possible. It's not a long trip to New York but I don't want her fatigued."

"I'll see to everything, sir, even to Miss McAfee's packing, though I understand that Charine will have clothes ready for her in the apartment."

A faint smile played around Dray's mouth. "That will be our little secret, Wilkins. I'll be back early, but I have to hurry."

"A small salad is in the dining room, sir. You have time for that."

Dray didn't bother to argue. In minutes, he had demolished the salad and was out the door to his Ferrari.

It was still early evening when they went aloft in his plane, Dray unreasonably happy because this was Luna's first time in a private jet. "Would you like to learn to fly, darling?"

"Yes, I would. It's wonderful up here."

"We'll start lessons for you right after we return from our honeymoon." He felt her glance on him. "Where would you like to go?"

"Ah, Dray, I can't go anywhere right now, my caseload is brimming over with ASAPs."

"Uel tells me that he, Barb, and Gretchen can handle it for a time, so pick a place."

"I . . . I don't know."

"I'll take you anywhere in the world as long as it's private."

"Your house?"

Dray's glance held hard amusement. "Right now my place is a zoo and you know it, but since you want to play games, I'll surprise you."

"I won't be able to take much time."

Dray caught her uneasy glance and felt damned irritated. "Why don't we talk about a safe subject for a while." He reached one hand over to hers and unthreaded her fingers. "Tell me what drew you to the Air Force."

"Well, they made me a very good offer when I passed the bar in D.C. . . . and I had an uncle who was career Air Force, Cletus Lyons, my mother's older brother. He was my idol when I was young and I wanted to be just like him."

"I think you mentioned him to me when we were in Germany."

Luna's smile wobbled for a moment, then she nodded. She didn't like the memories of Germany. "I might have. He was very dear to me. It was a blow to my family when he was killed."

"Yes, you said he had an accident of some kind."

"It was very bizarre. He was supposed to testify before a Senate hearing on crime, actually. The night before the hearing he surprised a burglar in his apartment, there was a struggle, and he was shot."

"Good Lord, that's terrible, darling. Your family must have been devastated."

"We were. Then Mother was killed. . . ." Luna's voice trailed off.

Dray took her hand. "Then we'll have to hurry along and begin our own family so that you'll have our children and me as your dynasty."

Luna gave a shaky laugh, catching the sudden frown that was quickly erased from Dray's face. "What were you thinking just then?"

"What?" Dray shot an amused glance at her. "You're observant, Counselor. I was just recalling something Darius told me. You remember my uncle, don't you, Luna?"

Luna nodded, glad that he was holding her hand. The world didn't seem so cold and distant when she was connected to Dray. "I like him very much. He's led a very interesting life and is very intelligent."

"Very, more so than most people suspect. He has a computer-clear mind and can hold more than any machine when it comes to facts. He once told me about a scandal during the Nixon administration after the Watergate incident. It seemed there was an ongoing investigation at that time into selling secrets to the Russians, but it was glossed over when two of the key figures who were going to testify were eliminated. . . ."

Luna nodded, her hold tightening on him. "That could have been my uncle. I was very small at the time and never did get all the details, but it could very well hook up with the same investigation. Wouldn't that be a coincidence? You're frowning again."

"Darling, I was just thinking."

"Dray, don't protect me with evasions. I hate that."

Dray nodded. "I'm not an alarmist, but could that have anything to do with the problems you've had—the trashing of your apartment, the assault in the park?"

Openmouthed, Luna looked at him. "What happened to my uncle? Is that what you're saying? That there could be a connection?"

"Yes."

"That's reaching, Dray. I can't imagine what the connection would be. I was a child when my uncle died; our last names are different. I have nothing that belongs to him even, except a small box with a diary in it and some favorite tapes of his."

"Have you ever played the tapes or read the diary?"

Luna shot him a sharp look, not even noticing the fleecy clouds and azure sky as Dray banked in a turn. "I read some of his diary, but there was a great deal of personal shorthand I didn't understand, so I just put it away. I never played the tapes. I have a record player but I never bothered to get any other components."

"Would you mind if I played the tapes and looked at the diary?"

"Dray, do you really think there's a connection?"

Dray shrugged. "It sounds farfetched, but there might be."

Luna was taken aback. Though they made desultory conversation about the same topic and others, she couldn't stop thinking about what Dray had said about believing there was a connection between her uncle and what had been happening to her. It was too bizarre!

Then they were making their approach to La Guardia Airport, the vista of Manhattan in the distance.

"What do you think?" Dray asked.

"It's wonderful. I landed at Kennedy when I returned from Germany, but I never did have a chance to go into the city."

"Tonight we'll do the town, New York style."

Luna exhaled a deep breath as Dray set the plane down with scarcely a bump, the buildings and people on the ground flying past them as they braked on the runway. "You love New York," she said.

"All of it, not just the Big Apple, but the mountains and rural areas of which we have many, upstate, downstate, there's much beauty in New York."

"We won't have time to see it all."

"No, but we'll make a couple of stops upstate. Each time we come back you'll see more of the state, and you'll begin to understand how great it is to live here."

"You sound like a travel agent." Luna smiled at him, then her attention was caught by the men who manuvered under the plane even while it was still moving. "That could be dangerous."

"Yes, but these people know what they're doing."

In minutes they were out of the plane and boarding a helicopter.

"Where will it land?"

"Not too far from an office I have down at the end of Broadway. We'll stop there first and then we'll go uptown to my apartment. I'll have the driver take us through Little Italy so you'll be able to see the Italian restaurant where we'll be dining this evening. It's called Forlini's, and their pasta is excellent."

"Ummm, pasta, I love it."

"I know. The body is beautiful and perfect, but I still want to put a little more meat on your bones." Dray slipped his arm around her waist and pulled her back as she was about to go down the steps to the tarmac. "Wait, let me go first, they're steep." Dray dropped down and turned to face her.

When Luna took the first step down, two hands came up and gripped her waist.

"Dray, put me down," Luna whispered, conscious of the laughing baggage handlers who were looking their way.

"Never. I love holding you, Luna McAfee." Dray laughed at her, their eyes level, his gaze holding hers. "I want to hold you always."

"I think security is heading this way on the run," Luna told him tartly, smothering an answering laugh.

"And you'd let them arrest me." Dray's tongue touched her lower lip.

"Like a shot." When had she developed a wheeze in her voice?

In minutes their luggage was transferred to a helicopter and again they were aloft.

"This is another first for me," Luna mouthed into Dray's ear. "I never realized how speedy they are."

Dray chuckled. "It knocks me out to be able to introduce you to new things. Marriage is going to be a series of new things for us, Luna."

"Yes, it will, since I've never had a husband."

"What did you say, darling? It's a little hard to hear."

"Nothing important." Luna lost her trend of thought as the air vehicle moved toward the tip of Manhattan. A first-class sighting of the refurbished Statue of Liberty had her gasping with delight. "I suppose you have to be an American to be affected by her, but she makes me want to cry."

Dray hugged her. "She's one special lady."

In minutes they were going down and landing with very little fuss.

It was a fast elevator ride to the street.

Before Luna could quite get her land legs, a liveried chauffeur was there, handling their luggage and doffing his cap to her as he handed her into the stretch limo. "Goodness me, this is not the way storefront lawyers travel."

"This is not done at taxpayers' expense either, love. My family's business takes care of all my trips." There was a grim look to him when he spoke, as though he weren't responding to her at all.

"You didn't have to tell me that, Senator Lodge."

"Thank you, darling." He cuddled her close to him on the short trip to his building.

Dray's office was a spacious corner suite overlooking the harbor, the rooms high and spacious.

While Luna wandered from window to window looking at the marvelous view of lower Manhattan and the business district, Dray made numerous phone calls, always managing to smile at her whenever she looked his way.

All at once her attention was caught by a file on the T-shaped desk marked GERMANY. Blinking, Luna stared at the file, glancing up to see that Dray had his back to her. Flipping open the cover, she stared at the first page, catching her name, rank, and serial number. A dossier!

Turning a few more pages, she saw the word *Germany* a few more times, then Washington, D.C. Had Dray known where she was all along?

Closing the folder, she moved away from the desk toward the window, staring unseeingly at the panoply of sky and water at the tip of Manhattan.

When she felt arms slide around her, she stiffened.

"Did I startle you, darling? Sorry." Dray kissed her neck, then turned her in his arms, his lips touching her cheeks, hair, and eyes. "What are you thinking about? You're a million miles away."

She was about to point to the folder when she saw it was gone from the corner of the desk. Looking back at him, she stared at him for long moments. "There was a folder on your desk a moment ago about me. I wondered about it." For a moment she thought she saw a hesitation, then Dray's ready smile went over her.

"Yes. I had a great many people looking for you, darling. You were hard to find." Dray kissed her again. "Would you like to look at the folder?"

"No, it's not necessary." If there was a nagging voice deep inside her that told her to scan the folder, she wasn't going to listen to it. "I don't need to see it, I trust you, Dray."

"Finally." Scooping her up into his arms, Dray carried her to the big overstuffed couch in one section of the room that faced the floor-to-ceiling window. A low table in front and a bar to one side made it an efficient corner for entertaining. Dray cuddled her close to him, raining kisses over her face.

"Do you know how happy it makes me to hear you say you trust me?"

"I do trust you." Luna ran her fingers up his face, pushing the uncertainties to the basement of her mind.

"Shall we go, darling? I'm anxious for you to see the apartment. I hope you'll like it."

"Not as much as I like your place in Georgetown, I'm sure."

Dray laughed, leading her from the office and to the private elevator that sped them to the street.

The ride through the clangorous, raucous, crowded, high-towered Big Apple was mesmerizing to Luna. "It's downright awesome, isn't it?"

"Yes." Dray chuckled. "I'm here several times a year but it's always new, yet still the same. It's a separate planet that isn't even on Earth."

Luna nodded. "I can feel the difference. It's beautiful and ugly, it's stupid and yet it has the most intelligent life forms. Can we sightsee?"

"Of course. We'll be here two days before we go upstate to the farm. There's not time to see much, but we'll pick a few of your choices and home in on them. Tonight we'll be dining in Little Italy. Be prepared to eat well."

When they pulled up in front of the cream-colored building with the balcony wings buttressing it, Luna stared at the doorman. "Isn't that Central Park over there?"

"Yes. Dutton, this is Miss McAfee, my fiancée. She will have a key to my place and will come and go as she pleases."

"As you say, Senator. How do you do, Miss McAfee?"

"It's nice to meet you, Dutton."

The elevator whisked them directly to the penthouse, the doors opening into the foyer done in caramel- and cream-colored marble, the crystal chandelier glittering richly.

Luna's gaze touched the curving staircase to the second floor that hugged one wall, the satiny sheen of a French cloth wall-covering done in cream and pale caramel weave. "It's lovely."

Dray laughed, very pleased because she liked his home. "Come upstairs and I'll show you the bedroom."

"Said the spider to the fly," Luna murmured, amusement and irritation at her reaction to him in her voice.

Dray cocked his head at her. "I've nicked you somehow. What is it?"

Luna inhaled a shaky breath. *I'm ready to fly up the stairs to your bedroom, lock the door, and keep you to myself for a hundred years, that's what's driving me crazy!* What would Dray say if she said that? "I suppose I'm overwhelmed by it all, but it is beautiful."

Dray took her hand and led her up the stairs, managing her piece of luggage with the other hand. "This is the master suite." Dray pointed. "In there are the sauna, hot tub, and exercise equipment. Downstairs there are two other bedrooms at the back."

After they had toured the eight-room, two-story apartment, Dray led her back to the master suite. "In here, darling. The bathroom's yours. I'll use one of the ones downstairs."

"But that's silly. This is yours." Luna was talking to air. Dray had disappeared after bringing up her cases.

Dray showered in the capacious bathroom, thinking of Luna in his circular tub, perhaps doused in bubbles. "Damn!" he muttered as his body hardened at the thought.

Thinking of what had happened at the office that day brought a frown to his face. Luna had seen the file!

What the hell was John Talbot thinking of to have that lying on the desk? Not that anyone was ever in his office but him and his staff. Still, it wasn't good security. He had specifically stated that the file was to be top secret. There was plenty of innuendo in that file, some documented, some not. In the wrong hands it could make trouble for him . . . and for Luna.

Getting out of the shower and slinging a towel around him, he went to the phone. "Father? Yes, it's Dray. No, I wouldn't have called this number if I didn't want it to be between us.

From now on, I only want you, Chad, Bret, and Luna's friend Uel in on this thing about Luna, and of course Ahmed's people. No, there's no one I suspect, I just want maximum security on this. And, Father, I want you to talk to Darius again about what he knows about Colonel Lyons. He'll know to what I refer. Listen to him, Father. In fact I would like Darius to coordinate this investigation."

When Dray replaced the receiver, he had a feeling that someone had just walked on his grave, that danger was closing around Luna.

With the towel still around him he left the suite on the run, taking the stairs to the master suite two at a time. Flinging open the bedroom door, he stalked across the room to the bathroom, banging the door open. Where was she?

Sprinting down the short hall of the suite to the exercise room, he watched Luna's mouth open in surprise as he headed toward the hot tub.

"Dray, what is it? You're white."

"I missed you." He flung off the towel and slid into the water, reaching for her as though she were his lifeline.

"What happened?"

"Nothing." For a moment the future flashed before his eyes, a future without her. Cold sweat broke out on his body, even in the heated water. The specter of danger was hanging over her, taunting him, and he would damn well deal with that. There were too many menacing figures in Luna's life, and most of them nebulous, unknown. How long would it take to pinpoint the peril and wipe it out completely? Whatever it took, he would do it.

"Dray! You're squeezing me to death."

"What? Oh, sorry, darling."

Luna stared at him. What was bothering him? Did he know she'd seen the dossier? He must suspect she'd noticed it, perhaps perused it, since he'd picked it up and put it away. Why hadn't he mentioned it? What could be in the dossier that he wouldn't want her to see?

"I find this erotic in the extreme, love. How do you feel?"

"Every time we're together it's erotic," Luna told him, shooting him a sharp glance when he chuckled.

"Very true, Luna, my sweet."

Luna felt his hand slide between her thighs, and her lungs tightened and refused to function. Every intention she had of pushing him away and keeping him at arm's length until she knew what he was trying to hide from her went out the window at that feathery, moist abrasion. As his finger gently probed the opening, her body spasmed in answer, wanting more. Whatever barrier she should have put up was dissipated in the heat that Dray generated.

"Luna, darling," Dray whispered, pulling her over his body, fitting her over him, gasping his delight when her exciting flesh imprisoned him. "Don't move . . . not yet." Dray was dizzy with the power she had over him. "I'll explode."

"Sorry," Luna told him in sinuous response, not a bit repentant. About time she dealt a few hands that they played. "I do like this very much."

"Damn you, Luna, you're a vixen." Dray's silky laugh signified surrender to her. Then it was her turn to gasp as he took her in gentle savagery, his body twisting under hers so that the sweet rough massage within set fire to her.

"Dray!" With a grasp born of desperate need she clung to him and closed her legs around his waist. There was no planet but the one she shared with Dray, there was no life but theirs. "I can't believe this."

"Darling, believe it, because you're pulling me apart." With convulsive need he held her as the age-old force took them captive. With a groan and sigh, Dray felt her release even as he was pumping his life into her.

For long moments they held each other, loath to unfetter the aura that imprisoned them.

"Luna, I want you now as I've always wanted you, and will want you into eternity. Let's get married tomorrow."

Luna gasped. "I can't. You live in New York, I live in Silver Spring."

Dray laughed harshly. "Since we don't travel by Conestoga

wagon I think we can arrange something. We'll do what any other couple would do in similar circumstances, we'll make adjustments. Many people do. It's not a long commute from New York to D.C. I usually manage it several times a month now. You would be an added incentive to me in making my roll calls."

"You have a very good voting record and you know it," Luna told him tartly, not able to tamp down the happiness that was swamping her at the thought of being married to Dray.

"Yes, I know it, my precious, but it surprises me that you do." He leaned over her, lifting her body so that he could take her warm, supple breast into his mouth. "I wonder if you know how that knowledge pleases me."

Luna inhaled a deep shuddering breath, aware that he could see the color rising in her face. "When I arrived in Washington I looked up your record."

Dray cupped her face, staring into her eyes, then he put his face back to her breast, pressing his mouth there. "Did you miss me, Luna, when we were apart?"

"Now and then," she answered faintly. There were some hours in the day when she hadn't thought of him, mostly between four and six in the morning, her optimum sleeping time.

Dray stared at her. "Still hiding from me?"

"Yes." Truth burst like a rocket between them.

Dray's face twisted. "I hated hearing that, but we're getting things out in the open. We need to do that."

"Something like sucking a giant lemon." Luna cuddled close to him.

"Or packing a sore with salt."

Heads together, they laughed.

"Have we a chance, Dray?"

"Better than most, love. At least we know ahead of time that we have to be wary of others in a relationship, that the dangers can come from without as well as within, darling.

Experiencing that was painful, but it can give us an edge now."

Then why didn't he share with her what was in the dossier? That question went around in her head like a chiding, childish voice.

"Look at the time, lady. Time to dress. We are going to do Manhattan." Dray rose to his feet and stretched, his lissome, well-muscled body quivering with good health. "I like having you here, Luna. It feels very right." He grinned down at her. "But I can't stay in here, because if you stand up and I take one look at you, we'll be making love again. I'll dress in the other room of the suite. Check the closets. You'll find clothing in your size."

"What?" Luna sat bolt upright in the tub, the water sluicing away from her body.

"Damn you, Luna, I told you not to do that," Dray said softly, his eyes glued to her. "Lord, my sweet, you are a voluptuary. I'll see you in twenty minutes." Dray grabbed at the towel he'd discarded and stalked from the bathroom.

"Now wait a minute, I'm not . . . Twenty minutes! You're crazy." Luna stumbled out of bed, fully intending to ignore the closets and get her own garb from her suitcase.

Rubbing on her body the emollients that lined the tub, she then toweled herself dry, pushing her fingers through her hair to loosen some of the steam-tightened waves.

Striding into the bedroom with only a bath sheet around her, she headed right for her suitcase. As her hand poised over the closure, she looked over her shoulder at the mirror-fronted wall of closets. "Oh, what the hell, I can look."

Inhaling a deep breath, she pressed the button and watched the wall disappear and a magnificent array of women's apparel appear. "Dray! You wild man. Where did you get such wonderful taste in women's clothing?" she whispered. Immediately she imagined a group of statuesque women slinking around Dray. "Stop it, fool," she groaned out loud. "I don't elieve it, why am I thinking it? Dray, you're spoiling a crazy woman, but I love you for it."

Luna suddenly frowned. Was it really possible to be this appy? Could she trust that it would last, or would everything rash around her as it had before?

Chapter 13

Manhattan was a crystal city glittering as if on royal command with diamonds, emeralds, rubies, and sapphires. The royal crown was the black satin sky strewn with stars.

"It's wonderful, isn't it?" Luna whispered to Dray as they sat close together in the limousine taking them downtown once more to the fascinating section of the island known as Little Italy. The silky new underwear she'd donned at the apartment was her size, but her loss of weight when she was overseas made the lingerie a trifle big, and she had the sensation of sliding around in it. Still, it had been wonderful to wear it under the silky suit in palest coral.

"What? Oh, yes, it is." Had there been someone watching them when they came out of the apartment building? Dray was used to people stopping him and asking to speak to him or sign an autograph. Maybe that was what it was, and maybe he was getting paranoid because of the many incidents involving Luna.

He forgot his angst when he heard her sigh as they alighted from the taxi. "You like it?" Dray directed a greeting to a waiter called Anselmo.

"It is another world."

When they entered Forlini's, Dray saw her salivate and swallow. "This place always makes my mouth water."

"I'm hungry," Luna told him, surprise in her voice.

Dray chuckled. "Of course, darling, and you will love the pasta."

Luna was on her second glass of wine, feeling light-headed at the unaccustomed alcohol when Anselmo reappeared with a table-sized platter of a variety of pasta dishes for another customer. Salivating at the glorious sight, Luna sighed. "We should probably have a memorial service for my waistline before I lift my fork."

"Darling, you're far too thin."

"Maybe I'm smaller than I thought. The lingerie in the drawer was a little big, but I couldn't resist the silk." She lifted her wineglass in salute then sipped a bit more.

"I have never come to this city when it didn't enthrall me." Except for the time he'd arrived from Germany with no idea of Luna's whereabouts. Then he'd been a quiet madman, ready to dismember anyone who approached him.

"Somebody walk on your grave? You looked pensive."

"Trying to decide where to take you dancing. Maxim's or Hobby's. The music is excellent at both places."

"I'll let you decide."

Dray was aware of her withdrawal from him; knew she had sensed that he had been hedging with her. Someday he would tell her about those lost months after his return to Germany, but not now.

Luna pushed away the black thoughts. She was having a good time. Forlini's was a delight. The problems could go to ground for just one evening. "I can't decide what to order, Dray. It looks like I would love the whole menu," she told him helplessly. "How can you laugh?"

"Easily." His grin widened when she leaned over and soft-slapped him on the jaw. "I wish you would repeat that when we get home . . . when we're nude and together on my bed." Grinning when she muttered his name, her face reddening, he gestured to the hovering waiter, speaking in rapid Italian.

Luna didn't speak the language but she thought she understood. "Did you tell him to get me everything?" Her hand went out instinctively to halt the waiter.

"*Sì, signorina,* how may I help you?"

"It's all right, Anselmo, the *signorina* thought that I had ordered the complete menu."

"No, *signorina,* I bring you a choice. You will like."

"I'll weigh seven hundred pounds by morning." Luna rolled her eyes at a laughing Dray. "You don't understand, I love the stuff. Pasta is a weakness with me. What if I eat until I burst? You'll be guilty of being an accessory to murder, not to mention your friend Anselmo and the entire establishment."

Dray leaned forward and took her ring finger, touching her engagement ring with his lips. "I wouldn't like you to be overweight, because I love your body and always want you in perfect health. I also know damn well it wouldn't make a difference to the way I feel about you." His teeth nipped the tender flesh. "How does it feel to have so much power?"

"You should know."

"Do I have power over you, sweetheart?"

"Too much," Luna muttered, just as the waiter put a table-sized antipasto between them.

Dray shot a wry look at the waiter, who beamed at them. *"Grazie,* Anselmo." Then he looked at Luna. "We'll talk again about this, but I know there's no sense trying to come between you and your food, so eat."

"Very funny." Luna speared a pepperoncini, then grabbed for the mineral water. "Good Lord, they are pure acid."

"Umm, I like them."

Luna watched between horror and amusement as Dray ate one after the other of the hot peppers, seemingly unscathed. "You will have no stomach at midnight."

When the pasta came, Luna was bemused by the array of entrées that Anselmo had arranged for her.

"Eat, darling," Dray encouraged her, all at once feeling uneasy, as though someone were staring at him. Putting down his fork, he dabbed at his mouth, turning as though to study the other patrons of the fine restaurant. He saw no one looking their way, nor anyone he knew, but he couldn't rid himself of the sensation of being watched.

"Dray? Why are you frowning?"

"Ah, was I? Sorry, darling. Here, let me cut you some bread."

He was doing it again! Hiding something from her, and she had no idea what it was or why he was doing it.

"Dray! Never mind the bread. Tell me what's on your mind."

"I don't want to spoil our evening together." The smile twisted his mouth. "I've had the feeling that we've been watched since we left the apartment."

Luna's laugh had a lemony sound. "I've had that sensation more than once since the children and I moved into your place, but I put it down to paranoia. You think it's more?"

Dray shrugged. "Probably not. I'm afraid I've been touchy about people being around me since your apartment was trashed."

Luna pushed back her plate. "Whether we're being followed or not, I'm glad we came here. The food was wonderful, but now I feel I should jog ten miles."

Dray signed his name to the check and rose to his feet. "We won't jog, but we will work out. We'll walk around the area and get an Italian ice for dessert before we go dancing."

"Dray! I couldn't."

"Then I will and you can have some of mine."

Luna was entranced with Little Italy, delighted when Dray conversed with the people in Italian, pleased that most everyone knew their senator. Though many spoke to him, they did not try to crowd him, and it was a very relaxing stroll.

"There's our car. Shall we go, darling?"

Luna noticed how he looked around him before he followed her into the limousine.

In minutes the powerful car had shot them back uptown and they arrived at the new "in" place for dancing. Hobby's was glitzy and spacious, the decor all gold diamanté, yet there was a laid-back air to it that was appealing.

"We'll never get a table," Luna gasped when she saw the hordes of patrons, many standing and obviously waiting.

"Calling ahead helps." Dray smiled at her and nodded to the woman in the figure-hugging lamé dress.

"And it doesn't hurt to be a personal friend of the proprietor," Luna snapped. "What's her name?"

"Hobby."

"Original."

"Tummy upset?"

"No. Actually I would like to dance." Luna shot a challenging look at the willowy brunette with the figure that should have been registered with the police, who was looking at Dray as though he were the specialty of the house.

Dropping her purse on the table they were led to, she turned and started walking toward the rather large dance floor.

"Wait up. Why are we running, darling?" Dray whispered into her hair as he took hold of her body and swung her into his arms.

"We should be dancing, not conversing," Luna told him tartly, her body abrading his in fierce heat. "Is she your mistress?" Damn, she hadn't meant to ask him that. "Don't answer."

"Hobby and I had a very interesting liaison before I met you, then when I came back from Germany we were a twosome for a time, but it just didn't work."

Luna smothered a gasp of pain not unlike the feeling of having her insides in a vise. Picturing Dray with another woman was masochistic to the max, and she fought the image with everything in her. "Shall I tell you about the men in my life?"

"Please don't, I have no inclination toward self-flagellation." Dray's tight smile went over the gyrating body in front of him. "You still dance better than any woman I know."

"Thank you."

They danced to tune after tune—fast, slow, languorous, rock, big-band sound.

"What a repertoire," Luna sighed, when they finally left the floor.

Dray ordered drinks for them, then slid around so that he was closer to her. "Let's get married right away, Luna."

"As soon as you tell me everything that's in that dossier you have on me, we can talk about it." She could feel Dray freeze up on her, withdraw. "It's funny that you want a commitment from me, but that you don't feel a need to confide in me."

Dray turned so sharply, the heavy table rocked. "That's not true. I assure you it has nothing to do with confidence." He inhaled and looked at his folded hands on the table. "I thought we could protect you better if you were left in the dark about certain things, but I suppose you're right; I have to tell you everything."

Luna felt a frisson of fear and had to batter down a strong wish to tell him to keep what he knew secret, but she was silent.

"Luna, I know you thought that what had happened to you, the park incident, the trashing of your apartment, and the other happenings, had something to do with the Skinner case you've been working on for quite some time."

"I'm sure I'm right."

"That may be true, Luna, and I'm inclined to believe that it does, but persons working for me have discovered a rather nebulous link, at present, with . . . your uncle, Colonel Cletus Lyons."

"What? How can that be? Uncle Cletus has been dead for years."

"Seven, to be exact; in a jeep accident in England, according to the records. He would have been flying home to Washington the next day to testify at a trial. And you are his only living relative."

"Yes, my cousin and my aunt were in another accident in the Channel some time ago, when the ferry overturned and so many were killed. The authorities were never quite sure it wasn't sabotage." Luna's words were mechanical. Her brain was concentrating on Dray, her skin goose-bumping with all the unsaid things between them.

"Do you have his papers, Luna?"

"His papers? My uncle's?" She felt like an owl repeating

everything, but she was off balance, her mind floundering in quicksand. "I have some things, I told you, a few notebooks and tapes, but most of what belonged to my aunt and uncle I sold. My cousin survived the wreck for several weeks and it took a great deal of money to sustain the high-level care she needed."

"I know," Dray said quietly, wincing when she looked at him warily. "You think I've been underhanded with you."

"You've been secretive." Luna swallowed the lump in her throat. "I don't like to think I've put myself in harm's way again. Germany is still a very fresh memory."

"Dammit, Luna, we've come so far. Don't throw it all away again. Trust me this time. Spare us both that other hell."

"How dare you blame me for that? You were friends with Hetty and you had come to the country to help him. My evidence disappeared. It had never done that in any other trial."

"Damn you, Luna," Dray whispered, his face contorted, his insides twisted in pain. "You know I had nothing to do with that."

Luna shook her head. She had trusted him, but now it was like a burning sensation on her skin when she recalled Germany. "Maybe there's too much between us, Dray." As she said it she felt a despair she'd never known. Life would be a desert without him. Living in his house in Georgetown had taught her that.

"I'll never leave you, Luna, you'll have to throw me away."

For long moments they stared at each other.

"I won't do that." The words were wrenched from her.

Dray put his hand out to her, only halfway, watching as though mesmerized as her fingers entwined with his. "Someday there won't be specters between us, Luna, but until then I suppose we'll have to wrestle them one at a time, as they arise."

Luna nodded. "Will you tell me what you know?"

"Yes."

Luna watched his face contort with thought, as though

what his brain was computing was painful to him. "My uncle was no traitor."

Dray nodded, squeezing her hand. "That's a fact." He glanced around the room and moved closer to her. "The people who work for me suspect that he may have been killed . . . and your aunt and cousin as well."

Luna hadn't expected that. It was a punch to the solar plexus. Her body felt limp, breathing was painful.

"That's why I insist we marry soon, Luna. I can protect you."

Luna pictured her apartment after it had been vandalized. If people were after her, they could as easily turn on Dray. "I don't think I want to . . ."

"Forget it." Dray's granite-etched features were echoed in his voice. "No backing out, I won't let you."

"Oh? And will you drag me to the altar, Senator?"

"If I have to, I will. Let's dance. We communicate better to music than with words."

Once they were on the floor again, it was like the first time; they danced to every tune and rhythm.

Later, when New York was still alive and kicking but the night was waning, they were driven home in the limousine.

Luna went right to her room with just a whisper of good night to Dray.

Going right to the bathroom, she stripped off her clothes, hanging them up one by one, feeling that she was both freezing and boiling, her body quaking in reaction.

Face turned up to the stinging spray, she let the cool water pummel the agitation from her. Barely noticing a sudden rush of air, she kept her eyes closed.

"I thought I'd join you."

"What? Aagh, I got a mouthful of water." Luna coughed over and over, swiping at her eyes so she could see Dray. "Get out of here, Dray."

"No. I came to tell you that we're marrying tomorrow. If you put up a struggle, I'll call every tabloid in town and tell them you're pregnant with my child. Turn around and I'll wash your back."

"Wha—? Who in blazes do you think you are? Stop that, you're pushing me against the tile."

"Then behave yourself, Luna. I've taken all the crap I'm going to take from you, and you will damn well listen to reason or see yourself plastered across every cheap rag in the country."

"You wouldn't dare! You're a senator. Aagh, turn off the water."

"No. And as to my reputation, I'll have you know that I don't stint on my constituents in any way, I have a good voting record, my interest in them is—"

"I know all that, but you should be like Caesar's wife, no stain . . . stop it, get out of my shower." When Dray's hand, holding the loofah sponge, whorled across her buttocks, Luna's body arched like a bow, bringing her in contact with the tile wall again. "Will you get out of here before I'm maimed?"

"No. I've been too easy on you, Luna, cosseting you when I should have been bashing you."

"Cosseting me? Where in the world . . . Did you say bashing? It would be a cold day in hell when I let you bash me, Senator. Now you listen to me. . . ."

"No. I've done that and I don't like what you say, so I'm not listening. You're not the only one who's determined."

"Hah! You're a bullheaded, arrogant New Yorker."

"Then believe that this New Yorker will take no more guff from you."

"All right, if you won't get out of here, I will." Wrestling past him was no small chore.

"Umm, do that again. Your backside is like velvet."

"Lecherous lawmaker. I have a good mind to let your constituents know just what kind of senator you are . . . a low-life ogler." Luna whirled to shake her finger at him and slipped.

Dray's arm shot out, steadying her. "Easy. You'll be better

once you're married. I understand marriage is very calming for a woman."

"Twit! Don't you dare pull that macho talk on me."

Dray stuck his face right up to hers. "And you know damned well that I'm not a sexist, so stop trying to throw a spanner in the works. We're getting married."

"You may regret it, Senator," she told him stiffly, flinging a towel around her and heading toward the door.

"Wait, you forgot to oil your skin. I'll do it." Dray whisked the bath sheet from her body and grabbed a container of fragrant oil.

"I can do it myself," Luna told him faintly, her eyes fluttering closed as he rubbed the emollient on her form in long, gentle strokes.

"Don't deny a man his joys," Dray told her, his accents hoarse. "You are beautiful, my own."

Luna whirled around, looking up at him. "I don't want to marry you. You could be in danger married to me."

Dray's rubbing motion was stilled. "So that's it. That's why you've been throwing up new barriers, tossing nails under my tires; you're worried about me." Dray placed the plastic bottle of emollient down with a crack that should have split the bottle up the middle. "Get this straight, Luna McAfee, woman and storefront lawyer. I don't know what's ahead for us, if it's going to be easy or hard, smooth or rough; but whatever it is, we'll do it together." He shook in slow, gentle rhythm. "Do you honestly think that I would let you walk in harm's way without my protection?"

"You belong to the people of New York." The words fell from flaccid lips. Luna had already surrendered to the fire in his eyes. She couldn't walk away from him even when she knew she should be galloping. "Senators are often targets, it isn't fair for you to be one because of my family."

Dray laughed. "And what makes you think I'll be safer with you out of my life? Most of Washington and New York know that I want you, darling. It's the worst-kept secret on the continent."

"I could ride shotgun for you." Hope was a small geyser in her.

"You could indeed. Tomorrow we drive upstate and get married. Then all the clothing at Charine's I ordered for you can come home to rest."

Luna stiffened. "I don't let anyone buy me clothes. . . ."

Dray leaned down and kissed her ear. "I'll be your husband, dopey."

"Oh. That's right. Husbands can buy things." She beamed up at him. "That's different."

Dray swallowed. "Don't do that."

"What? Smile?"

"It knocks me out, lady, it's so beautiful. I've waited so long for you to smile naturally, without fear or reproach." Dray touched her nose. "You're blushing."

"I've never reproached you."

"Your eyes have."

"Yes." Luna swallowed. "I'm not afraid when I'm with you."

"But you have been afraid and very hurt at times."

Luna nodded. "That's why I'm so devoted to Uel and Barbara. They helped me through so much."

Dray nodded. "They're good people. My father says that he has asked a few of his cronies to send a little business that way."

Luna's mouth dropped. "But . . . but we're storefront lawyers. We handle the poor and almost poor. Wouldn't that be corporation law?"

Dray shook his head. "There are multitudes of legal matters that involve the corporations of my father's friends and associates. You and Uel's expertise could be very valuable."

"Dray, that's silly," Luna said weakly, not daring to tot up the revenues such a move could mean to Lopez, McAfee and Lopez. "But it would be wonderful. It would give us the added freedom to take on more legal help."

"Not to mention finishing off Gretchen's education."

"Yes." He touched her hair. "Shall we go to bed, my lady?"

Luna nodded, her eyes locking with his when he bent his head and kissed her.

Their mouths were still together when he lifted her and carried her to the bed.

"What's the latest on the problem with the storefront lawyer?"

"Nothing, sir, it's being handled."

"And what does that mean?"

"Ah, nothing can be done now, sir. She and the senator are in New York."

"I see. Then what I heard about a failed confrontation was true? Speak up, man."

"There was such a happening. It was clumsy."

"Yes, it was. I want that journal that belonged to Lyons, and I want it fast."

"Yes, sir, but if it's in a safety-deposit box, how could we get it if the lady JAG was killed?"

"I have that all taken care of, don't trouble yourself with it."

"Did the copies of her signature help?"

"Yes. Now I want you to get into her private papers. Somewhere there must be a list that tells which bank her uncle used. I'm betting it was Hervey's Bank."

"Hervey's, sir? That doesn't seem likely. That's one of the oldest banks in the D.C. area, and very prestigious and correct. I can't imagine military personnel using it."

"The JAG lady's grandmother was a Hervey. I'm sure she isn't even aware that she's in line for a sizable share of the bank." There was a rustling of papers. "It's amazing what turns up among personal papers. The JAG lady is the last surviving member of her family."

Skinner caught his breath at the sardonic tone. He wished, not for the first time, that he knew who his mysterious boss was, and had been for the past thirty years. He seemed to know everything and everybody but he had never revealed himself. What a coup if he could find out the identity, then he could make some real money if he had a hold over—

"Are you listening, damn you, Skinner?"

"Oh, yes, sir, I am."

"You've missed your chance in New York. When she comes back to D.C., she'll no doubt move back in her own apartment. . . ."

"I think they're living together, sir."

"They have been, but that's no problem. The family will be hard put to accept her when the "facts" come out about the Hetty trial. Get hold of the man who was so useful to us in Germany."

"Yes, sir."

"And, Skinner? Stop screwing up, I don't like it."

"Yes, sir." Skinner held the phone away from his head when the receiver cracked dead in his ear. "Bastard! Maybe you won't be Mr. High and Mighty forever."

"You wanted to see me, Father."

"Yes, Chad, I did. Dray is in New York right now. He and Luna are getting away for a few days."

Chad grinned. "My future sister-in-law, you mean."

A reluctant smile crossed the older man's face. "Yes. To tell the truth, I wouldn't be unhappy about it. She's good stuff and she handles herself well."

"Uncle Darius says she's cut from good cloth."

His father looked up sharply. "Is he here? Why didn't you tell me right away, Chad?"

The door to the study opened behind Chad. "No need. I'm right here." Darius stared at them myopically, his glasses slipped down on his nose, his ubiquitous fishing hat askew on his head.

"Uncle, I sometimes think you have the ability to catch the airwaves."

"Years of training." Darius's rather vapid expression hardened when it fixed on his brother-in-law. "I've been able to get access to the files on Cletus Lyons. Close your mouth, Chad, you'll attract flies."

"Uncle, I hope you don't mean secret files. Military files?"

"Better than that, and don't ask any more, because I won't answer."

Chad rolled his eyes toward his father. "We could be looking at a sizable term in a federal slammer."

"Chad's right, Darius. It's very chancy, not to mention what it could do to Dray's career."

"He doesn't have to know about this until after we connect all the dots."

Chad looked gloomy. "If you think you can put one over on Dray, Uncle, think again."

Darius Mallory shrugged. "I know the boy is sharp."

"Tell us what you discovered, Darius." Dray's father indicated the chair on the other side of his desk.

"It's about what I thought it would be. Cletus Lyons was like Caesar's wife, without stain. The man was a patriot, honest as they come, and by the number of medals he had, brave." Darius leaned back and steepled his hands. "His accident seemed nothing more than that on the surface, but I'll bet it wasn't."

"Why?"

"He was to testify at a closed special Congressional hearing the very week of his death."

"Too coincidental, Uncle?"

"I'd say so. I took the liberty of contacting a man I know. He does very sophisticated surveillance. Everyone who had anything to do with the colonel at that time in Germany will be watched."

"Germany? Wasn't that where Dray met Luna?"

"Yes," his father said roughly. "Do you think there's a connection, Darius?"

"There's always a connection in this type of work; the problem is to find the link." Darius stared at his steepled hands. "All at once I wish Dray and Luna were back in D.C. At least we could put some people on them."

Chad leaned forward to stare into his uncle's face. "Do you think they could be in danger?"

"There's always peril if the enemy is unknown."

Dray's father bit his lip, looked from his son to his brother-in-law. "Do you think this reception we're having for them could spell trouble?"

Darius smiled, looking like an aging cherub. "I think it's the best thing to do. Who knows what we might flush out?"

"Skinner is going to be taken off the list."

Darius shook his head. "Better to keep all the foes under your eye, then let them try to come up behind you."

"What poet said that? Edgar Allan Poe?"

"I said it, just now," Darius said testily, shooting an irritated glance at his nephew. He pulled a wrinkled piece of paper from his pocket. "These are a few more names you might invite."

"Gil Hetty? Gad, Darius, the man's a cutthroat."

"True, and he seems to be hand in glove with Skinner; but neither of those men has the intellect to run the type of organization this is shaping up to be. There has to be one strong man at the helm, but I haven't found him yet."

Chapter 14

"I can't believe you're sincere, Dray," Luna said, feeling stunned.

"I am. I have the license in my pocket. I know just the town. It's a beautiful place called Blayer, New York. It's tucked into the mountains and the justice of the peace said he would be glad to perform the ceremony today."

"You called him," Luna breathed faintly.

"Yes." Dray leaned over and covered her tightly threaded hands with his. "In less than two hours you'll be Mrs. Perrin Draper Lodge."

Luna looked out at the crisp but warmish day. May was beautiful in New York. Everything was leafing out. The forsythia and tulips were gone, but the lilacs were everywhere. Today was her wedding day to Dray.

Luna was barely aware when they drove along Fifth Avenue, blinking when they stopped in front of a gold-scrolled shop with the name CHARINE on the window. "Are we going in here?"

"Yes, darling, we are. I thought you might like a new outfit for our wedding. Our appointment with the justice of the peace isn't until three o'clock, and it isn't a long ride once we get out of the city."

"But, but, Dray . . ."

"Shh, indulge your husband-to-be. I have a little shopping to do down the avenue, so I'll be back with you in an hour or so."

Luna felt herself being shepherded into the shop. It was

similar to the place in D.C., only larger and more opulent-looking.

The diminutive but dynamic owner seemed to be conjured from Luna's mind, she appeared so rapidly. "Ah, Miss Muck-Fee, it is so very good to see you. I have the very garment for your wedding. The rest of the things will be sent to you."

"The rest?"

"Shh, darling, go with Charine." Dray kissed her slowly, savoring her mouth.

"I should tell you," Luna told him breathlessly when she was able to move back from him, "I break out in a rash when I'm in a place with no price tags."

"I'll buy you some salve." Dray kissed her again and left the salon.

"*Vite, vite,* Miss Muck-fee, this way if you please."

"I'm coming." Luna felt a stirring of interest as she glanced at the many swatches of material she noticed in the one large workroom that she passed. Charine's was a beehive of activity.

An hour later Luna felt as though she'd been through a cyclone. Twirled, whirled, pinned, and prodded, she was sure that nothing could be accomplished in such chaos.

"Ah," Charine murmured, nodding as the circular dais on which Luna stood revolved slowly. "That is it. It is perfect. Look at yourself, Miss Muck-fee."

An attendant pushed a button and the coved wall became a mirror.

Luna expelled a sigh as she gazed at the peach-colored silk suit with the slightly fitted jacket, the hemline just touching the knee.

"The silk blouse is cream, as will be your shoes and bag, Miss Muck-Fee. Do you like what you see?"

"Thank you, madame, I do."

"*Bien.* Now, you will have the shoes you need in moments, and your hair will be done by Henri, *hein?*"

"My hair? Madame, I always do my own hair."

"It is your wedding day, Miss Muck-fee," Madame said sternly.

Once more Luna was disrobed, dressed in the clothes she'd been wearing, and escorted from the dressing room along a corridor to a connecting inner foyer. When the far door in it was opened she was in a beauty salon. At the end of the long room Luna could see a door to a side street, which must have been the main entrance.

A woman met her as she stepped through from Charine's. "Welcome to Henri's, Miss McAfee. Henri is waiting."

"All right." Luna was bemused by the number of persons who seemed to know her name and what was expected of them on her behalf.

Sometime later she was led back to Charine's through the connecting door. Now her slightly waved hair, heavy on her shoulders, was layered from the crown, emphasizing the delicate strength of her heart-shaped face.

When she was finally made up by an attendant and helped into the peach-colored silk with the matching shoes and bag, she had to smile at a beaming Charine. "I feel like a glitzy Cinderella, madame."

"And you look like Venus, Miss Muck-fee. If you ever decide to model, come to me, *hein?*"

"Thank you." Luna felt as though she were gliding when she went out to the plush foyer to meet Dray.

Stretched out in one of the Louis Quatorze chairs that looked too fragile to hold him, Dray had had his eyes on the curtain that closed off the back. He saw Luna the moment she came through.

Rising to his feet, he stared at her. "You're too beautiful, wife-to-be. Are you real?"

Luna nodded, her vocal cords paralyzed by the heat in his eyes.

"Shall we go?" Dray looked past Luna to the diminutive designer. "Thank you, Charine. She's wonderful, isn't she?"

"Ah, yes, indeed she is." The designer chuckled. "It was a delight, Senator."

Back in the car, Dray took her hand and lifted it to his mouth. "You're a very bewitching bride."

"Thank you. Are we going back for the driver?"

Dray shook his head. "No. This is a time for us and no one else. I've told the judge who will be marrying us to obtain the witnesses at the last minute. After it's over we'll give a statement to the judge, who will in turn give it to the press. We're going to be alone."

There was so much to say, but the words wouldn't come. Thinking about being married to Dray was a narcotic. Children! They would have bourbon-colored eyes and silver-touched blond hair. Her heart did a slow spin in her chest at the thought of holding such children. Children? More than one? Yes.

Getting out of Manhattan and heading north was not the hassle it could have been, but Luna wasn't even aware of their progress. She was caught up in the delightful daydream.

Even when the city faded behind them and stretches of country appeared, she was cobwebbed in the happy future she was weaving with Dray at the center.

"Hey, lady mine, come back to me. You have been carrying on a very lively discussion in that head of yours. Care to share it?"

Luna was going to hedge. "I was thinking about children," she blurted.

"Ours?"

"Yes."

"I would love a little girl with red-blond curls."

Luna delighted in the picture of Dray holding the hand of such a child. "I'm afraid they don't come prepackaged, just add water and there's your order. It's generally a surprise."

Dray reached over and clasped her hand. "There's nothing wrong with working on it . . . until we get it right."

"I have a feeling we could end up with twelve children." Luna laughed, the smile fading when she saw the scowl on Dray's face. "I was just kidding."

"Having so many children is very risky to your health, and we're taking no chances with that."

"It was a joke."

"A not very funny one. Before you ever have children we will make sure that you are capable of having one easily, without complications."

Luna stared at him, the rock line of his jaw, those tough lips pressed tight together. "Dray, there are no guarantees in this world. . . ."

"We'll have one before you get pregnant."

Luna opened and shut her mouth. "First we should get married."

"Right." Dray's features lightened. "How do you like the ride?"

"I never knew that New York was so beautiful and had such lovely mountains."

"We're entering the foothills of the Catskills, but there's also the Adirondack range. The Winter Olympics a few years back was held at Lake Placid, a very lovely place. We'll ski there this coming winter."

"I can see you don't love your state, Senator. You sound like a travel brochure."

Dray nodded. "I feel like one sometimes. People know New York City, which is wonderful, but they don't know that we have sizable dairy farms, that animal husbandry is a thriving industry here, and that we have large farms of all types that manage to feed many people in this country and the state."

Luna moved closer to him, stretching across the console to kiss his ear.

"What was that for? I loved it, but we could get into an accident."

"You care. I like that."

"Thank you, wife-to-be." Dray lifted her hand and kissed the palm. "Now, why don't you put your head back and close your eyes. You didn't get too much sleep last night."

"Neither did you, Senator," Luna shot back when he chuckled.

"That's true, but just thinking about last night energizes me, love."

Luna rested her head against the upholstery, watching him. Sleep took her like a soft gloved hand.

"Luna, darling, wake up, we're here."

"Oh, sorry, I didn't mean to do that, since you must be as tired as I was."

"Actually I'm not tired, just eager to be your husband." Dray helped her from the car, grinning when she stared around her.

"What a picture-perfect town. Everything is white, with the green mountains in the background. Where are we?"

"Blayer, New York. It's a village really. Do you like it?"

"Very much." She turned around and saw the colonnaded home in front of them. "Is this the judge's place?"

"Yes. Let's go in, we're a little late."

"I feel wrinkled and a little messy."

"You look beautiful. Here."

Luna took the ring box and opened it; the gold swirl of the masculine wedding ring glinted in the sunlight. "I didn't think you'd want to wear one."

"I do. It was made at the same time as yours and from gold given to me by my grandfather."

Luna blinked at the sting of tears in her eyes. "How lovely."

When they walked into the two-story foyer of the Greek Revival structure, a crisply dressed housekeeper directed them to double doors on the right.

In minutes Luna was introduced to the judge and the witnesses. Almost before she realized what the judge was saying, the ceremony was over and she had on her third finger the wide gold band that was a smaller replica of Dray's.

Back in the car, she couldn't seem to take her eyes from the ring.

"What are you thinking, Mrs. Lodge?"

"It doesn't seem real."

"It is, Luna, it is."

"It's been such a long and twisting road, I can't believe we're here."

"So the tabloids have been salted with this information, have they?"

"Every one of them, Mr. Skinner."

"I don't want anything failing this time. I want you to mention Germany. Did you get the records from Hetty?"

"Yes, but I think you should be careful on this one. He doesn't seem too stable to me."

Skinner scowled. "You're right about that, but what can we do? We need the information he has. Besides, his father throws substantial business this way and he's useful to us."

"I don't know what Mr. Big would say about that, sir."

"Listen to me, Beech, I've had enough about Mr. Big, as you call him. He doesn't direct my life, and one day he'll realize it."

"Yes, sir."

"I called because I think you should know that he's become somewhat recalcitrant, sir. You said I should watch for that."

"Yes, I did. Thank you, Beech. You've done a good job. Just let things ride until after we get the situation settled with the senator and his lady friend. How is Skinner's court settlement coming?"

"They found for the plaintiff. He's going to have to cough up some money and property. That could be making him edgy. That lady JAG is clever."

"She is no longer in the military."

"Sorry, sir, I know that. It's just that she is always referred to in that fashion."

"So she is. She is also becoming a thorn in my side that I would like removed."

"Do you want me to see to it, sir?"

"No, I'll handle it."

"From now on just refer to her as McAfee, that's her name."

"Ah, sir, we were not able to ascertain whether she had a safe-deposit box or not, but we do know that the information you wanted was not in her apartment, and I don't think she would keep it on her."

"It could be kept in her law office."

"You want us to look there, sir?"

"If what we plan doesn't scare her off, you'll have to do it. I'm not too happy about the way things are going."

"We'll get the information, sir."

"You damn well better, you're getting paid enough."

Luna was overwhelmed at the outpouring of affection shown Dray when he visited some upstate cities. Hands reached not only for him but for her as well, as they went down a wire fence that edged a shopping mall where he was to give a short speech. "And this isn't even an election year for you. Senator. I'm impressed," Luna murmured to him.

Dray grinned at her, then turned to the crowd as he led her forward. "And this is my wife, Luna McAfee Lodge. We came home to New York to be married."

The cheers and laughter that greeted the oft-repeated remark had a calming effect on Luna. She did indeed feel at home among the open-faced New Yorkers, both the city people and those who lived off the land. It was quite obvious that Dray was popular with his constituents.

Luna had a real urge to know the New Yorkers better.

That night they went to an old country inn that boasted that George Washington had indeed slept there. Since inn after inn in the original states often stated this, Luna was skeptical.

"Darling, would I lie to you? I tell you that he stayed here, wooden teeth and all."

"Oh? Did he leave them behind?"

"Ah, no, he needed them, I understand."

Luna laughed out loud, happier than she could ever remember being. Then she remembered Washington. "I should call Uel and Barb . . . and poor Wilkins, with the children and the dog . . ."

"Don't worry, darling. We'll call when we get to our room."

When Dray was picking up their reservation Luna wandered around the small lobby, looking at the many Revolutionary War artifacts hanging on the walls. She passed a paper kiosk, barely glancing at the myriad headlines until she caught her own name. Like a sightless person she paid for the tabloid and retraced her steps, unaware when Dray approached her.

"We're all set, darling. Do you want to look around before we go to our suite?"

"No."

"What is it? You sound hoarse. Are you coming down with a cold?"

"No." Blindly she preceded him up the wide staircase that split at a landing and went left and right to the second floor. Another narrower stairway went upward to the third level.

"This way." Concerned at the tight, withdrawn cast to her features, Dray said no more until they were in the suite. He directed the attendant to place their luggage on the rack and leave. Then he faced his wife. "All right, now what's wrong?"

She brandished the paper. "I don't know, I'm afraid to read it. Oh, Dray, I could ruin your career if I bring scandal on you." Tears sprang to her eyes.

Dray pulled her into his arms, feeling her body shudder. "Stop that. Nothing is going to separate us or get to us. You're mine and I'm yours and we'll handle anything and everything that comes along. Now, shall we read the paper together?"

Luna nodded mutely, sitting beside him on the bed, in the curve of his arm.

LUNA MCAFEE, FORMER JUDGE ADVOCATE GENERAL, THE MISTRESS OF ENLISTED MAN, HELPED HIM DESTROY EVIDENCE FOR A PRICE.

AT THE SAME TIME THE LADY WAS PARAMOUR
OF WELL-HEELED SENATOR FROM NEW YORK.

"Oh, God, where do they get this stuff?"

"What they don't dig out of the slime they make up, darling." Dray threw the paper down after he'd finished, hugging
her tightly. "They will not get away with printing this garbage
about you. I'll sue."

Luna could feel his body shake. Fear magnified as she pictured what an angry Dray could bring down on himself if he
went head to head with the tabloids. Scandal would mush-
room. He could be ruined. "Dray, don't take them on, try to
battle them. It could be fatal to your career. I shouldn't have
married you."

"Don't say that." He gripped her shoulders. "Our marriage
was the first step in beating these people. Nothing can stop us
if we stay together. No one can split us apart unless we let
them."

Hope was like an atom in her insides. She touched his face
with one finger. "The Mean Machine, that's us."

"Yes." Dray gave a hard laugh. "And we'll beat them into
the ground, wife of mine, I promise you that." He gave her a
hard kiss. Then he pulled back from her, picking up the paper
again, scowling. "Dammit, who is feeding these lies to these
rags? That's what I'd like to know." Lifting her chin, he
kissed her again, his tongue intruding gently and dueling with
hers. "Just don't think it's just your court cases that have
given birth to this. I have enemies too."

"I know." She pressed closer to him, welcoming the
warmth of that strong body. "So much doesn't make sense to
me. Chuck Skinner is the logical person to have a grudge
against me because of the way the judgment went. But in
reality, why would he bother? He has ample funds to pay off
the judgment, so why risk his reputation in such a way? Raymond Hetty is another factor. I saw Hetty at the courthouse
one day, but he would have no reason for vendetta." Luna
shook her head. "Why imply that I had an affair with him?

What good would that do him? He walked away from his court-martial clean as a whistle. No other person comes to mind." Luna shrugged. "Even if Skinner paid off twice as much as we're asking, he can well afford it. It doesn't make sense that he would draw attention to himself by causing more trouble."

Dray looked thoughtful. "Maybe there's something here that's hidden from us. And maybe that's the way we should approach our attack on them, because attack we will, wife of mine. We'll bring them to their knees." Dray kissed her hard, his mouth teasing hers, his body urging her backwards to the bed.

Chapter 15

Despite the glaring headlines of the tabloids, the honeymoon was a delight to them.

Luna was letting down her barriers with Dray, however slowly. In many ways she was being as open with him as she'd been when they first met in Germany.

They crisscrossed the state, and on the last evening before they would return to Manhattan for one day before returning to D.C., they stayed in a rather glitzy resort in the Catskills. Their suite looked out at the mountains with a hot tub right in front of the windows.

"Shame on you, Senator. You're not supposed to be cavorting in front of a window with a naked lady."

Dray kissed her shoulder, her skin steamy and fragrant. "And you were not supposed to put Chanel #5 into this water. I hope this wears off by tomorrow. I don't want the breakfasters at Hilltop to desert the room." Dray pulled her onto his lap, letting her body down gently on his aroused one. "You have a permanent effect on me, wife."

"It would seem so. Ummm, I do love this." Luna wriggled her hips gently, smiling when her husband groaned.

"Now your smile is disappearing, darling." Dray moved his own body inside her. "Damn, it's wonderful."

"Yes." Luna gripped him tightly, leaning forward to press her lips to his.

Bodies and mouths locked, they were swirled upward into the cyclone, hot tub and Earth left behind them, passion meshing them for all time as they reached the pinnacle of physical love.

"Nothing ever could be as great as that, Luna mine."

In slow, languorous delight, they left the hot tub, rubbed each other with oil, then dried each other. Arms around each other, they went to bed to begin the love ritual all over again.

It was a pain-filled delight for Luna to accept that there would be no life without Dray, that to live and be happy she had to cling to him, keep him, cherish him all her days.

It was Sunday in Manhattan and they would be leaving the city in a few hours. They walked the short distance to the Metropolitan Museum, then strolled the periphery of Central Park before returning to the apartment, packing, and driving to the airport.

The man in the nondescript black car seemed to be watching their every move. When their car moved into the traffic, he followed.

Monday in D.C. was drizzly and a little cool for May.

"Kiss me good-bye."

"I've kissed you good-bye four times, Dray." Luna laughed at her husband, very reluctant to leave him, though she had a host of things to do at the office. "One more, then I have to run."

"All right, but I think I should have two."

They kissed and held each other tightly.

"They do that a lot," Tommy told Amy as the two children walked around them, watching them.

"I know. How do they breathe, Wilkins?" Amy looked up at the chauffeur as he took her hand.

"It takes practice, child, and you will have to wait until you are older to attempt it."

"I don't think I want to do it. I might lose my bubble gum." Amy's voice drifted into Dray and Luna's aura.

Luna pulled back from Dray and smiled down at the staring children, aware that her face was getting redder by the minute. "Would you like me to take them in my car, Wilkins, since I will be going in that direction?"

"It's no trouble, madam. I will drop the senator at his office and then go from there. I took the liberty of gassing your new car, madam."

"New car?"

"Get going. You'll be late. Here are the keys, love." Dray kissed her again, then followed the children and Wilkins out the door.

Luna stared and stared at the dark green Jaguar, not really believing it was hers even when the door unlocked and the engine turned over. "Dray, you fool, it's beautiful," she whispered, engaging the gears and swallowing at the leashed power as she pulled away from the curb. Could she crawl to work through the back streets?

The Jaguar was not hard to drive, but Luna felt as though every car in D.C. were aiming at her.

By the time she reached Silver Spring she had trotted out a few cuss words that were generally alien to her. Still she had managed to reach some semblance of sangfroid and felt more confident than at first. Not trusting the car to the street, she parked behind the building.

"Good gravy, Marie. Is that a Jaguar? Luna, have you been into the petty cash?" Gretchen stood in the doorway to the office, arms akimbo.

Luna laughed when she locked the door of the sleek pale green car. "Dray gave it to me."

"Does he pass them out like business cards, maybe?" Gretchen lifted her chin, her mouth tight. "Congratulations. I saw the wedding announcement in the paper. Nice of you tell your friends."

"Dray never even told his family."

"Oh." Gretchen was only slightly mollified. "You have a high stack of messages on your desk and a woman has been calling all morning but she won't give her name."

Luna nodded as the two of them walked down the short corridor to the small office. Luna stared at her desk and rolled her eyes at Gretchen. "I see the place is still a zoo."

"You've got that right. Oops, there's the front door. I'd

better see who's there. By the way, both Barb and Uel are in court this morning."

"Thanks. Unless it's a hanging, don't disturb me. I should go through these messages."

"Right."

Luna had been working on her briefs for over an hour when the phone rang. "Luna McAfee speaking." She and Dray had decided that it would be proper for her to keep her maiden name for professional reasons. But she was tempted to tack the Lodge onto her name, and maybe she would in time. "Hello? Is anyone there?"

"It is I, Stenzi Heilmann." The voice, in stilted English, quavered over the wire. "I cannot talk long, but I am coming to America to help you. Do not tell anyone I am coming. My son is dead. Good-bye, Luna McAfee."

"Stenzi? Stenzi. Wait! For God's sake don't hang up." Luna stared at the instrument, the buzzing signifying that the connection had been broken. Stenzi Heilmann! A voice from the past. What had she said about her child? Luna recalled that Stenzi had been pregnant, and though the woman had never told her, Luna had assumed that Raymond Hetty was the father. Stenzi had been so caring of her unborn child, so protective, and now it would seem that she had lost it somehow.

Gretchen stuck her head in the door. "You have a consultation, Luna. What's wrong? Shouldn't you hang up the phone?"

"What? Oh, yes. I just had the strangest phone call from a woman I haven't seen in a long time."

"Oh. Do you want me to cancel your eleven o'clock consultation?"

"No, I'll take the appointment. Let me know when Barb and Uel return, will you."

As usual the troubles of prospective clients absorbed her and she didn't even notice the passage of time. Instead of the hour that should have been allotted to them, it was well past midday before Luna ushered them from her office to the reception area, where Gretchen would set up a file for them.

Barb and Uel came in later in the day, and the three partners took the time to go over the cases pending.

"So! Are you ever going to tell us about your wedding, or are we supposed to guess?"

Luna shot a quick look at Barb. "You're testy. Are you angry with me?"

"She wanted you to have a shower and all the trimmings, plus a wedding reception for three thousand at the Mayflower Hotel." Uel chuckled when his wife glowered at him. "Me, I'm thankful you ran off, child. It's cheaper for me this way."

"Uel! How can you talk that way?" Barb was incensed. "It wouldn't have been three thousand, just an intimate group of our friends."

"Fifteen hundred?"

"Uel, stop teasing her." Luna rose from her chair and went to her friend, putting her arms around her and hugging her. "If I had planned anything at all, it would have included you and the Good Humor Man there. You know that."

"Yes, I do, but I need to sulk about this for a while, Luna. Gretchen and I had such high hopes." Barb hugged her back. "I almost had a fit when you called from New York."

Uel saw the arrested look on Luna's features. "Why the sudden start, partner? What's up?"

"Speaking of calls, I got one myself today, from Stenzi Heilmann."

"What? The woman in Germany who was going to testify for you and then disappeared?"

"The same. She said something about coming here to help me."

"And you don't know what she means?"

"Honestly, Uel, I don't. Raymond Hetty won't be retried, so I don't see how she would be able to help me with clearing my name, assuming that's what she meant."

Barb looked from one to the other. "Is this about the mysterious time in Germany that Uel won't discuss?"

"Yes, but I think it's time he leveled with you, Barb. Tell her everything, Uel."

"Tonight I will, pet." Uel patted his wife's knee. "Will you tell Dray?"

"Yes, because I'm hoping that he can help me locate her if Stenzi does manage to get into the country. I don't know where she would get the money to get here. Her family didn't have money, and she'd lost her job the last I heard."

Uel rose to his feet. "I wouldn't worry about it until she gets here." He turned to leave her office, then paused. "By the way, thank your in-laws for inviting us to this shindig on Friday, the invitations were beautiful."

"Dray and I just found out about it ourselves, but I think it's very kind of them."

"But you're still nervous."

"Uel, you say the most outrageous things to Luna. She won't be nervous, will you?"

"I hate to admit it, Barb, but Uel is right. I'm feeling very jumpy about Friday night." Luna smiled at the dark-eyed, dark-complexioned woman. "Even with my best friends there."

"That settles it. You need to shop for some new duds. Gretchen and I are going to Gillian's to get something. Why don't you come with us?"

"Thanks, I will. I can use the diversion." She rolled her eyes at Uel when he chuckled.

"What makes you think you'll be able to get information out of her at the bash her father-in-law is giving?"

"Because I'm going to tell the senator's wife a few home truths about her husband's career. We shall see what will happen then."

"How did you get an invitation to this party?"

Chuck Skinner looked at the other man. "Don't be a fool. All things are possible with connections, and I have them, more than I'll ever need."

The man facing Chuck Skinner shivered, thinking that Skinner had a cold smile.

* * *

"Sorry to disturb you, Senator, but I didn't want to give you my report over the phone." Peevy moved into the room, a smile flashing on those normally morose features. "Incidentally, congratulations on your nuptials. I've seen your lady's picture and she's a beauty."

"Thank you, she is." Dray rose to his feet, noting how the man called Peevy closed the door firmly before turning to face him once more. His glance ran around the room as if to probe every cranny. "How are you, Peevy? Looking for bugs?"

Peevy cocked his head in a way that made him look like a cautious sparrow, the quick movements and the brown suit and shoes all carrying out the illusion. But the eyes were different. There the sparrow became the hawk, with the predatory bird's acuity and intelligence. "Could be."

Dray waved him to a chair. "Why do I get the feeling that you've discovered a great deal?"

Peevy took the seat and placed a bulging briefcase on the desk between them. "Senator, you and I go back a long way, to your university days, when you hired me to help a friend in trouble."

Dray nodded, a cold clamminess assailing him as the other man proceeded to take out folder after folder. "Speak up. I want it all and straight."

"I think your wife may be in grave danger."

Dray's chair crashed to the floor as he surged to his feet, leaned over the desk, and seized the shirtfront of the other man. "How, who, and why?"

"Relax, Senator, I've already put some men on her. Would you let go of my tie? It's my only silk one."

"Sorry." Dray released the man, picked up his chair, and sat down, his brooding stare never leaving the detective. "Go on."

"First of all, Charles Skinner. He's a vindictive man, Senator, and very unwilling to part with his money, according to very reliable sources." Peevy opened a folder and placed half-glasses on his nose. "Since your wife began petitioning the courts to get him to help his first wife financially, a good deal of his public and private life has surfaced, some of it in the tabloids. This has angered the lobbyist. To many people this first wife is a surprise. Skinner had kept her and his two children by her a deep, dark secret." Peevy looked up. "You've been keeping those two kids of his at your place, haven't you, Senator?"

Dray nodded, evincing no surprise at Peevy's knowledge. He would have had somebody watching the house and the children would have been spotted. "They'll soon be joining their mother, now that she's back on the mend. When she's completely well, she'll be working on my staff here on the Hill."

Peevy's mouth pursed. "I would suggest that you stick to your original plan of getting Mrs. Skinner and her family out of the way for a while."

Dray was suddenly still. "Is he the danger to my wife?"

"I'm pretty sure he's part of it."

"Go on."

"I think this investigation is getting intricate and dangerous, that there is a real scam here involving government officials and people like Skinner." Peevy paused, his mouth tightening. "Your wife was anxious to have Mrs. Skinner and her children given protection. I think she's right, but I also think she could use some, Senator. I'm sorry to say this, but I think your wife could be the target of some very nasty happenings. For one or more reasons she has stepped on some pretty high-placed toes by the look of it. I wish I knew more."

Dray inhaled deeply and nodded. "I've had the feeling that something was afoot that involved more than the court case she'd been trying. Does your investigation show that it might include her uncle, Colonel Cletus Lyons?"

"Sooo, I wasn't wrong when I had an inkling that there was another investigation going on at the same time. Does this include your uncle, Darius Mallory?"

Dray nodded. "I want you at the reception my mother is

having so that you can talk to my family about this. Peevy, I want all the stops pulled on this one. My wife is top priority."

"I know, Senator." Peevy coughed. "We traced that car that almost hit you and your wife, Senator."

"And?"

"It's registered to a leasing firm that's owned by a holding company with hidden ownership. You know, one of those things where everybody has a piece but where there's no name to pin down on a deed or lease. I've run into this before, and I'll tell you that it's usually a cover for something. I'll keep digging."

Dray felt a cold hand squeeze his insides. "Do that. I want whoever it is out in the open where I can see him. I can't fight the unknown." Dray drew in a shuddering breath. "It's like dueling a cobweb, hitting out at nothing. We have to know more, who the people are, what type of network."

"I think you've hit it on the head, Senator. I think we're dealing with a group and that it's far-reaching and powerful.

"Whoever is orchestrating this operation is damn cool and smart enough to pull off anything; but finding the culprit is one thing, proving it is another matter." Dray stood up and began pacing his office. "Could there be a connection between what has been happening to my wife, and her uncle, Cletus Lyons?"

Peevy stretched his neck so that he could keep the senator under his eye. "Does your wife have any papers on her uncle? Did he keep a journal or anything like that?"

"Possibly. She told me she has a few of his notebooks and tapes." Dray turned and paused in front of Peevy's chair. "My uncle feels that Cletus Lyons's death was not accidental, Peevy."

Peevy whistled low. "Then this could be an old operation, something that is threatened by what your wife either knows or has access to, Senator."

"Yes." Every drop of his blood turned to ice at that moment.

* * *

Luna talked to Uel and Barb about the other cases they had, and finally had most of them in order. "You two go home, I have a few things to finish."

"Don't stay too late," Uel admonished, leaning over Luna's desk and kissing her on the forehead.

"I am going to bed before the sun goes down this evening," Barb promised, smothering a yawn. "And tomorrow you, Gretchen, and I are going to Gillian's and get new duds for the reception. I'm going to splurge." Barb grinned when her husband groaned.

Luna was still chuckling after her friends had left. She liked being alone in the office. The quiet was very conducive to cogitating, and she needed to ponder the new client's quandary. A neighbor's garage built four feet onto their property! Good Lord, didn't anyone ever hear of surveying?

When the front-door chime sounded signaling that someone was there and wanted entry, Luna was irritated. Maybe if she waited very quietly in her office the person would go away. After the fourth chime she rose, muttering to herself. No matter who it was or what the problem was, tomorrow was going to be her answer.

Looking through the slats of the door blind, Luna stared at the woman facing the door. At least Luna assumed it was a woman. Despite the rather balmy May weather the person wore a long voluminous coat, a scarf swathed around her head and lower face, and despite the waning sun, dark glasses. "We're closed," Luna called through the door.

"Captain McAfee?"

Luna paused, a cool dampness running over her skin. "Yes."

"Let me in, please. It's Stenzi Heilmann."

Luna was frozen for a moment, then her hand went to the lock, dialing the release of the alarm system and freeing the night lock. Flinging back the door, she stared openmouthed at the older-looking woman who pushed past her and turned to stare at her.

"Close the door, Captain."

Luna slipped the night lock on again as a precaution before she faced the woman, who'd made no effort to remove any of her heavy clothing. "Stenzi, is it really you?"

A nervous jerk of the woman's head was the only answer.

"Come back to my office, we can talk there." Again Luna closed the door so that the two women were enclosed in the tiny office. Luna watched as the other woman removed her glasses, scarf, and coat. Still the woman was unrecognizable. Gone was the svelte blonde with the laughing eyes and curvaceous figure. In her place was a heavyset woman with dull eyes, a putty cast to her skin.

"I look different to you, I know, but all has not gone well with me. All there is in my life now is a need for justice, and that I will have before I die."

Luna reached out to Stenzi, feeling the quiver in the arm under her hand. "Sit down, please. It will only take me a moment to make coffee. I'll make a call and then you and I can have a long talk."

Dray paced the study in his home, wishing that Luna was with him. When the phone rang he grabbed it on the first ring. "Luna?"

"Ah, no, Senator, this is Elmo Behrens, Luna's friend from law school. Ah, I wanted to tell her that I have a place for her friend and two children if the need is still there, and they can go to the safe house tomorrow."

"Thank you, we'll handle it at this end. Tomorrow, you say. We'll be ready."

Dray felt a cold perspiration coat his body. Why didn't Luna come home? Why the hell had she put her calls on hold?

He dialed again and it rang and rang, then the after-hours message came over the wire. Good, she must have left the office and was on her way home.

Luna drove through Georgetown with Stenzi's words ringing in her ears.

"He threatened my unborn child, Captain McAfee. More than once he said that he would kill the baby when it was born if I ever tried to testify against him." The stilted English had a staccato horror in it. "I could not endanger my unborn child, so I went into hiding so that I would not have to go to court . . . but still Raymond Hetty beat me. When my son was born, the doctors . . . they say he was not strong, that he had been damaged in the womb. Now he is dead and I will have justice. That is what I live for now, and I will tell you everything I know so that he can be put in prison."

Stenzi described the secret storage areas that Master Sergeant Nichols and Hetty were in charge of, how they systematically pilfered military sundries and padded invoices.

Luna had perked up when Stenzi told her that the bosses were in the United States.

"Hetty told me that he and Nichols took their orders from Washington. Sergeant Nichols had been working with the bosses for many years. Hetty said that nothing could touch them."

So the black-market supply ring had to have been in operation for a long time. The pipeline of money, information, and sundries must be one of long standing, with powerful backup, involving persons with clout. Luna ruminated on all that Stenzi had told her, imagining the mushrooming business getting its start after the Second World War. It was an established, slick operation. Had Hetty's protection at his court-martial been part of the black-market network? It was like dropping a penny in a fountain, the ripples kept spreading outward.

Perhaps Stenzi's appearance was the first step in clearing her name. Luna had a wary hope that it might possibly happen, that Hetty could be the keystone to building a case that would do just that.

As Luna drove into the alley behind the Georgetown home and pulled up to the garage, she activated the electronic door opener. Once inside, she pressed the gadget again, locking the big door behind her and unlocking the back door of the garage that opened to the enclosed backyard. This action also turned on the yard lights and garage.

Getting out of the car, she gripped her briefcase, which held the cassette that Stenzi had spoken into while in the office. It was a precious lifeline to vindicating herself.

Luna had passed through the door to the yard and was on the winding brick walk when she heard a noise to one side of her. Wariness born of all her "accidents" had her turning and crouching, bringing the briefcase up like a weapon. Before she could take further evasive action a hand came up to grip her mouth.

Survival had her pulling back from the smothering hand, her fingers clawing at the grip, calling out in desperation. "Lance!" Then she was struggling with her assailants with all her strength. There were two of them and they were overwhelming her; she couldn't get her breath to call out again.

Through the roaring haze of red, strangling in the savage holds, she heard the bang of a door as though someone had slammed through it. Then with an angry roar the dog flung himself at the two men who were holding his lady, teeth and paws flashing in furious retaliation. The gentle lamb was a lion.

Finding herself put aside for a moment, Luna screamed again before gripping her briefcase like a weapon and swinging at the person nearest her.

The man turned, his face revealed by the bright backyard beacon. Raymond Hetty!

Then Dray was there with Wilkins, and a shot was fired and the two men were running away, scrambling up a ladder placed against the high fence and over the side. Sounds of footsteps running down an alley were followed by an engine coming to life and a car screeching away.

"Lance, sit," Wilkins demanded, reaching for the infuriated animal, who wanted to chase the men.

Dray gabbed for Luna, pulling her close, putting her behind him.

"They're gone, Senator." Wilkins flung the ladder to th

ground. "They must have come onto the grounds this way. I'll check the security system. Come, Lance," Wilkins ordered the dog, who sniffed the ladder and growled.

"Darling! Luna, are you all right?" Dray turned to her, enfolding her in his arms.

"I am now." Luna cuddled to her husband, her body quaking in the aftermath, feeling the answering shudder in his. "Ray Hetty was one, and I think the other was . . . Nichols." Her chattered words were almost indistinguishable. "I didn't see his face, but I discovered tonight that he was part of a conspiracy in Germany . . . that he probably was the one who destroyed my evidence against Hetty."

"What? Darling, are you sure?"

"About seeing Hetty, yes. I'm not dead sure about Nichols, but I would bet he was the other man." Stenzi's words about the collusion of the two men ran around in her head.

Dray picked her up in his arms, carrying her to the back door, just as Wilkins returned to it. "Wilkins, put on tea for Mrs. Lodge, then call the authorities." Dray looked down at her. "No more of this. I'm pulling out the stops. I'll get the bastards no matter what it takes."

"I've called the security people, sir, and they are doing that as we speak. The tea will be ready for Mrs. Lodge in moments, sir."

Luna put her hand up to her husband's cheek. "Are you sure you want to bring the police into this? It will be in the papers and . . ."

"Do you, a strong woman and advocate, think those two men should get away with accosting women?" At the quick shake of her head he leaned down and kissed her mouth. "I'll kill them in a hundred different ways they haven't thought of for what they tried to do to you." Dray kissed her again, cutting off her interjection. "Don't worry, I won't use a gun. There are other ways to take down a man and I'll use every one of them."

* * *

By the time the police finished talking to all of them, Luna was exhausted and glad to go up to bed.

Standing under the stinging spray of the shower with her husband massaging her body with a loofah sponge, she finally began to relax.

Turning off the water, Luna stared up at him through the beads of moisture. "Thank you, I feel better now."

"No more working late in the office for you. You can bring your work home and take care of it in the library."

"I didn't tell you that I had a visitor tonight, did I? Stenzi Heilmann stopped at the office."

Dray frowned, his brain throwing myriad facts around his mind. "The German girl who lived with Hetty! I thought she was dead."

Luna shook her head as Dray rubbed emollients on her damp body, then began drying her hair. "She disappeared, and since she had been my star witness against Hetty, the case fizzled. It seems she'd been threatened that harm would come to her and her unborn child if she testified. Her son died a few months ago as a result of trauma done to him in the womb, which Stenzi attributed to Hetty." Luna leaned her head against his shoulder. "The doctors told her that the terrible beatings she suffered could well have contributed to the baby's ill health. Now she wants to pay back a few scores by revealing things to me about Hetty. It seems that he and accomplices, Nichols for one, were into the black market in Europe. She gave me some addresses to warehouses where the materia stolen from the U.S. government was stashed."

"And she's going to retaliate against Hetty by revealing what she knows to you." Dray whistled softly and handed her a satiny nightgown.

"Why should I wear this? You'll only remove it."

"And that I enjoy very much. Put it on, darling, you look wonderful in this peachy color." Dray kissed her on one shoulder. "I'm going to put every gun I have at your dispos on this, darling. We will get Raymond Hetty and his cohorts. Umm, that peach hue makes your skin glow."

"It's apricot." She smiled at him lazily, loving the heat in his eyes. Their lovemaking was always great, improving each time they were together. It was a contiuing shock to Luna that her love for Dray never leveled off, but grew, expanded, deepened.

"You're mine, and I won't let anything happen to you."

"I know, and I won't let anything happen to you."

Arms around each other, they strolled from the bathroom into the bedroom.

Dray turned her to face him when they were next to the huge bed. "Kissing you is high on my list of favorite things to do."

"I like it myself." Pushing back from him after the lingering embrace, Luna clambered onto the bed, sitting Indian fashion in the middle of it. Facing her husband, she placed her hands in her lap.

"What is it, darling? You look nervous."

"Edgy, maybe. I want to tell you something, Dray."

Sitting down near her on the bed, making no attempt to cover his nakedness, he watched her in a relaxed fashion with only a tinge of wariness. "I'd rather make love, but I'll be patient."

"So would I—rather make love, I mean. Wait, wait," Luna pleaded when he reached for her. "I want you very much, I generally do." Luna sighed.

"Don't look so gloomy about it."

"I am. You see, I want children, maybe three, but I also want to continue my storefront law."

"Fine. Even if and when we move back to New York, you can have an affiliate office wherever we reside."

"I never thought of that. I was sure you would want me to go into your firm."

"No, but I might want to go into yours one day. I like the concept and I think I would find it challenging."

"Oh, Dray, I love you." Luna threw herself into her husband's arms, knocking him back on the bed. When he was so still, she moved back and looked at him. "You're white. Did I hurt you?"

Dray shook his head, the hands going over her trembling a bit. "That's the first time you've said you loved me since our time in Germany."

"Is it?"

"Yes, my darling, it is, and I've waited so long to hear you say it. I thought I never would."

Luna went lax against him, her mouth barely touching his. "But you must have known that I loved you, that I wanted you. I married you."

"I wanted to hear it."

"I'll say it all the time from now on, Senator."

"Please." Dray let his hand slide up over her backside under the satiny nightgown. "I do love your skin." In gentle pressure his hands opened and closed on her buttocks. Then they began a whorling motion, each movement taking the material higher on her body. "I want you, Luna, and tonight I won't be taking precautions, darling."

Luna laughed out loud. "Good, because I haven't been."

Dray chuckled, sliding her down his body so that his arousal touched her. "As you can see, I'm ready."

"So am I." Wriggling downward, she felt him penetrate her and she sucked in her breath in joy.

"Darling, don't. That feels so good when you do that." Dray's ragged laugh shivered over Luna's skin. "You're very potent."

"Why are we talking?"

"It keeps me from exploding."

"My darling husband, I want you to explode."

Dray gripped her, moving deeper into her. He sighed when her body entrapped his in a golden rhythm. Turning quickly, he slid her under him and with tooth-clenching restraint he moved, gently massaging her insides until she melted with him.

Love took them; conquered them. There was no more conversation, only the aura they'd made for themselves that pulsated through them. Again and again the climax was like an atomic explosion that mushroomed them from the planet into the ionosphere. Their world enclosed them.

With her head on his shoulder, Luna sighed. "I wish we could always stay like this."

"We can, darling, and we will."

Chapter 16

But Dray was wrong. The next day the papers had the notice that two men had been taken into custody and charged with attacking the wife of the junior senator from New York. Both Luna's and Dray's pictures were in the paper, along with those of Raymond Hetty and Nichols.

"This might prejudice anything I planned on doing to clear my name."

"Your name is cleared, darling, but we will dissipate the cloud that hangs over your spirit, I promise you. Go to work, Luna, and don't let this throw you. I will be calling the district attorney's office and telling him that we will be cooperating in every way to put the men behind bars." Dray was going to tell her about the private detective watching her, but he decided to wait until Peevy had given his report. There had been a security breach somewhere. Those men had got into his yard undetected.

"Up the rebels." Luna tried to smile at her husband, but she felt a nameless dread, as though what was happening could invade their lives. Clinging to him, she kissed him over and over, her mouth open on his.

"This is wonderful, darling, but neither of us will be leaving this house in about five more minutes," Dray said huskily.

"I don't want to leave you."

"Luna, darling." Dray scooped her close to him, his mouth fixed to hers.

"Ahem, Senator, I think that the committee meeting you were anxious to attend will be starting in under an hour, and you did say you wanted to speak to some people first." Wilkins stared woodenly at a spot just past Dray's right shoulder.

"What? Committee? Oh, right." Flushed, his hands moving convulsively on Luna, Dray stepped back. "I have to go, darling," he told Luna regretfully.

"I know. So do I." She leaned up and kissed him. "I should be with you when you give a statement to the press."

"Not to worry. I intend to make sure that the people know that this will be a joint statement from the two of us." He kissed her nose. "We will stop this once and for all. Good-bye, darling, have a good day."

Luna was to think of those words in the days ahead when the papers were emblazoned with her picture and Dray's. All the nasty details of the Hetty court-martial were thrust to the forefront of the news.

When the phone rang at her elbow, Luna jumped. "Hello."

"Are you going to hide or fight?"

"Stenzi, I recognize your voice. Why don't you come into the office where we can talk again?"

"It looks as though there will a trial because those men accosted you, and that they will do it very quickly. With all they are saying about you, will you not fight them?"

"I'm going to fight them all, Stenzi."

"Then I will help you."

When Luna replaced the receiver she put her chin in her hand, brooding about Stenzi Heilmann. What a beautiful girl she'd been, and now she was an embittered woman. Raymond Hetty should be in prison forever for what he'd done.

As her fingers played over the embossed box on her desk that held a barometer, a clock, and a colorful Air Force insignia, her mind shifted to her uncle, Colonel Cletus Lyons, who had owned the desk ornament. It was right in front of her, and her doodling fingers played over the surface, lovingly. What a fine man he'd been, caring, interested, filled with the joy of life, but dedicated to his country and family. It had all seemed so wrong to lose her aunt and cousin, then have her uncle killed in an accident. All the family she'd had, gone.

When Luna felt the insignia move she was surprised and more than a little dismayed. The desk set was all that she had left of her uncle's things.

Vandals had broken into his home shortly after the accident that had killed him, and this was the only thing that had survived the resultant fire. Arson had been the cause, but the culprits had never been apprehended. Luna had sold the property once the estate had been settled.

Luna tried to push the embossed front of the insignia back into its wooden holder but it seemed to unscrew from the face. Then it fell forward in her hand. Taken aback, she stared at the small, shallow cavity in the oak wood. A dull sheen caught her eye, and she poked one finger in and brought out a key with a small metal tag attached with her uncle's name and the Brairly Bank of Washington stamped on it.

Glancing at her watch, she ascertained that it was too late to phone the bank, then she recalled that it was Friday.

Reaching for a phone book, she dialed Brairly's information number. "Yes, it does have a number on the key," Luna told the woman who instructed her that the last three numbers were the code of the Brairly Bank located on K Street. "Yes, thank you, I can find it. Good-bye." Luna rang off, pushed the briefs she'd been working on into her top drawer, then grabbed her purse and keys.

It still gave her a jolt to drive the beautiful sports car that Dray had given her, but at the moment she was too enamored of her quest to do more than be grateful that she had so much power under the hood.

Breaking a few traffic laws and earning a few curses from other motorists as she wove in and out of traffic, trying to beat the six o'clock closing at the Brairly Bank, she prayed she wouldn't be stopped.

Screeching into the parking lot, she smiled weakly at a security guard, who shook his head and frowned at her.

Once in the bank she went right to the down escalator with the large sign that directed persons to the basement for safety-deposit boxes.

Signing next to her uncle's name, she noticed on the register that she had been designated her uncle's cosignee for the box.

Following behind the person with the matching key, she felt a sense of foreboding coupled with anticipation.

"There you are, ma'am." The attendant turned his key, then the box was in Luna's hands.

She went into a private cubicle and opened the box. There was a note and a journal.

LUNA, BE CAREFUL, CHILD. THIS IS MY LEGACY TO YOU, THAT YOU BE HONORABLE AND LOVE YOUR COUNTRY AS I HAVE TRIED TO DO. MY ENEMIES ARE CLOSING IN, BUT THERE IS ENOUGH IN THIS NOTEBOOK TO DESTROY THEM IF I DON'T GET THE CHANCE TO DO IT MYSELF. BE CAREFUL. YOUR UNCLE.

Luna stared at the journal, flipping through it quickly. When she saw the name Skinner, she paused and read a few paragraphs. It seemed that Skinner was linked to a network of people, that there was a buying and selling scheme involving government sundries.

Some of the people her uncle thought of as dishonest, even traitorous, were high on the list of honored Washington guests. Military ordinances were stolen and sold to the highest bidder. Whether that bidder happened to constitute a threat to the United States didn't seem to matter. Selling to the highest bidder was what mattered in these transactions.

There was mention of way stations and drop-off points in Europe and Asia, where the arms, foodstuffs, even clothing, were stashed and dispersed to the buyers, who paid high prices for the American specialty goods.

Feeling both ice-cold and feverish, Luna looked around her steel cubicle, even squinting at the light fixtures in paranoid fashion. The thought of being watched made her shiver.

Slipping the journal into her briefcase, she patted the leather. Discussing this with Dray was the first thing to do.

"I tell you, my man followed her to the Brairly Bank and just barely kept up with her. She drove like a wild woman, he said. He didn't see her go down to the safety-deposit section, but he did see her come out of there."

"Skinner, why didn't you have the man waylay her? She might have been carrying the record that her uncle kept."

"On K Street, with a million people around including joggers who might have given chase? Not a chance."

"Bungler. I'll take care of this myself."

When Luna reached home she was bubbling over with her find, eager to know more of what was in the journal her uncle had kept. She parked her car in the garage and ran across the small yard and through the back door. "Wilkins! Is the senator upstairs?"

"No, Mrs. Lodge, he's sent a message that he would be late and he would go right to his parents' home and dress there, so that he wouldn't keep you waiting. I'm to drive you to the farm, ma'am."

"Oh." Luna stared at Wilkins, wilting a little in disappointment.

"May I help, Mrs. Lodge?"

Luna looked down at her briefcase, then up again at the houseman. "Yes, perhaps you can. Does the senator have a safe or a place where he keeps his most important papers, Wilkins? I need to squirrel something away that's very vital to my future." She nodded her head sharply. "Dray and I have to go over this as soon as possible."

"We'll put it in the study, Mrs. Lodge. The senator has a locked desk and . . ."

"Oh, I don't think I would want to go into his things, Wilkins."

The retainer smiled. "He has told me that you are to have

access to everything, madam, including his desk. You have a
key on your key ring that will unlock it."

"I do? Oh, you must mean the little one that Dray gave me
with the house key."

"That's it, Mrs. Lodge. Come this way and we'll lock up
your papers now."

"How do you plan to handle this?"

"Don't worry, Skinner, it will be taken care of, by me."

"What if she has what you want and shows it to her husband first?"

"I'm banking that she won't think she has time. You just
make sure that you break into that house and get the journal.
I'll take care of the senator's bride."

Wilkins didn't mind being alone. He'd driven Mrs. Lodge
out to the farm and now he was free for the evening. His own
apartment in the home was roomy and pleasant. He'd walked
the dog and now it was a pleasure to sit in his quarters with
the dog at his side.

Lance had become a friend and companion to him.

"What is it, old boy?" Wilkins looked down indulgently at
the growling animal. When the animal's deep-throated growl
turned to a snarl, Wilkins dropped the book he was reading.

Getting to his feet, he went to the console on the desk and
pressed the many switches that checked the alarm system.
One of the lights turned red! Something or someone had tam-
pered with the system at the back door and shorted it out.

Kicking off his house slippers and switching off the lights,
he snapped his fingers at the dog and grasped a blackthorn
walking stick that had belonged to his Scottish grandfather.

Moving quietly, he left his own suite of rooms and entered
the main part of the house through the kitchen.

Now Lance was angry, threatening sounds issuing from his
throat as the dog crouched in an attack position.

Wilkins bent low too, relying on his knowledge of the house
rather than risking putting on a light.

All at once with a tooth-baring growl the dog launched himself across the kitchen.

Wilkins moved fast and switched on the kitchen light. Before he could aid the dog he was struck. As he went down he heard muffled curses and Lance's cry of pain.

Dray was beginning to get a bit edgy. He hadn't expected to arrive at his parents' place before Luna. As he was excusing himself from an acquaintance to go to the library and call Wilkins, she walked in the door.

For a moment he could only stare as she paused on the threshold and looked around her. He saw the hint of shyness in her smile and the hesitant moves she made. If only she could see how she glowed in the peach strapless dress with the hem ruffle that just touched above her beautiful knees. The low-heeled peau de soie slippers of the same hue emphasized her long, slender legs.

Dray's mouth went dry just looking at her. He wanted her! Then she turned and saw him, and the smile that began in her eyes and smoothed its way down to her velvet mouth melted him.

Walking toward her with his arms outstretched, he was totally unaware of any of the other two hundred and more guests who were moving easily through the palatial home and its grounds. All he wanted to do was hold her, love her. It was a pang to accept how much he missed her when he was apart from her during the day.

Other eyes watched the tableau, the electricity between the two people.

"Our daughter-in-law is quite beautiful, isn't she, Haddon?"

"Melanie, she is exquisite."

"We love her."

"It doesn't bother you what the rags have been saying about her?"

"Oh, it bothers me. I would like to tear a strip off the person that gave that story about her to the *Tattler.*"

Haddon laughed. "Good for you. I never believe anything they write." He frowned for a moment.

"You're thinking about Dray and how it could affect him, aren't you?"

"It crossed my mind."

Melanie patted his arm. "You've always been Dray's champion." Then she frowned. "You know the world better than I do, Haddon. What do you think? Could it damage Dray?"

"Take that worried look off your face. I think Dray's constituents would forgive me anything at this point." Again he looked serious.

"There's a 'but' in your voice."

"Luna strikes me as fragile. How would she hold up if a scandal touched Dray? I wonder if she could live with herself."

"I never thought of that." Melanie touched his arm. "You don't think she could do herself an injury, do you?"

"Perhaps not. After all, she did live through a rather traumatizing time when she was in Germany and she seems unscathed."

"But no one really knows what another person is thinking, do they, Haddon?" Melanie's eyes went to her daughter-in-law, her face softening. "She is a dear girl. Perhaps she carries all of this inside herself."

"That could be the case."

"Could you speak to her, Haddon? You have a such a diplomatic way about you. She should turn to us if something is bothering her, and I want her to know that, but I don't want to be the bothersome mother-in-law."

"Of course I could talk to her, my dear. She was going to get in touch with me anyway to talk about something. When we're conversing I'll just try to draw her out a bit and manage to tell her what you want her to know."

"Thank you, dear friend."

Haddon patted her hand. "Ah, here's Perrin. No doubt I'm keeping you from your guests and he's come to chastise me."

"I heard that." Perrin Lodge shook hands with March. "We've done a few of these in our time, haven't we?"

"Too many. Ah, here comes your brother, Melanie. I don't think I've ever seen him in evening wear before this moment."

"It took tears and threats from his sister to do it." Perrin laughed with Haddon.

"Talking about me, are you?" Darius smiled benignly at the company, blandly accepting his sister's piercing scrutiny. "And I've only had my underwear on for a week, Melanie, so I should be all right, unless of course we get a nor'easter."

"Darius, for heaven's sake, behave yourself." His sister's acerbic response didn't entirely mask the affection she had for her elder sibling. "You do look nice this evening."

Darius bowed from the waist. When he looked up his gaze was on Haddon March. "And how is the Marlin Limousine Service doing, Haddon? I understand that you took that over about five years ago. I remember using it myself when I was working in the D.C. area."

"Why, Haddon, I didn't know you owned a limousine service." Melanie patted his arm in mock censure.

"Not to mention all the shipping, trucking, and car-leasing outfits that were purchased in the same package," Darius interjected blandly, bringing his brother-in-law's gaze on him. "I understand your overseas transports are doing extremely well."

"Mallory, you sound as though you've been running a check on me."

"Do I?" Darius's cherubic look didn't change when he stared right back at the entrepreneur. Then he smiled sweetly. "I guess it's a habit. Done it to all my friends."

"Darius! You haven't! That's awful, and don't do it anymore. You're no longer with the Agency." She pouted at her husband. "Must we talk shop? Tonight is very important to Dray and Luna."

"Whatever you say, my love." Perrin kissed his wife's

cheek, then nodded at Dray and Luna, who had just danced past them. "Don't they look good together, Haddon?"

"Yes, and if we hurry we can catch the last of this dance, Melanie."

"Good idea." Melanie crooked her arm into Haddon March's, looking over her shoulder at her husband and brother. "Mingle, you two."

"Yes, we will, dear." Perrin watched the other two as they walked away. He spoke without looking at his brother-in-law. "What's the matter with you? Are you trying to spark Haddon's temper? You know he's a private man and wouldn't appreciate anyone nosing into his affairs."

"Too late, I've done a bit of checking since we discovered that the vehicle that tried to strike Dray and Luna was from his limousine service. Admittedly the service is often used by Skinner and his cronies, so it could be a blind alley, but I was able to discover that Haddon March has made several fortunes since the Korean War. He was part of the lay personnel negotiating the peace settlement."

"Which means nothing. Everyone has known for years that Haddon has made millions on speculation. His consulting firm specializes in helping clients make good investments overseas." Perrin gave his brother-in-law a sharp look. "Business is his life. He never married or had children, and gave every effort into making his investments grow. He is very respected on the Hill."

"Maybe it means nothing, but it looked interesting." Darius shrugged.

"I admire your perception, Darius, and your suspicious nature, but I've known the man since we were in the Second World War and Korea. He's smart, but there's no odor about him."

"I've been wrong before. Come along, Perrin, let's mingle before my sister comes back and lectures me."

"Does Dray know any of this?" Perrin asked.

"Some. It was working with him that got me started on this."

"I think we should talk to him. I don't want your suspicions to fire up Dray. He's edgy enough about Luna to leap at anything."

Darius sighed. "I suppose you're right. I've always been too damned suspicious."

"That's true." Perrin Lodge clapped his brother-in-law on the back affectionately.

"Ah, that was very nice, Melanie."

"Thank you, Haddon. Oh, we stopped next to Luna. Dear, your dress is lovely. The cream-colored jade jewelry you're wearing is wonderful with it."

"Thank you, Melanie. Hello, Mr. March."

"My dear, you must call me Haddon, we're almost family."

"Fine, I will, Haddon."

Melanie turned to speak to a friend, then gestured to Dray to speak to the person.

"We seem to be on our own for a few minutes, Luna. Perhaps you would like to walk in the garden. We could discuss what it was you wanted to speak to me about when you called my office so many times."

"Thank you. I appreciate that." Luna was surprised at the strength in the hand that took her elbow. Haddon March was tall and ascetically thin, he didn't look powerful. "Actually, I don't think I need much more for my case. But perhaps you could tell me if you know anything about the Skinner investments. We unearthed some rather strange ones; one had your name on it. The Whalley Import Antique company."

"Ah, yes. Whalley's. A wonderful place. I sold out my interest in it some time ago, but I realize that it's good business to keep a name like mine on the letterhead." Haddon March stood back to let her precede him through the French doors to the terrace.

Luna smiled and nodded. "It is, indeed."

"The garden is beautiful, isn't it? I always loved the old-fashioned lanterns that Melanie has strategically placed among the flowers and shrubs. Those came from Whalley's

They also give off enough light to show me your lovely face. I am sorry that I can't help you with Skinner's investments, but I will ask around the capital about him, if you'd like. Something could surface. Would you excuse me, Luna? I have to leave early so I should make my excuses to the guests. May I escort you back to the ballroom?"

"No. I'll go back in soon. The May flowers are so fragrant that I think I'll just enjoy them for a while."

"I don't blame you, I would like to linger here too. Good night, my dear. I hope to see you soon again."

Luna looked after the man who was such a close friend to the Lodges and wondered why she always had the feeling of talking to a wall when she conversed with him. No doubt years of being a canny businessman had given Haddon March the ability to hide himself even when he seemed to be talking freely.

Her thoughts turned naturally to the Skinner case because of the conversation she'd just had. She blinked as the paper she'd received from her case investigator flashed in front of her eyes. Hadn't it mentioned something about Haddon March's being an owner of Whalley's? Had it said he'd sold it off years ago? Maybe it had. She couldn't quite recall. Haddon March had dabbled in so many companies and he seemed a success at everything he touched. Even if a few of the mergers involved Skinner, it wouldn't make March guilty of anything. The man was just a past master at making money.

Straightening up, Luna stared into the blackness. She was so absorbed in her own thoughts that she paid no attention to the snap of a twig, the whisper of a leaf, the night owl singing high in the branches of an oak.

Then the hair stood up on the back of her neck. By the time she'd turned in alarm, the hand was already encircling her neck, cupping her mouth, the sickeningly sweet smell wafting up her nose. Her struggles died and she went limp.

"Hurry, let's get her out to the car."

"Yes, sir. You were smart to let me drive you this evening. Without the two of us, she might have been harder to take out."

"Shut up and hurry."

Chapter 17

"Dray, can we speak to you?" Perrin Lodge put his hand on his son's shoulder as he stood at the edge of the floor, scanning the room.

"I was looking for Luna. I want another dance with my wife."

"You sound like a bear with a sore paw. Is your wife too popular?"

"Yes, Uncle Darius, she is, dammit. Where is she?"

"No doubt strolling on the terrace or through the gardens with a guest. She is the coguest of honor," Perrin told his son, chuckling. "And I used to think I was bad with your mother."

"You were," Darius said blandly. "My father threatened to shoot you on sight if you ever interrupted another meal. And he hosed you down one summer evening when you were serenading Melanie."

Perrin Lodge smiled ruefully when his son raised an eyebrow in his direction. "True. Unfortunately your uncle has a photographic memory. Let's go in the library, shall we?"

Dray was reluctant. "I suppose I can find her when we're through. Lionel"—Dray gestured to the houseman—"when you see my wife, will you tell her I'm in the library."

"I will." Lionel nodded woodenly. "I'll look for her."

When the door closed behind the three men, Dray really looked at his father and uncle. "Something you don't want anyone to hear?"

"Darius has turned up a few interesting things along the way." Perrin Lodge nodded to his brother-in-law, who proceeded to fill Dray in on the things uncovered by his investigation.

"Skinner seems to be in the thick of more than one scam. The man's crafty in some ways, clumsy in others." Darius tapped his chin with his index finger.

Dray stared at first one man then another. "Peevy has been turning up interesting things on Skinner as well that seem to run parallel to your investigation, Uncle." Dray's face tightened. "If there is a connection between Skinner and high-level crime, Luna could be in danger. She's been hitting pretty hard at Skinner in court. Maybe he feels that he doesn't want any of his private life surfacing because some of his shady connections might show. Luna could be a real problem to him." Dray's face whitened and he hit the palm of his hand with his fist.

Turning to the phone, he dialed rapidly. "Wilkins? What? When? Are you sure? Whatever it was, get it out of my desk and bring it out here. I can't find Mrs. Lodge at the moment. Hurry." Dray slammed down the receiver, his brow creased with concern

Then he shot a sharp look at his uncle. "Luna's relative, Cletus Mallory, was killed shortly before he was to testify before a committee about black marketeering. At the time, Skinner's name kept cropping up throughout the hearing, though nothing was ever proved." He took a deep breath. "According to Wilkins, Luna brought home something she wanted put in a safe place. If it is about Skinner, maybe she could be in jeopardy. Why the hell was Skinner invited here tonight? I didn't want him."

Perrin Lodge stared at his son. "We had the feeling he was on your list. Your mother and I didn't ask him."

Dray left the room on the run, the two men at his heels.

"Uel, will you stop rubbernecking that way? People will think you've never been to a society party," Barb admonished her husband, excitement heightening her color and giving even more sparkle to her lustrous brown eyes.

"I haven't," Uel said absently. "Where's Luna? I saw her going out to the terrace, but that was some time ago."

"You're still worried about her, aren't you?"

"Yes, she's had too many close calls lately. I don't like it. My skin crawls when I think there's someone after her, but I'm damned sure I'm right."

"About what?" Gretchen ambled up to them, her hand entwined with Harry Lemke's.

"Uel is sure that Luna is in danger." Barb's lip trembled.

"Tell me who it is," Harry rumbled.

"I wish I knew. I'd go after him myself, but I think Chuck Skinner is involved, and Hetty, a man Luna tried to prosecute in Germany. . . ."

"What's going on? Look at Luna's husband. Is he ready to bite through steel, or what?" Gretchen was round-eyed as Uel whirled and strode across the room, intercepting Dray.

"It's Luna, isn't it?"

Dray hesitated, then nodded. "Do you know where she is?"

Uel shook his head. "But I did see her go out on the terrace a while back. I'll help you look for her."

In minutes Dray had informed the security personnel that his wife might be missing, and though the party went forward, a search was begun in earnest.

"Nothing," Perrin Lodge informed his son some time later. "A black limousine was spotted leaving the grounds but nothing seemed unusual about it."

"I'm calling the police."

Haddon March strolled toward them from a group that was close to Melanie Lodge. "I'm going to make my good-byes, gentlemen." The smile faded from his face and he looked searchingly from one to the other of the men in front of him. "Is something wrong, Dray? You look positively white."

"That's the man who was talking to Luna." Uel pointed.

"I don't believe we've met. I'm Haddon March. . . ."

"Have you seen Luna?"

"Why, yes, Dray, a short time ago. We went out to the

terrace and talked, then I left her because I wanted to make my good-byes to my hosts. She was just enjoying the flowers and the lovely spring night. She's probably still out there. Shall I show you where we were?"

"Please," Dray answered, already moving toward a pair of double doors leading to the terrace that girdled the house.

"Wait, Dray. Is there anything I can do?"

"If you're leaving, Haddon, you might keep a sharp eye out on the grounds."

"Of course I will. I'll call in the morning to see how she's feeling before I go to my meeting. Good night, Perrin, Darius."

Perrin Lodge nodded abruptly and followed after his son.

Darius Mallory moved closer to March. "If I recall, you were involved in the Calumet Scandal."

"I was a business adviser of Henry Calumet, that was all. When I discovered he was skimming I cut my ties with him." March's society smile twisted a bit. "You still get your facts mixed, Mallory."

"Not all the time." Darius smiled benignly when Haddon March grinned, then strolled across the room toward the front foyer.

Darius was about to hurry after his nephew and brother-in-law when he saw Wilkins come from the back of the house, a bandage on his head, looking grim and white-faced. "What happened to you, man?"

"Sapped by intruders. I have the feeling they were after something special, but the dog must have tripped one of the interior alarms and they scattered."

"That's quite a dog," Darius mused absentmindedly. "What's that you're carrying?"

"Something Mrs. Lodge brought home with her this evening. After talking to the police I began to wonder if it had been just a robbery or if they were after something specific. When I got the call that the senator wanted me out here because Mrs. Lodge wasn't to be found, and I told him about this, he said to bring this with me."

"Good man, give it to me."

Wilkins shook his head, looking obdurate. "I will give it to the senator."

"Tough nut, aren't you?" Darius cackled.

"Where is the senator?"

"On the terrace. Follow me."

The two men crossed the room and went out onto the terrace.

"There he is. Dray, come up here. Wilkins is here."

"I'm coming. Keep them looking for her, Father. Wilkins, Darius, come into the library."

Dray looked at the journal Wilkins handed him across the library desk, flipping through it, his jaw tightening, his eyes flashing lightning. Swallowing painfully, he handed the book to his uncle, who perused it quickly. "Where is Skinner? His name is all through this journal."

"And who is this Mr. Big referred to in here? Would that be Skinner?" Darius looked skeptical.

"I don't know. Right now I have to find Luna."

"You said Peevy and his people were watching the guests?"

Dray nodded. "If Skinner did leave, someone will be following him. How the hell did he get an invitation to this party if none of us gave him one?"

At the knock on the door, both men turned.

"This was left for you, sir." The butler handed him a single folded sheet of paper.

"Thank you, Lionel." Dray opened the note, staring at it blindly until his uncle took it from his hand and read it out loud.

SENATOR LODGE, YOUR WIFE IS INCOMMUNI-CADO FOR A FEW DAYS. I WILL NEED THE TIME TO FIGURE MY NEXT MOVE. IF YOU TRY ANY-THING AT ALL BEFORE I CONTACT YOU, SHE WILL BE SILENCED AT ONCE. CS

"Skinner has her." Dray's words were wrenched from his throat.

Chapter 18

Stenzi Heilmann had seen the man walk from the house and get into the Rolls-Royce. It seemed strange to see him drive himself. When he'd spent time in Germany he had always used a chauffeur. She'd never known his name, but Ray Hetty had worked for him. He deserved punishment, just as Hetty did.

Though she wasn't too familiar with the rented car she was driving, she managed to follow the other auto. Even in Washington a Rolls-Royce was not so common that it couldn't be noticed. She would go back to the house that she'd followed Luna to and tell her about this man, but first she should discover where the very important man lived.

Puzzled, she trailed him back to D.C. into a rather shabby neighborhood of warehouses with seedy-looking town houses squashed between them. Parking a city block behind the man when he stopped, she made sure there was a truck in front of her so that she could see without being seen. Why would such an important man go into such a place?

Surprised to see him come out again in such a short time, she followed him back the way they'd come, but this time he drove much faster and she couldn't keep up with him.

Stenzi drove around for a while, lost in the unfamiliar streets, then she saw a landmark she recognized and was soon heading back to the house where Luna had gone to the party. She wanted to talk to the man who had been so friendly with Hetty, but since she had lost him, she would go back and talk to Luna.

Driving laboriously in the unfamiliar American car, it took

her a little time to get back to the place called Merry Hill. Once there, she was stopped twice by security people, but they let her go when she said she had to speak to the senator.

Quite a few cars were departing, so that she was able to drive almost to the door and park.

"May I ask what you're doing here, miss? My name is Peevy."

Stenzi wasn't fooled by the mild manner. There was steel in the eyes. "I must see Captain Luna McAfee." She could see the man digest what she said, his eyes narrowing on her.

"Come with me."

The grip on her arm was surprisingly strong, but Stenzi didn't try to free herself. The important thing was to see Luna McAfee.

Peevy led her right down the main hall, not even stopping when Dray's mother called to him. He knew to the second when Dray's brother and sister made a phalanx behind him. Pushing open the library door, he faced three men, the senator, his uncle, and his father. "We should talk to this woman."

Whatever protest Dray was going to make died when he caught Peevy's grim look. "All right. Who are you?"

"Who are you?" Stenzi shot back. "I have come to see Captain McAfee."

Dray stiffened. "I'm her husband. Are you Stenzi, the girl from Germany whom Luna tried to help?"

Stenzi nodded. "I would have been here sooner but I followed the Big Man first."

"What 'big man'?" Darius Mallory's usually indolent voice sharpened.

Stenzi stared at him for a few seconds before answering. "I do not know any of you. I, what you Americans call 'stick my neck out,' but I tell you. I do not know his name, but he left here driving a Rolls-Royce. I saw him in Germany once. He had come to the apartment that I shared with Raymond Hetty. They thought I was not there, but I had come in the back way, through the kitchen. Hetty had told me that he had never seen the Big Man who was his business—how do you

say?—associate, but I knew it was the man because he called
him Mr. Big, no other name. I never told Hetty that I had
seen him." Stenzi rushed her words, then inhaled a shuddering breath as though she had not been used to talking so
much.

"Could you describe him to us?" Peevy took out a notebook.

"I can show you his picture. I took it when he went by the
kitchen window that day in Germany and have kept it because it was another tie to Hetty." Stenzi rummaged in her
capacious handbag, then brought out a dog-eared, faded
photo.

Dray sucked in a tight breath. "Chuck Skinner."

While the others muttered in anger, Darius sidled up to his
nephew. "That doesn't surprise you that much, does it?"

Dray stared at his uncle for a few minutes, then shook his
head. A bell went off in his brain as he turned to look at
Stenzi again. "You said you followed him."

"Yes, he does not live too close to here, and it took a while
to come back from the other place."

"What other place? Can you tell us where that might be?"

Stenzi's puzzled look was replaced by a searching one.
"Where is Captain McAfee? Has something happened?"

Dray nodded. "I will tell you all about it after we find her.
Will you help us?"

"Yes, she is my friend. She tried to help me."

"Then can you give us some idea where you were?"

"I followed the Big Man, thinking he would take me to
Hetty, but he didn't. It was just a factory of some kind. It
looked unused."

"Your English is very good." Dray felt his way with her,
though he felt a burning urgency, noting how she glanced
around constantly, her hands threading and unthreading.

"Thank you. I spoke English on my job at the air base.
That is where I met Raymond Hetty."

"Won't you sit down." Perrin Lodge pushed a chair toward
her and seated her.

"Miss Heilmann . . ." Dray began.

"Call me Stenzi, please."

"Stenzi, I know you don't know Washington, but do you think you could recall anything about the factory you saw?"

"I wrote down the street and number and I remember that it is off New York Avenue." Stenzi spoke slowly, looking down at the paper in her hand. "See, I have marked it."

Dray snatched the paper from her hand, mumbling thank you, his eyes perusing the rough map.

Wilkins and Peevy moved next to him, looking over his shoulder. "I know just the location, sir. I will drive you in the Rolls. It will be faster."

"I'll go with you," Peevy said gruffly.

"I'm going too," Darius said, blinking myopically. "Perrin, rouse the authorities and your children and follow us. Bret will be able to find the place. Hurry, Dray."

"Right," Dray said abruptly, ushering Stenzi ahead of him. "Father, call your police connection and tell him what we have."

"Hurry, son, I'll be there as fast as possible."

Her mouth was filled with sawdust. Why else would it be so dry? Opening her eyes was arduous, they were sticky and felt raw. Blinking, she tried to move and found that she was bound. Surprise held her immobile for a moment, then realization hit her and she remembered the party and someone grabbing her. When she tried to wriggle free, the ropes tightened, eliciting a groan from her.

"So, lady JAG, you finally woke up, did you?"

Luna stared up at Raymond Hetty, feeling her gorge rise. Swallowing several times in an effort to quell the nausea, she stared up at the man who had been her bête noire almost since their first meeting. "You can be put away for good for kidnapping, Hetty."

"You ain't got the winning hand here, any more than you had in Germany, lady JAG, so don't get uppity."

Luna took deep breaths. "Look, there's a chance you won't even be charged with anything if you let me go now. . . ."

"Don't jive me, lady JAG. You think I don't know you'd sink my boat if you could?" Hetty pushed at her face, knocking Luna backwards. "Umm, you got right pretty skin, missy. Maybe before we ice you, I should have some fun."

Frozen, Luna stared at him. Pushing back the fear, she tried to think. There was no reasoning with him, and it would be foolish to anger him. Greed! That was what had gotten him into the black-market world in the first place. From what she knew of Hetty there was no good way to handle him. He was nasty and unpredictable, volatile as nitroglycerin, and about as dangerous.

"My husband is a rich man. I imagine that he could double, even triple, what you would be getting from your bosses to return me to him."

"I'm afraid that won't be possible, Mrs. Lodge."

Charles Skinner looked angry. Luna guessed that he must have seen the thoughtful look on Hetty's face when she'd been talking to him.

"What are you doing back here?" Hetty quizzed truculently. "I thought you went home."

"Skinner, are you out of your mind? You get mixed up in a crime and you'll be sent away until . . ."

"Shut her up," Skinner snarled.

Hetty chopped downward, striking Luna in the forehead. "She's out now."

"Damn you, you should have taken care of her instead of bringing her here."

"I thought you wanted to find out where that wife and kids of yours were kept and put the arm on 'em."

"That was before I realized I was followed to my home. I figured I'd better get back here and get rid of her before I do anything else. I don't want complications." He hit the palm of his hand with his fist. "But I'll be damned before I pay any more money to that frump and her kids. I have expenses," Skinner said thoughtfully, not even looking at Hetty. "I could make the senator's wife talk before we kill her. If I get my hands on the papers the chief is so anxious to find, that could give me an edge. Yes. That might take care of things."

"Put me in a room with her . . . alone. I'll get it out of her."

"What?" Skinner came out of his reverie and stared at the man in front of him. "Damn you, wasn't the trouble in Germany enough for you? I told your father I didn't want you in this, but he insisted. The Chief won't be too happy if you bring the roof in on us again; and if she started screaming, someone could hear."

"That wasn't my fault," Hetty muttered sullenly. "Besides, nobody ever got to Stenzi. She disappeared."

"Lucky for you and all of us that she did. Now, how the hell am I going to get the lady lawyer to tell us where that journal is?"

"I tell you, leave me alone with her, I can make her talk. And if you like, I'll gag her while I work her over. She'll tell us everything when I get through with her."

Dray heard the last remark as he made his way up the wooden stairs to the second floor of the warehouse. Anger and fear for Luna's safety built in him like a whirlwind.

"Take it easy, Nephew. I heard it too, but we have to be cautious for Luna's sake," Darius warned, pulling a small-caliber gun from his shirt.

"He's right," Peevy whispered to Dray on his other side. "Stay calm."

"Come on, Skinner, give her to me. I'll bring her out of that faint and make her talk." Hetty's reedy voice sounded louder.

"All right, but keep her mouth shut."

"No more time, Darius," Dray breathed hoarsely, then he flung himself through the open door, registering the horror and surprise of his targets. Choosing Hetty in a millisecond decision was the right one because the man reacted almost immediately, trying to yank a gun from the shoulder holster he was wearing.

Dray hit him with everything he had, rasping fury in the attack sound he made.

The two men rolled to the floor, struggling furiously for advantage.

"Don't move, Skinner. I'll put a bullet up your right nostril if you do," Darius said conversationally.

"Who the hell are you? I don't know you. Get out of this warehouse and take that mad-dog senator with you."

"Bluffing won't work now. Stay where you are." Darius positioned himself directly in front of the man.

Peevy looked dispassionately at the two men on the floor, then moved around, out of Darius's line of fire, to frisk Skinner. "Stay still and be glad I don't throttle you," Peevy whispered sweetly, making Skinner stiffen to immobility.

With a savage chop, Dray flattened Hetty. In almost the same second he was moving toward the pile of rags that was a bed for Luna, lifting her in his arms and calling her name.

"Is she all right?" Darius didn't take his eyes off Skinner.

"I don't know. Damn them, I think they've hit her, there's a bruise on her forehead."

"See if you can bring her around, Senator. I don't like moving her if there's been more than a hit on the jaw. . . ." Peevy wrenched Skinner's arms around his back, slapping cuffs on him.

"Damn their souls." Dray went over her carefully, speaking to her the whole time.

Hetty opened his eyes, and in seconds knew the situation. Not moving, he scanned the room. The senator was bent over his wife, the other man was holding a gun on Skinner. Hetty could see his gun just a few feet away. When the older man risked a glance at the senator, Hetty, in one lightning move, found his gun and brought it up to bear on the older man.

"Hetty! You murderer, drop the gun." Stenzi faced him, a gun held in both her hands, aiming right toward her nemesis.

"Stenzi!" That shook Hetty. She would have to die with the others. He didn't fear that she could do anything to him. Positioning himself, he aimed the gun, watching as Dray turned in slow motion, his body curved over his wife protectively.

"Murderer!" Stenzi fired, freezing the others in the room, her bullet striking Hetty in the face, exploding his features, his gun firing into the ceiling . . . once . . . twice. "He killed my child and he would have killed everyone in this room."

Dray rose with Luna in his arms. "Give the gun to my uncle, Stenzi . . . and thank you. You did the right thing and you're a very brave lady."

Before anyone else could comment, the room seemed to fill with police.

"These people accosted us, Officer. Of course I will prefer charges," Skinner blustered, not sparing a glance for the sheet-draped gurney containing the body of Raymond Hetty.

"Just come along with me, sir. You'll get your chance to speak at the station."

Dray was reluctant to put his wife in the hands of the ambulance attendants, but his uncle persuaded him.

"I'm fine," Luna told him, smiling faintly. "I'm so glad you're here."

"Darling!" Dray felt his throat tighten at the whiteness of her face. "I'm with you every step of the way."

"I know, and I thank God for that." Tears welled and coursed down her face as her husband embraced her, cursing steadily in uneven cadence.

The trial didn't get under way until a few months later.

Dray's and Luna's testimony did much to nail down Chuck Skinner's coffin.

Not all Gil Hetty's bluster and money could cover up the fact that his son was a cold-blooded assassin and thief.

"You, sir, are as culpable as your son, and I am issuing a warrant from this bench for your arrest," the judge told Gil Hetty sternly, effectively silencing him.

"Prosecution calls Luna McAfee Lodge to the stand."

"Yes, it is true that I have been trying through the courts to gain an equitable financial settlement for his wife and his children by the first marriage. Chuck Skinner has consistently refused to obey the court order that he must make payments; instead he tried to intimidate and cow them. It was then we had to find a safe house for them."

"And isn't it also true that Hetty colluded with a Sergeant Nichols and the base commander, Colonel Encorvado, to destroy the evidence, and that those two men are both in custody, charged with that crime and black marketeering?

"I object. That is hearsay, since neither man has been convicted of the charges. This witness has a vendetta against the deceased Raymond Hetty and she is seeking to make my client look bad because she was unable to make a case against Hetty in Germany. My client maintains that Raymond Hetty was brutally murdered by the people who are plotting against him."

"Your Honor, prosecution will prove that Chuck Skinner was indeed involved in kidnapping, assault, and in a worldwide operation of stealing from the United States government."

The court erupted with newsmen rushing out to telephones.

Piece by painful piece the German trial was exposed. When Master Sergeant Nichols was called to the stand, the prosecutor, bolstered by testimony given by Luna and by the journal kept by her uncle, attacked with every gun port open.

"So you admit that you were the person that destroyed the evidence collected by the then Luna McAfee?"

Sergeant Nichols's eyes flicked around the courtroom as though looking for an escape hatch. At the prodding of the prosecutor, who mentioned perjury, he whispered, "Yes."

Again voices rose in agitation and excitement, and Skinner muttered urgently to his lawyer.

The trial lasted for many days. When the verdict was announced, Chuck Skinner was convicted, as was the deceased Raymond Hetty implicated, along with Nichols and Encorvado. A bench warrant was issued to Gil Hetty.

"I'd feel better if we'd been able to make Skinner open up more," Dray mused to Peevy.

Peevy nodded, as did Darius Mallory. "There's a bigger skunk in the woodpile somewhere, probably in Germany. Maybe he'll go to ground now."

"I wonder," Darius pondered, tapping his chin with one finger.

Chapter 19

That night, when Luna and Dray were alone in their bedroom, he looked over at her. "It's been rough on you, hasn't it, darling?"

Luna smiled at the man who'd turned her life upside down and sideways. "Actually it was a catharsis. Until the moment when Nichols admitted culpability, I hadn't realized what a burden that time in Germany had been." She sighed. "I never suspected our commanding officer. Now, because of you, I feel free."

Dray didn't move any closer to her, but he had the sensation of their bodies being pressed together. "I love you, Luna McAfee Lodge."

"I know, and that's what the real freedom is, that somehow you've managed to take my burden, simplify it, then wipe it out." Luna stepped closer to him, her one hand coming up to touch his cheek. "Are you a magician?"

"You give me power, Luna mine. I've always considered myself a strong man, but since meeting you, I realize that I'm both stronger and gentler because of it. I can leap tall buildings, Luna, but I can also cry because you've wreaked the havoc of love in my life."

"I hope New Yorkers appreciate their senator."

"Going to campaign for me the next time I come up for election?" Dray grinned at her. He had decided not to tell her of his fears that the man behind the criminal activity had not been caught. Maybe he would disappear, or go to ground, as had been intimated.

"It will be the toughest campaign ever waged."

"Up the rebels. Kiss me, wife." He had Luna safe in his arms and he would keep her that way.

Luna stood on tiptoe, her body not quite touching his, her lips soft and supple on that tough mouth. "I have something to tell you, husband."

"Ummm, great. Talk later," Dray told her, his mouth moving on hers, his tongue jousting with hers.

Luna pulled back a fraction. "Can't we put this off for just a fraction of time?"

"A fraction of time and no more. I don't get enough loving. I need your body to hold me fast."

"Dray!" Luna laughed breathily. "You say the most outrageous things."

"You mean because I love the feeling I get when your body surrounds me, when you breathe, or talk, or whisper. Darling, it's the ultimate high, and I can see us doing it when we're in our nineties and it will still put me in a tailspin. Of course, I think we might shock our children, but then they'll be along in years and might not notice." Dray ran his mouth down her neck, his arms coming up to clasp her hips and move her closer to him, whorling her middle on his aroused body.

"That's what I wanted to talk about."

"What?" Dray lowered his head, his chin edging away her clothing from her breast. His mouth moved slowly toward the nipple, his breathing becoming ragged.

With one quick movement, he bent and scooped her up in his arms, carrying her to the bed, placing her on it and going down next to her.

"About children."

Blinking his eyes, Dray tried to focus on her. "What did you say? I think I lost you. Were you talking about Amy and Tommy?"

"No, but I think they're very happy in their new home. Actually, I was talking about our children."

"Oh." Dray grinned at her. "I don't think it's that important now, but if you'd like to start a family this instant, I think it's a good idea."

"Too late." Luna nuzzled his neck.

"For what?" Dray was moving down her body, his mouth heated and passionate.

"We've already made a baby. In about seven months we should be able to see him or her."

"Huh?" Dray was still massaging her body with his one hand, his being filled with passionate emotion. "What? Luna, did you say that—Are you pregnant?"

"Give the man a cigar."

"Honest?" Dray felt an elation, fear, love such as he'd never experienced.

"Dray, I see tears in your eyes. Is something wrong?"

"If you're healthy, everything in the world is wonderful. Darling, I can't believe it. Is it true? Have you been to a doctor?"

"Yes and no, but I'm going to make an appointment tomorrow. Uel has a friend at the Georgetown Medical Center about whom he brags constantly, Dr. Adelsen."

"Is he the best?"

"It's a woman, and she's given papers on the subject of birthing and has lectured around the world. Uel says her first love is delivering children. Sound good enough?"

"She sounds marvelous. Damn! It's exciting." Dray kissed her hard, grinning. "I suppose you'll want Uel and Barbara to be godparents."

Luna nodded. "They are the best people in the world."

"I agree, but right now I'd like to make love to my wife." He gave her exposed breast a gentle, searching kiss, his head moving downward. Lightly his thumb moved over the damp nipple as his mouth continued past her abdomen. Kiss after kiss was pressed into the muscular softness of her stomach. The minuscule fine hairs on her skin were electrified by the moist abrasion, the muscles contracting at the embraces.

Blowing against the soft down that preceded the reddish-golden triangle at the apex of her body, he whispered soothingly to her. "Easy, darling," Dray pleaded, his voice cracking when her body arched in sensuous reaction. His open mouth pressed against her, his breath intruding, warmly giving, loving.

Crashing combers of sensual shock shuddered through her as his knowledgable tongue entered and touched in tactile electricity. Her body rippled and thundered to the core in passionate shock, the undulating sensation giving rhythm to her body.

Sliding up her form, Dray entered her with a gentle ferocity that rocked both of them, thrusting them into the maelstrom of passionate love that controlled them and flung them to the farthest stars.

Dray leaned over his supine wife. "You can't be sleeping."

Luna opened one eye. "I'm just savoring what we had. Wonderful. Haven't you ever heard of an aftershock? I'm in one of them."

"Are you happy, Luna mine?"

"Happier than I ever thought anyone could be."

"Will you be unhappy having a child when your career is so fulfilling?"

"No. And when our baby is small, I'll work out of the study . . . if I have time." Luna smiled lazily at him. "I understand babies can be a twenty-four-hour job." She reached up to touch Dray. "I'm too possessive to give my baby over to anyone else. I would resent anyone but one of us seeing the first smile, hearing the first word."

"That's why they have those carrier things. Take the baby to work."

Luna laughed. "That would be fatal. Barb and Gretchen would get nothing done."

"We'll work out something." Dray touched her nose. "I do know that you will have a battery of helpers around the clock. I will not let you tire yourself." He kissed her mouth. "As I said, we'll work out something."

"Yes, we will, won't we." Dray would always be there for her to aid her in anything, she knew that with a lover's clarity. He was her love, her bolster, her friend.

* * *

Three weeks after the trial Luna was walking along the street in Silver Spring. She'd had to park down the avenue, away from the office, because there had been no empty parking places closer.

When she walked in the front door, Gretchen shot her a sharp look, then rose from her desk and followed her into her office.

"What's up, Gretchen? You look as though you have a secret."

"The senator's office called and said that he'd be picking you up for lunch." Gretchen sighed. "He is so romantic."

Luna frowned. "Oh? I thought he had a full agenda. Did he give you a reason why? I could have sworn he'd said that he was up to his eyes today."

Gretchen shook her head. "No, but isn't it nice of him? By the way, is it still on for Friday dinner at your house, Luna?"

"Yes, I hope you and Harry can make it."

"We can. Uel and Barb are coming too."

"Good." Luna smiled at her friend and coworker, thinking that she'd never seen her look so glowing. "You and Harry getting serious?"

"I think so. He makes me feel very good about myself, Luna."

"That's the magic touch." Luna lifted her friend's hand. "No one should feel better about oneself than you, Gretchen. You've come a long way, and it looks as though you'll be in a position to take the bar next year."

Gretchen's mouth dropped. "You don't mean it."

"I do. Barb, Uel, and I were talking about it. Your comprehension is great and you have the feel, your confidence in your legal ability is growing by leaps and bounds." Luna grinned at her. "For instance, the Leber case that you handled so well."

Gretchen nodded. "I did, didn't I?"

"I had better get moving. Send in the Lovetts the moment they arrive."

"Is that the surrogate-mother case?"

Luna nodded. It was almost on the tip of her tongue to tell Gretchen to give the case to Uel or Barbara. With her own precious child growing inside of her, she was very sensitive on the subject of children. Luna sighed. The Lovetts deserved to be heard. Besides, she didn't want to make an announcement yet. She and Dray wanted to savor the news together before they let the world know they were having a baby.

The morning flew by with case after case. The Lovetts were late, so that they were the last people she saw before lunch break. Shaken by the tragedy of the couple who'd wanted a child and had paid to have a woman impregnated with the husband's sperm, Luna listened to them describe the heartbreak of an about-face. After the birth of the child, the natural mother decided she wanted to keep it. Now the case would have to be tried in open court. Maybe she would give this one to Barb or Uel.

Going out the front door, it surprised her to see the Rolls-Royce and not the Ferrari that Dray had driven that morning. Stepping wearily into the back, she had another surprise. Wilkins had not gotten out and opened the door for her, and he was wearing his uniform, cap and all. "Is the senator meeting us somewhere?"

Luna was in the act of smothering a yawn when she heard the door locks click into place. When the window between the front and the back slid up and locked, Luna straightened in her seat. "Wilkins?"

The man in front whipped off his hat, throwing a glance over his shoulder. "Do be quiet, Mrs. Lodge."

"Haddon March! Why are you driving our car and what are you doing? I'm to meet my husband . . ."

"Afraid not, *I* gave that message to your receptionist. You have ruined my life, Mrs. Lodge."

"I have? What are you—"

"Be quiet. I don't want to talk now. You'll know everything a few minutes before you die. And incidentally, this is my car." He reached behind him and pulled down a black curtain, and clicked off the speaker system between the back and the front.

Luna could still see out the side and back windows, though they were tinted, but she had never felt such isolation in her life.

Though Dray had not discussed it with her, she had known that he had suspected that another, higher member of the syndicate had been involved in stealing the government sundries. It was like a slap in the face to accept that it must be Haddon March who was pulling the strings. Why else would he be kidnapping her? All the coolness left her as memories of that last frightening time, when Skinner and Hetty had taken her, mushroomed in her mind. She fought the trembling that shivered through her, calling on every bit of strength that she had not to cave in, to figure out how to free herself.

Luna recalled her uncle's journal and how he had referred to a "boss" time after time, and how careful he'd have to be to apprehend him. The "boss" was highly placed in government and a friend to congressmen. Though Skinner had been apprehended and tried, her uncle's journal repeatedly mentioned the "boss." Why hadn't she concentrated on the journal more? There must have been some mention of Haddon March, even if it was veiled.

The car moved rapidly out of D.C. into the countryside.

The area looked familiar to Luna. Then she realized that it was the Virginia countryside where her in-laws had a home. They passed Merry Hill! Luna stared out the window until they passed the property.

"Senator? Sorry about calling you from the caucus." Peevy was tight-lipped and edgy.

"Is it my wife?"

"Yes, sir. You obviously didn't pick her up for lunch. My man checked with her office and the woman, Gretchen Taylor, said that your office called and—"

"Not true," Dray interrupted hoarsely.

"Don't worry, Senator, my man's on the car. He called me from his autophone."

"Where are they headed?"

"Virginia. Wait a minute, don't go off half-cocked. She's being watched." Peevy dialed a number and spoke tersely into the phone.

Dray drummed his fingers on the table in front of him, feeling as though he were bleeding to death.

The detective replaced the phone on the cradle. "They've headed into Haddon March's place. I'm going out there now," Peevy told him in colorless accents. "I want to be on the road in case he reverses himself."

"Fine. I'll get a copter." Dray dialed quickly, getting his brother-in-law's private line. "I want the company chopper and get it here fast, I'll explain later. I'll provide the clearance." Hanging up, he called Senate security and described what was happening in short, terse terms.

Calling to an aide, he gave instructions to be taken to the caucus room as he left. "And I've already spoken, so it's a matter of discussion now." Dray left on the run, down the corridor and stairs, not braking his pace until he was out-of-doors.

Waving to the security people who were clearing an area for the copter, he waited impatiently until he saw the machine circle and land. Then he sprinted the short distance and vaulted in next to the pilot.

"Good luck, Senator," one of the security men called to him.

"I'll need it," Dray muttered. "Take off, I'll direct you, Thomas."

"Emergency, sir?" the pilot quizzed.

"Yes. Do you have firearms on board?"

The man nodded woodenly.

Dray shrugged out of his suit coat, tossing it behind him, then he went through the small storage cupboard indicated by the pilot until he came up with an automatic handgun. "Are these legal?"

The pilot nodded. "I have a license."

"I'm taking it."

"All right, sir. There's another one in there, bring it out for me, please. I'll back your play." The pilot, who'd been an employee of the Lodge family for many years, spoke in flat, emotionless tones.

"It could get hairy, Thomas, I don't think . . ."

"I flew choppers in 'Nam, sir, if you recall. I'll back your play."

"Thank you."

Dray couldn't sit still. The copter was crawling. They passed Merry Hill, then they were on March's grounds. "Put this down behind those trees, Thomas. I don't want him to be suspicious. He's used to seeing my father come home in one of these, but he might wonder if we parked it too close to him."

"Right, sir. I've landed here before with your father. There's a path through that pine brake, sir."

Dray nodded. "I know the way."

As soon as the copter touched down, Dray was out of it and running, crouched and alert.

Dray wasn't even sure that Thomas was behind him as he sprinted over the rough ground, through the pine brake, using every bit of cover he could muster.

He heard dogs barking but didn't see any of them. When he heard a rustling noise off to the right, he turned, bringing up his hands in attack position.

"It's me, sir. Russell, from Mr. Peevy's agency. All's quiet in the house and those dogs are penned, sir, but I think the gate can be electronically released to free them if our man ever gets suspicious."

Dray nodded to the man's whispered information. "We're going in, Russell, and fast. We won't wait for Peevy."

The other man hesitated, then nodded. "All right, sir, how do you want to handle it?"

"Thomas, go up to the door, ring the bell, and keep ringing it until it's answered. I'm going around to the side of the house where the library is. That's his particular hangout. Russell, you follow behind Thomas and rush the door. Let's go."

"Take it easy, Senator. This man could be dangerous."

"I'm sure he is," Dray answered grimly, then moved quietly away. Luna, Luna, Luna. All of his life was wrapped up in one wonderful woman. Losing her would be like cutting himself in half with a rusty knife.

The barking increased. Dray loosened the gun at his belt and moved from tree to tree. If Haddon March had been alerted, things might get sticky, but there was no way Dray wasn't going in there and find his wife. Why didn't Thomas ring that front-door bell?

At that moment the bell chimed and the dogs retaliated in shrill ire that anyone should be on their property.

Dray vaulted from the ground and over the stone terrace wall, landing catlike in front of the terrace windows.

Readying himself, he thrust feet first with all the power at his command at the closure of the French doors, setting off an alarm and sending the animals into a frenzy. The frame gave with a splintering crash.

Dray landed on his feet in the library, his head swiveling rapidly, finding Luna at once where she was tied to a chair. Haddon March was at her side, a pistol at Luna's head. "Give it up, March. We have enough information on you to put you away for two life terms."

"I suppose it is over," the soigné criminal concurred smoothly. "I should kill your wife, Senator. If it hadn't been for her, I might have gone on for years," Haddon mused softly. "A cohort of yours leaning on my bell?"

Dray nodded. "You haven't a prayer."

"Did you know that I've had this operation since Korea, when I was there with your father as an infantryman? He never knew. The operation was sloppy, but I could see the great potential. I made my first million before I was rotated home. I wanted you to know this, Dray." Haddon March's smile was vinegary. "You see, I was always fond of you, never had time to marry, never wanted anyone that close to me. You were like the son I'd never had." It was as though Haddon didn't hear the front door splintering, the back door being forced open. "You could have had it all, Dray. I'm a very wealthy man."

"No thanks. Let my wife go."

"Ah, yes, the illustrious Luna. You love her, don't you? She botched up an international syndicate for me, but I told her that, didn't I, my dear?"

"Dray, leave," Luna pleaded, dry-mouthed.

"Not polite to interrupt, my dear. I had every intention of replacing Ahmed on the throne with his cousin Ahoud, you know. That would have eased things for me in the Middle East. Abdul worked for me as well. Too bad Ahmed had him executed." Haddon stiffened when people pounded on the library door. "No, stay where you are, Dray. This gun has a hair trigger. You wouldn't want to lose your bride." Haddon March touched Luna's face with his finger, laughing when she flinched. "I will give you a free one, Luna McAfee. Colonel Encorvado, who was also in my pay, kept a journal as well. I'm sure his wife would give it up for a sum. He keeps names, I don't do that. When Nichols stole the evidence you'd gathered against Hetty, it was the colonel who got rid of it. Burned it in the incinerator."

Luna gasped, but said nothing, her eyes going to her husband, pleading silently for him to be careful.

March looked around when the heavy oak door began to split from the blows of an ax. "We should have fed Hetty to the dogs, he was no good to us. That woman who testified against him was an albatross from the beginning. Hetty was my one weakness. I should have killed him." With bland interest March watched the hand come through the door and turn the lock. Then he lifted the gun, put it into his mouth, and fired.

Luna screamed even as Dray was diving through the air, putting his body between Haddon March and her.

"My darling, are you all right?" Dray kissed her, turning

her away from the gory sight on the Herez carpet and untying her bonds.

"I'm fine, but my wrists hurt from the ropes." As soon as she was free she put her arms around her husband's neck. "You shouldn't have come through the terrace. He might have killed you."

All at once the place filled with emergency attendants and police.

Dray answered some questions and then announced that he was taking his wife to the hospital and that if they needed any more information, they could follow him there.

"Dray, thank you," Luna looked up at him from the circle of his arms as the helicopter lifted them into the sky.

Dray looked down at her, shaking his head, swallowing hard. "All I've ever wanted to do was protect you, yet since we met again you've had more ugly confrontations with people than anyone should have in two lifetimes."

Luna saw how his mouth trembled, even though he tried to smile at her. "Darling, don't." She turned more into his arms and clutched him to her. "It's over now."

"It has to be, Luna mine. If anyone else accosts you, I'm going to kill him." Dray buried his face in her neck. "I was so damned scared that he might have done something to you."

Luna held him tightly, toying with the idea of telling him nothing, then realizing that Dray would have to know what had occurred and that she had no right to keep it from him. "He was coldly manic, raging but frosty. And there was surprise in his voice as though he'd thought he could have gone on forever, that no one was smart enough to catch him."

"Until you became the thorn in his side. You surfaced, and the danger from your uncle was there to threaten as it had done so many years ago. It must have been a shock to him when he connected you in Germany, trying Hetty, with your uncle, who had been on his trail so many years ago."

"I'm going to look in my uncle's journal again. I'll bet there's mention of March, even though it may be coded."

Luna kissed her husband's cheek. "I think he began to make a connection between my uncle and me when I was on the Skinner case."

"All that damned time when we thought he was such an upstanding citizen, he was running a thieves' operation that would have put Al Capone to shame."

Thomas made a circle, the radio began to crackle, then they were setting down near the Georgetown Medical Center.

"Dray, I don't need a doctor." Luna looked at his set face and sighed. "All right, but there's nothing wrong with me."

"Thank God."

When Luna was about to step to the tarmac, Dray swept her up into his arms. "Thanks, Thomas. I want you to contact my father and brother and give them a rundown on what happened."

Thomas grinned. "I will, Senator. Feel free to call on me anytime if there's trouble."

"I will. Thanks again."

Dray steamrolled into the emergency entrance of the hospital, giving orders, demanding to see Luna's doctor on the double.

Luna was torn between laughter and irritation when he froze an attendant with a glance when the man was about to question him. "Darling, do stop it."

Dray looked down at his wife blankly. "I want to see that you're given every care."

Luna was about to remonstrate with him when she saw the lines of strain around his mouth, as though he were keeping a volcano tamed within him. She said nothing.

In short order she was examined by the doctor with her husband staying with her, listening intently to every word that the medical personnel exchanged.

"Your wife is in excellent shape, Senator. There's no need for concern."

"There's every reason for concern. I want her to have a smooth pregnancy and an uncomplicated delivery."

"Of course." The doctor bit her lip and nodded.

Luna almost laughed out loud at the struggle the doctor was having in containing her mirth. "Let's go home, husband."

Chapter 20

In the months that followed, the Haddon March scandal precipitated a fact-finding committee to investigate the corruption in the sundries portion of government. When the scope of the man's power was laid open to the nation, the people were shocked and outraged, realizing the extent of the thievery that had put a hole in the taxpayers' pockets. The outcry brought changes, so-called fail-safe methods, a new checks-and-balances program that would thwart such high-level stealing before it could flower.

"Do you think that all those recommendations can stop the pillaging of military and government stores, Dray?"

Dray shook his head. "A crooked mind will come up with a squeeze play that will work for a time, but I don't think that any big-time, long-term operation will work for some time because of the public outrage over this one. The American people took a real licking on this, with their tax money going right into the hands of the pirates." Dray cuddled her close to him, loving the moments before their fire at night. His hand lay possessively on her swollen middle. "I can't believe it's December and that our baby is due this month."

"Don't count on it, Senator. First babies can be capricious, they arrive when they choose, early, late, sometimes even on time."

"I can't believe this isn't tough on your body. If the doctor hadn't said that she couldn't detect another heartbeat, I would say we were having twins."

"And I can't believe what a folk hero you've become to the people in D.C. and in New York. Your work in airing the corruption and the way you've helped Stenzi and Veli Skinner have captured the hearts of the people, my husband." Luna could see the telltale red on his cheeks. Dray, despite his courage and great ability in all matters of law, was modest. She really didn't need any more reasons to love him, but since their marriage, Luna had seen many other wonderful facets to the man she needed and wanted so much.

Dray kissed her nose. "As long as I've won your heart, I'm happy."

Luna touched his cheek. "You know how I care for you, Perrin Draper Lodge."

"Yes, I do, and it never fails to make me happy, Luna. You've brought so much into my life. I don't know if I'll ever be able to show you just how much I need you."

As always, they retired early. Luna tired easily as she approached the last weeks, not finding many comfortable positions for her cumbersome body.

Many nights Dray sat up with her when she couldn't sleep, and they played cards or talked until she could get some rest.

"Did I tell you what I miss most being pregnant, Dray?"

"Ice cream?" Dray slid the nightie over her body, loving the look of her as she faced him.

"Making love." She smiled at him serenely. When he closed his eyes as though in pain, she chuckled.

"Not funny, Luna mine. I want you so much sometimes, I think I might shout your name out when I'm in the Senate. I mean it, I pinch myself so that I'll concentrate on the world around me, not on you."

Delighted, Luna fell into his arms, feeling so relaxed with him, quite aware that he was as intensely interested in her bulbous form as he was when it had been svelte and slender.

In the night, Luna's eyes popped open and she knew at once she was in labor. Lying there as quietly as she could, she began the breathing exercises that she had been taught. Each time she moved, she caught her breath. Dray was so quick to pick up on her wakefulness and he needed his sleep. Tomorrow there would be an important caucus for a bill that he and a colleague had introduced. He had to be there.

The sun was coming up as the sky went from pale gray to a cold pinkness tht signaled it would be clear but cold in the capital.

Luna bit down on her lip as another pain took her.

"Luna? Darling? Are you uncomfortable? You stiffened." A bleary-eyed Dray came up on one elbow, focusing on her, sleep leaving him at once when he noticed the strained look on her face. "You *are* in pain. Why didn't you waken me?"

"Darling, they aren't that bad. And you have that caucus today. . . ."

"Luna, I'm not leaving you. Here, let me time the pains for you."

In minutes Dray was on the phone talking to the doctor, despite Luna's protests.

Wilkins was tight-lipped when Dray carried Luna downstairs. "I will drive you, sir. It will be more comfortable for Mrs. Lodge."

"Wilkins, go back to bed," Luna pleaded, laughing and wincing when Lance paced around them, emitting short whuffs of concern. "Silly dog, go back to bed."

"He is worried about you, madam, as we all are. Unless it would be not what you want, I would like to drive you, madam."

"Please don't argue with him, darling, because I want him to drive us."

"All right. Have you my bag, Dray?"

"I have everything. Go to the kitchen, Lance, good dog. I think he wants to come."

Wilkins put the dog away, then helped Dray get Luna to the car and settle her comfortably in the back of the limousine, then he drove carefully but not slowly through the streets of Georgetown.

"Oh!"

"Darling, what is it?" Dray leaned over his wife, his hand massaging her middle.

"I think . . . the baby . . . is coming." Surprise was in her voice, then she gave a low scream.

"Wilkins, stop the car. Get on the phone and call emergency. All right, darling, I'm here. I have you."

"Dray! The baby . . . *owwww.*"

Moving fast, Dray stretched her out on the ample seat, then he removed her underthings and began counting for her. "Easy, darling, don't bear down anymore. I see the head. All right, push." To Dray's shock, the baby slid out into his waiting hands. "Luna, my darling, are you all right?" He placed the baby on her middle and leaned over her.

"The baby?" Luna gasped, trying to focus on the bundle on her chest.

"Don't worry about the baby, darling. He's fine. Listen to him, he's howling his head off. Wilkins, get moving, but drive safely."

"Yes, sir." Wilkins shot a quick look over his shoulder at the child lying on its mother's middle. "Congratulations, Senator, and to you, madam. We have a baby." The retainer's voice shook with emotion. "It's wonderful. Oh, dear, I think we'll have a police escort, sir."

"Good. Get going." Dray leaned over and kissed Luna. "He's messy but beautiful, darling. I think he looks like you."

"I want to call him Perrin Draper Samuel Lodge, Dray. Would that suit you?"

"Very much, darling. My parents will be ecstatic. How do you feel?"

"Light and triumphant. What a considerate child we have to hurry things along so." Luna laughed weakly.

"Oh, God, I love you. I'm so proud of you, and very happy. I'd dreaded you being in labor for long, agonizing hours, and now it's over and you didn't have to suffer too much."

The sheen of tears in her husband's eyes touched her, bringing her to the full awareness of how much he'd become a part of her. "Your son was no trouble, Senator. Now, maybe next time we'll try for a girl."

Dray leaned down and kissed her. "Not for a long time,

please. I want you fully recovered and strong before the next
one." He winced. "How can you talk of another child now?"

"I think you had more physical trauma than I did." Luna
laughed again, feeling stronger . . . free . . . and loved
. . . and content.

"Don't try to make a joke of it, I don't see the humor."

When the baby let out a yowl of protest, both his parents
chuckled and hung over him.

Wilkins steered the powerful car in the wake of the motorcycle policeman, his hands gripping the wheel at eleven and
one o'clock, his eyes glued to the road. A baby! What a mira-
cle!

The hospital had been alerted by the police and the staff
were ready for both mother and child.

Dray stayed with Luna while she and the baby were examined. Then when they were settled in a private room, he
phoned his family, not taking his eyes off his wife the entire
time.

Luna was drifting between sleeping and waking when her
in-laws arrived at the hospital. The baby was in a bassinet
near her, snoozing contentedly after sucking at his mother's
not yet full breast.

Melanie had tears in her eyes when she hugged her daughter-in-law. "After all you've been through from a man we
trusted, you still manage to produce the most beautiful baby
in the D.C. area. Darling girl, you must take a great rest.
Come out to Merry Hill and let us care for you."

"No! I have nurses around the clock for her, and we'll be
spending time on the farm in New York later, Mother, but I
don't want her far away from me," Dray told his parent,
earning an irritated glance from her.

"You are positively greedy with your wife, Perrin Draper,
isn't he, Perry?"

"He is, but I wouldn't have let you out of my sight after our
children were born, dearest. Remember?"

"That's true." Melanie frowned at her husband. "I hate it
when you're so sensible."

"I know." Her husband kissed her. "We'll come into Georgetown all the time to see the baby. We'll sublet a place nearby."

"Nonsense," Luna interrupted. "I insist that you stay with us, Melanie, then you can be near the baby all the time," Luna told her mother-in-law. "I know Barb and Uel will be there every chance they get, so—"

"Damn!" Dray interrupted his wife. "In all the excitement I forgot to call them. Barb will have a fit, she called this morning to see how you were and gave Wilkins the message that she was to be called if anything happened." Dray turned to the phone and dialed. "Uel? It's Dray. Yes, it happened. A boy. Beautiful, almost nine pounds. His name is going to be Perrin Draper Samuel Lodge. Yes, after you, his godfather."

Dray turned to his wife when he replaced the receiver. "I think he was crying."

Luna nodded just as the nurse entered, picked up the child, and placed it in his mother's arms. Looking down at the babe in her arms, she smiled. "Uel will be a very special godfather."

"I like that young man. I've talked to my board of directors about getting him a seat on it. We need his acumen and perception."

"Thank you." Luna smiled shyly at her father-in-law. "I know he won't let you down, sir."

"I wish you would call me Father, my dear—or Perry, if that's too—"

"I would like to call you Father."

"Thank you, Luna. You honor me." Perrin Lodge leaned over and kissed his daughter-in-law while his wife dabbed at her eyes and whispered, "It's so sweet."

"More people attended his christening than they did the last inaugural," Dray complained to his very slim wife as they looked out over the gathering at Merry Hill.

Luna leaned against her husband and nodded. "I wonder if we'll be able to pry Uel away from his godson. He's told everyone who will listen that the baby smiled for the first time when he picked him up in the hospital."

Dray nodded. "My mother walks behind him, telling everyone that it's true because she saw it happen."

"Do you think they'll ever believe the baby had a gas pain?"

"Not easily. Uel told me he's already working on Sam's entrance into law school."

"What if he wants to be a drummer or a rock star?" Luna felt lazy, happy, and complete.

"It could be a problem." Dray looked down at her. "*You* are looking especially beautiful today."

"And feeling especially sexy." Luna stared up at her husband, chuckling when he flinched.

"Don't say that, darling, I'll have to be packed in ice."

Luna let one finger score down his chest. "Maybe not. The doctor said that all was a go for me to resume relations with my husband." She pouted outrageously. "But if you have a headache, I'll understand."

Dray looked around at the group. "Come along. They won't miss us for a while. Uel is still expounding on my son's many virtues and my mother is hot on his trail."

"Dray! Where are we going? We can't leave our son's christening party. I meant we would have our wonderful encounter this evening." Luna was both amused and horrified when her husband swept her up into his arms. "We can't disappear into your parents' house like this. Can we?" she quizzed hopefully, looking over his shoulder at the throng, who were paying no attention to them.

"Of course we can, but we're not going there." Dray strode across the manicured lawn until he came to one of the golf carts that the Lodge family kept on the property.

There was a nine-hole golf course for the use of family and guests, and the carts were for those who needed them.

Dray lifted her into one. "Hang on, darling."

"Where are we going, you mad, impetuous fool? We are parents now, we have to be more decorous."

"We are being decorous, we're married, aren't we? And we're going to a place that was given to me by my grandfather when I was a young man so that I could have my privacy. I think the old reprobate kept his ladies there at one time. Father never said that, but my mother often pursed her lips when talking of her father-in-law. Rumor has it he was quite a boy."

When they reached the stone house that Dray told Luna was well over two hundred years old, Luna was enchanted. "It's beautiful. We should come here more often, Dray."

"Whenever you like, lady mine," he told her huskily, stepping out of the cart and lifting her to the ground, keeping his arms around her as they strolled down the winding path to the door.

When he reached up to the lintel and took down an old-fashioned key, he turned and grinned at her. "You'll be my first seduction here, Luna mine."

"And your only one," she told him pertly, smiling when he nodded.

He lifted her again and carried her across the threshold, not releasing her, but kicking the door shut behind them. Then he strode to the steep, narrow stairway that led upward to the bedroom that was the entire upper story. There was a small bathroom off the bedroom.

Placing her on the bed, he followed her down, smiling into her eyes. "My recurring dream is undressing you, my love."

"Do get on with it." Luna swallowed as the heat of her own passion began building. "I do love you so much, it frightens me to think that we might never have found each other again after that brief encounter in Germany."

Dray shook his head. "No, we would have come together at some time, darling, it was our kismet to belong to each other." Dray peeled the clothes from her body, kissing each portion of skin that appeared, his breath ragged as he muttered love words to her over and over again.

Luna clung to him, the world forgotten in his arms.

"Our brief encounter is forever, darling," Dray muttered as he entered her, her hoarse cry of joy matching his.

The world fell away and the brief encounter became forever.

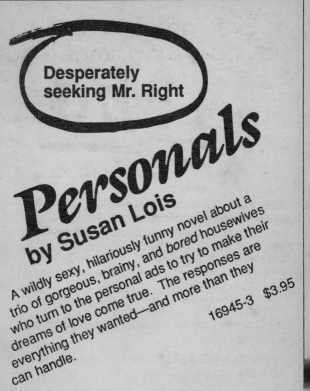

Desperately seeking Mr. Right

Personals
by Susan Lois

A wildly sexy, hilariously funny novel about a trio of gorgeous, brainy, and bored housewives who turn to the personal ads to try to make their dreams of love come true. The responses are everything they wanted—and more than they can handle.

16945-3 $3.95